AUTUMN

Also by David Moody from Gollancz:

Hater
Dog Blood

AUTUMN

DAVID MOODY

GOLLANCZ
LONDON

Copyright © David Moody 2010
All rights reserved

The right of David Moody to be identified as the author of this work has been asserted by him in accordance with the Copyright, Designs and Patents Act 1988.

First published in Great Britain in 2010 by Gollancz
An imprint of the Orion Publishing Group
Orion House, 5 Upper St Martin's Lane, London WC2H 9EA
An Hachette UK Company

A CIP catalogue record for this book is available from the British Library

ISBN 978 0 575 09127 6 (Cased)
ISBN 978 0 575 09128 3 (Export Trade Paperback)

1 3 5 7 9 10 8 6 4 2

Typeset at The Spartan Press Ltd,
Lymington, Hants

Printed and bound in the UK by CPI Mackays,
Chatham, Kent

The Orion Publishing Group's policy is to use papers that are natural, renewable and recyclable products and made from wood grown in sustainable forests. The logging and manufacturing processes are expected to conform to the environmental regulations of the country of origin.

NEATH PORT TALBOT LIBRARIES	
2300019829 6	
HJ COM	09-Nov-2010
AF	£12.99

www.davidmoody.co.uk
www.orionbooks.co.uk

Prologue

Billions died in less than twenty-four hours.

William Price was one of the first.

He'd been out of bed for less than a minute when it began. He was halfway down the stairs when he felt the first stabbing pains around the inside of his mouth and the back of his throat. By the time he'd reached his wife in the living room he couldn't breathe.

The virus caused the lining of his throat to swell at a remarkable rate. Less than forty seconds after initial infection the swelling had almost completely blocked his windpipe. As he fought for air the swellings began to split and bleed. He began to choke on the blood running down the inside of his trachea.

Price's wife tried to help him, but all she could do was catch him when he fell to the ground. For a fraction of a second she was aware of his body beginning to twitch and spasm, but by then she'd also been infected.

Less than four minutes after infection, William Price was dead. Thirty seconds later and his wife was dead too. A further minute and the entire street was silent.

1

Carl Henshawe was more than three-quarters of the way home before he realised anything had happened.

The early morning sun was low on the horizon as he drove back from the Carter & Jameson factory just north of Billhampton. He'd been there since just after four, fixing an insignificant repair which had hardly warranted him being called out in the middle of the night. Simpson – the wily bastard who ran the night shift there – was too tight to pay for new machinery and too smart to have his own men fix the problem when he could call someone else out. He knew the maintenance contract inside out, better even than Carl's employers. Never mind, he thought to himself as he tried to drink a cup of coffee with one hand, tune the radio with the other and still keep the van moving, being on twenty-four-hour call paid well, and Christ, did they need the money. He loved his family more than anything, but neither he nor Sarah had been prepared for the extra expense of having another mouth to feed. Gemma, their perfect little girl, was costing them a fortune.

Damn radio. Must be something wrong with it, he decided. One minute there was the usual music, interspersed with inane chatter and drivel, the next just silence. Not even static. The final notes of the last song faded away and were replaced with nothing.

The sun flashed through the tops of the trees, blinding Carl intermittently. He knew he should slow down, but he wanted to get home and see Gemma before Sarah took her to nursery. He shielded his eyes as he took a tight bend too fast, then slammed on his brakes as a small, mustard-yellow-coloured car raced towards him, careering down the middle of the road. He swerved hard to the right to avoid impact and braced himself as the van bumped up the verge at the side of the road. He watched in his rear-view mirror as the other car continued forward, its speed undiminished, before clattering up the kerb and thumping into a wide oak tree.

Carl sat unmoving in his seat and gazed into the mirror, unable for a moment to fully comprehend what had just happened. The sudden silence was unbearable. Then, as the shock slowly began to fade and the reality of the situation sank in, he got out of the van and ran over to the crashed vehicle. His mind was racing; his focus entirely self-concerned. *It'll be his word against mine*, he thought anxiously. *I wasn't concentrating. If he sues and they find against me, I'll probably lose my job. As it is I'll have to explain why I . . .*

Carl stood in the middle of the road and stared at the body of the driver, slumped forward with his face smashed into the steering wheel. His legs heavy, he took another couple of nervous steps closer. The car had hit at an incredible speed, making no attempt to either slow down or swerve. Its bonnet had hit the trunk so hard it had virtually wrapped itself right around the tree.

He opened the door and crouched down, his face level with the driver. He knew immediately that the man was dead. His empty eyes stared at him, somehow blaming Carl for what had just happened. Blood was pouring – not dripping – from a deep gash on the bridge of his nose, and from his mouth, which was hanging open, pooling under the pedals in the footwell. Suddenly nauseous, Carl leant over the crumpled front of the car and emptied the contents of his stomach in the grass.

Got to do something. Phone for help.

He ran back to the van and grabbed his mobile from its holder on the dashboard. *It's easier knowing he's dead*, he thought, trying to convince himself, and feeling guilty for even daring to think such thoughts. I can just tell the police that I was driving along and I found the car crashed into the tree. No one needs to know that I was here when it happened. No one needs to know that I probably caused the accident.

No one was picking up. Strange. He looked at the phone's display and dialled 999. Plenty of battery power left, and the signal strength was good . . . He cancelled the call and tried again. Then again. Then again. Then another number. Then the office. Then the number of the factory he'd just come from. Then his home number . . . Sarah's mobile . . . his dad's house . . . his best mate . . . and got nothing. No one answered.

Get a grip, he told himself, trying not to panic. There had been no other traffic on the road since the crash. If no one's seen you here, his frightened and flawed logic dictated, then no one needs to know you were ever here at all. Before he could talk himself out of it, he got back into the van, started the engine and began to drive away. Maybe he'd call the police anonymously later, he decided, trying to appease his guilt. I don't even need to tell them about the body. I'll just tell them I've seen a crash at the side of the road.

A mile and a half further down the road, Carl spotted another car, but as he neared it, he saw that it had stopped, parked at an awkward angle across the dotted white line, straddling both lanes of the road. The driver's door was wide open and the seat empty. As he pulled up alongside the car, he saw there were three people inside: a woman, the mother, maybe, in the front, and two children in the back. Their frozen faces were filled with agony and panic. Their skin was grey, and he could see trickles of blood running down the chin of the boy who was nearest to him. He didn't need to look any closer to know that they were dead.

As he drove off, Carl found the lifeless body of the missing driver a few yards further along the road, sprawled across the tarmac.

Carl slammed his foot down on the accelerator and raced away, his head spinning, hoping every time he turned a corner that he'd see someone alive who could help him, or at least explain what had happened. The further he drove, however, the more obvious it became that in the space of a few minutes, everything had been changed for ever.

The level of Carl's panic and fear was such that he'd seen more than another fifty lifeless bodies – bodies which had all looked to have simply fallen and died where they'd been standing - before it occurred to him that whatever had happened here had probably happened to his family too. He drove back home at a dangerous speed, swerving around the corpses in the streets, abandoning the van outside his house and running to the front door. With his legs shaking, a sick feeling in the pit of his stomach and his hands trembling, he forced the key into the lock and shoved the door open. He shouted out for Sarah, but there was no reply. The house was cold and silent. He slowly walked upstairs, almost too afraid to open the bedroom door, tormenting himself with unanswerable questions: *If I'd driven faster, would I have been home in time to help? If I'd wasted less time with the corpses at the roadside, would I have been here for them when they needed me most?*

His heart pounding, he went into the bedroom and found his wife and daughter lying dead together. Gemma's head hung over the edge of the bed, her mouth open wide in the middle of a silent scream. There was blood on Sarah's white nightdress, and on the bedsheets and floor. His eyes stinging with tears, he begged them both to wake up, pleaded with them, shook them and screamed at them—

Carl couldn't stand to leave, but he couldn't bear to stay there either. He kissed Sarah and Gemma goodbye and covered them with a clean sheet before locking the door and walking away from his home. He spent hours stepping between the hundreds of bodies outside, too afraid even to shout for help.

2

Michael Collins stood in front of a class of thirty-three fifteen- and sixteen-year-olds, tongue-tied and terrified. Under his breath he cursed Steve Wilkins, his idiot of a boss, for forcing him to do this. He hated public speaking and he hated kids, teenagers especially. He remembered having to sit through things like this when he was at school. 'Industry into Schools' days they used to be called: days when, instead of listening to their teacher drone on for hours, kids were instead made to listen to unwilling volunteers like him telling them how wonderful the job was, no matter how much they really despised their work. Michael hated compromising himself like this, but he didn't have any choice. Wilkins had made it perfectly clear that his performance today would be directly linked to the quarterly bonus he was due to receive at the end of this month. Wilkins had come out with some bullshit about how his middle managers were 'figureheads of the company'. Michael knew that in reality, his middle managers were just there for him to hide behind.

'You gonna say anything?' a scrawny kid in a baseball cap sneered. Michael tried to stay calm and not react, but the way his sheaf of notes was shaking was probably making his nervousness obvious to the entire class. Sadistic teenagers were always quick to seize on any apparent weakness.

'The work we do at Carradine Computers is extremely varied and interesting,' he began, his voice wavering as he lied through his teeth. 'We're responsible for—'

'Sir—!' a lad said from the middle of the room, waving his hand frantically in the air and grinning.

'What is it?' Michael answered, almost against his better judgement.

'I think you should just give up now, sir. No one's listening!'

The rest of the class – those who weren't reading magazines, drawing on their desks or listening to music through barely concealed earphones – began to jeer. Some at least tried to hide their sniggers behind their hands; others rocked back on their chairs and laughed out loud. Michael looked to the teacher at the back of the class for support, but the moment he made eye contact with her, she looked away.

'As I was saying,' he continued, not knowing what else to do, 'we look after a wide range of clients, from small, one-man firms to multinational corporations. We advise them on the right software to use, the systems to buy and—'

Another interruption, this one more physical as a fight broke out in one corner of the room. One boy had another in a headlock.

'James Clyde, cut it out,' the teacher yelled. 'Anyone would think you didn't want to listen to Mr Collins.'

Great. As if the apathetic behaviour of the students wasn't bad enough, now even the teacher was being sarcastic. Suddenly the stifled laughter was released and the whole room was out of control. Michael threw his notes down onto the desk and was about to walk out when he noticed a girl in the far corner of the room, who was coughing. It cut right through the rest of the chaotic noise, and sounded horribly painful – a rasping, hacking scream of a cough, which sounded as if each painful convulsion was ripping out the very insides of her throat. He took a few steps towards her and then stopped. Her choking was the only sound he could hear; the rest of the room had become silent. He watched as her head jerked forward, showering her hands and her desk with sticky strings of sputum and splashes of blood. She looked up at him, her wide eyes terrified. He realised she was suffocating.

Michael glanced at the teacher again and this time she stared back at him, fear and confusion clear on her face. She began to massage her own neck.

A boy on the other side of the room began to cough and wheeze. He got halfway out of his seat, then fell back again. A girl just behind began to cry and then to cough. The teacher tried to stand, but instead fell out of her seat and hit the floor . . .

Within thirty seconds of the first girl starting to cough, every single person in the room was tearing at their throats, fighting to breathe. Every single person except Michael.

Numb with shock and not knowing what to do or where to go to get help, Michael moved jerkily back towards the classroom door. He tripped over a student's bag and grabbed hold of the nearest desk to steady himself. A girl's hand slammed down onto his and he stared into her face, deathly white save for dark trickles of crimson blood which ran down her chin and dripped onto her desk. He pulled his hand away and opened the classroom door.

The noise inside the room had been horrific enough, but out here it was even worse. Screams of agony were ringing out through the entire school. From every classroom, and from the more remote places – assembly halls, gymnasiums, workshops, kitchens and offices – the morning air was filled with the terrifying noise of hundreds of children and adults suffocating, choking to death.

By the time Michael had walked the length of the corridor and was halfway down the stairs to the main entrance, the school was silent. A boy was sprawled on the ground at the foot of the stairs. He crouched down next to him and cautiously reached out his hand, pulling it away again as soon as he touched his skin. It felt clammy and unnatural, almost like wet leather. Forcing himself to overcome his fear, he rolled the boy over onto his back. Like the kids in the classroom, his face was ghostly-white, and his lips and chin smeared with blood and spittle. Michael leant down as close as he dared and put his ear next to his mouth, praying that he would hear even the slightest sounds of breathing. It was no use. He was dead.

Michael walked out into the cool September sunlight and crossed the empty playground. Just one glance at the devastated world beyond the school gates was enough for him to know that whatever had happened inside the building had happened outside too. Random fallen bodies littered the streets for as far as he could see.

He didn't know what to do. He considered his options as he walked: one, go back to work and look for people there? Two, try the hospitals and police stations? He decided on option three: to go home, change his clothes and pack a bag, then head deeper into town. He couldn't be the only one left alive.

3

Emma Mitchell felt depressingly sick, cold and tired. Everything was an effort this morning. The head cold which had been threatening for a few days had finally hit her hard and she decided to skip classes and stay in bed. She'd tried to study for a while, but gave up when she realised she'd started reading the same paragraph five times without ever making it past the third line. She decided to fix herself some food, but couldn't find anything to eat – her bloody flatmate had been taking her stuff again. She'd have to talk to her about it when she got back tonight, she decided. The last thing Emma wanted to do was go out, but she didn't have any choice. She put on as many layers of clothing as she could stand and dragged herself to the store at the end of Maple Street.

There were only two other customers in Mr Rashid's shop. Emma was minding her own business, haggling with herself and trying to justify spending a few pence more on her favourite brand of spaghetti sauce, when an elderly man lunged at her. She instinctively shoved him back, but then realised he was struggling to breathe. Her mind immediately began racing, sudden surprise and panic taking hold. *What do I do?* She was just a few terms into a five-year course of medical studies, she wasn't sure. Did she use her limited knowledge to try and work out what was wrong, or just use commonsense first aid to help? His face was grey-white and his grip on her tightened, so strong that she dropped her shopping basket and tried to prise his bony fingers off her arm.

Another noise behind her made Emma look back over her shoulder. The other shopper had collapsed face-first into a display rack, sending loaves of bread, rolls and pastries crashing to the ground. He lay on his back in the middle of the aisle, coughing, holding his throat and writhing in agony.

Emma felt the grip on her arm loosen and she turned back to face the old man. Tears of pain and fear ran freely down his weathered cheeks as he struggled to breathe. Her training slowly began to take hold and she leant across to try and loosen his collar – but she stopped when she saw the blood inside his gasping, toothless mouth. As he leant forward, it dribbled onto the floor, splashing her feet. His legs buckled and he dropped to the ground, his entire body shaking and convulsing.

Emma ran to the back of the shop to find Mr Rashid and call for help. She found him lying in the stockroom doorway, barely alive. His wife had collapsed in the kitchen. The tap was still running and the sink was overflowing, blood-tinged water collecting in a pool on the floor around her pallid face. By the time Emma got back to the front of the store, both of the men she'd left there were dead.

Outside, there were bodies everywhere. Emma stumbled onto the street, shielding her eyes from the blinding sun. Hundreds of people had fallen around her, and every face she looked into was ashen, each person's lips bloodied and red. They had all suffocated.

Much further ahead, perhaps a quarter of a mile, where the High Street crossed Maple Street, the road was covered in an unfathomable tangle of crashed cars. Nothing was moving but for the traffic lights which, oblivious to the carnage, continued to cycle through their routine of red, amber and green and back again.

Emma walked home, slowly at first, but then moving with more speed, stepping over corpses as if they were just discarded litter. She didn't allow herself to think about what had happened, already knowing, perhaps, that she wouldn't be able to find any answers – or even anyone else left alive to ask. She let herself back into the flat and locked the door behind her. She went into her room, drew the curtains on the nightmare outside, got back into bed and pulled the covers over her head.

4

By eleven o'clock on a cold, bright and otherwise ordinary Tuesday morning in September, more than ninety-nine per cent of the population was dead.

Stuart Jeffries had been on his way home from a work conference when it had begun. He'd left the hotel on the Scottish borders at first light, with the intention of being home by mid-afternoon. He'd had the next three days booked off as holiday and had been looking forward to sitting on his backside doing as little as possible for as long as he could.

Driving virtually the full length of the country meant stopping to fill up the car with petrol on more than one occasion. He'd passed several service stations on the motorway, but had decided to wait until he reached the next town to get fuel. A smart man, he knew the cheaper he could buy his petrol, the more profit he'd make when he claimed back his expenses. Northwich was the nearest town, and it was there that a relatively normal morning became extraordinary in seconds. Around him the busy but fairly well ordered lines of traffic were thrown into chaos and disarray as the infection tore through the air. Desperate to avoid being hit as the first few cars around him lost control, he'd panicked, and taken the first turning off the main road, followed by an immediate right into a virtually empty car park where he skidded to a stop. He'd got out and run up a muddy bank on the other side of the car park, where he'd stood behind strong metal railings and watched helplessly as the world around him fell apart in an impossibly short time, countless people dropping to the ground without warning, then dying the most hideous choking death imaginable.

Stuart Jeffries spent the following hours sitting terrified in his car with the windows shut and the doors locked. The unfamiliar vehicle had only been delivered to his hotel late the previous evening, but in the sudden madness and disorientation he'd found himself plunged into, it now felt like the safest place in the world.

The radio was dead and no one was answering the phone. The petrol tank was almost empty and he was still more than two hundred and fifty miles away from home. Completely alone, stranded in an unfamiliar town, surrounded by corpses and literally paralysed with fear. What he'd witnessed was unprecedented, inexplicable and terrifying.

Finally his bladder forced him into action. After sitting for what felt like for ever in the car he decided he couldn't stand it any longer. He left the warm, muffled safety of the car and stumbled out into the cool, late September day. Had it really happened? His eyes watchful, he stood and pissed against a tree, then slowly walked back towards the main road, surveying the devastation around him. Nothing had moved. Motionless cars still filled the carriageway; some had crashed, others just stopped. The wet and dirty pavements were still littered with lifeless bodies. The only sound came from the biting autumn wind as it blustered through the trees on either side and chilled him to the bone. Other than those corpses trapped in the mangled wrecks of crashed cars, there didn't appear to be any immediately obvious reason for the deaths. The closest body to him was that of an elderly woman, and it looked like she had simply dropped to the ground – one minute alive, the next dead. She still had the handle of her shopping trolley gripped tightly in one of her gloved hands.

Stuart thought about shouting out for help. He raised his hands up to his mouth but then stopped. The world was so eerily silent and he felt so exposed and out of place that he didn't dare make any noise. In the back of his mind was the very real fear that, if he was to call out, his voice might draw attention to his location. Although there didn't appear to be anyone else left to hear him, in his vulnerable and increasingly nervous state he began to convince himself that making a noise might bring whatever it was that had destroyed the rest of the population back to destroy him – paranoid, perhaps, but what had happened today was so illogical and unexpected that he wasn't going to take any chances. Frustrated and afraid, he turned around and walked back towards the car.

At the far end of the car park, at first hidden from view by overhanging trees, stood the Whitchurch Community Centre. It was a dull, dilapidated building which had been named after a long-forgotten local dignitary and built (and last maintained, by its looks) in the late 1950s. Stuart cautiously walked up to the front of the hall and peered in through the half-open door. He pushed it fully open and took a few tentative steps inside. This time he did call out, quietly at first, but there was no reply.

The cold, draughty building took only a minute or two to explore, because it consisted of only a few rooms, most of which led off the main hall. There was a very basic kitchen, a storeroom filled with tables and chairs, and male and female toilets. At the far end of the hall was a second, much smaller area, with a second storeroom leading off it. This room had obviously been added later, an extension to the original building, the faded and peeling paintwork slightly less faded and peeling than that of the rest of the Whitchurch Community Centre.

Stuart decided to shelter in the hall until morning. It wasn't a difficult decision: it was as safe a place as any in which to hide. Although not in the best of repair, the windows and doors were all intact, and it would be warmer than the car. He couldn't see any point in trying to get anywhere else, not right now: the only place he wanted to be was back home, but that was still several hours drive away and he didn't have enough petrol. He quickly convinced himself that it would be safer to stay put for now and to try and refuel in the morning – he could siphon it from one of the cars on the road outside if he had to.

Other than two bodies in the main hall the building was empty. Stuart forced himself to drag the corpses outside. Clenched in the hand of a grey-haired man who looked to have been in his early sixties he found a bunch of keys which, he discovered, fitted the building's locks. This, he decided, must have been the caretaker. And the well-turned-out, equally grey-haired lady who had died next to him was probably a prospective tenant, looking to hire the hall for a Women's Institute meeting or a Mothers' Union coffee morning or something similar. He heaved the stiff bodies awkwardly through the doorway and laid them down side by side behind the building.

Night was beginning to draw in. He flicked on the wall switch and was surprised when the lights came on. How long would they last? He didn't much want to think about that. If everyone was dead, he realised, then the power stations would eventually stop producing electricity. He had not the foggiest idea how power stations worked: it might last for weeks, but it might just as well be gone by morning.

He went outside and jogged to the end of the car park, where he looked out over the rest of the city. The streetlamps and other automatic lights – road and shop signs and the like – had come on as usual, but it was still unsettlingly dark. There was no illumination in houses, offices or shop windows, no headlights on the road. He went back to the hall and shut and locked the door. It made him feel marginally safer, less exposed. With a locked door between him and everything else he could, at least for a while, pretend that nothing had happened.

Just before nine o'clock Stuart's solitary confinement was ended. He was sitting on an uncomfortable plastic chair in the kitchen of the centre, concentrating on the buzz of the electric light above him and trying to block out the silence of the dead world around him. It was impossible to think about anything other than what had happened today and what might happen tomorrow.

Someone was outside. He jumped up from his chair and crept cautiously down the hallway, his heart thumping in his chest and his legs weak with nerves. Silence. Maybe he'd imagined it? Maybe he'd just wanted to hear something? He took another step closer to the door, and jumped back as the handle moved up and down, up and down: someone trying to force it open. His mouth too dry to speak, he fumbled in his pockets for the keys, then struggled to shove the right one into the lock. He finally pushed the door open and stood in silence, staring at the figure in front of him. Stuart reached out and grabbed hold of the total stranger outside. He was Jack Baynham, a thirty-six-year-old bricklayer who'd lived in Northwich all his life. Although they'd never met before, they hugged like long-lost friends. Neither said a word.

*

The arrival of another survivor brought sudden unexpected hope and energy. Neither man had any answers as to what had happened earlier, but for the first time they did at least dare to consider what they should do next. If there were two survivors, then it followed there might be a hundred, maybe many more. They had to let other people know where they were.

Using rubbish from three dustbins at the side of the hall, branches from a dead tree and the remains of a smashed-up wooden table, they built a bonfire in the centre of the car park, well away from the hall and Stuart's car. Petrol from the wreck of a sports car was used as fuel. Jack set the fire burning by flicking a smouldering cigarette butt through the cold night air, and within seconds the car park was filled with welcome light and warmth. Stuart found a CD, something classical, in another car and put it into the player in his. He turned the key in the ignition and it started, filling the air with sweeping, soaring strings which shattered the oppressive and overbearing silence that had been so prevalent all day.

The fire had been burning and the music playing for less than an hour when the third and fourth survivors arrived together at the hall. By four o'clock the following morning more than twenty shell-shocked and terrified individuals had reached the Whitchurch Community Centre.

Emma Mitchell had spent almost the entire day curled up in the corner of her bed with the covers over her head. She'd first heard the music shortly after midnight, but for a while she had convinced herself that she was hearing things. It was only when she finally plucked up the courage to get out of bed and open her bedroom window that it became clear that someone really was out there, playing music. Desperate to speak to someone else, to see another person, she threw a few belongings into a rucksack, locked up her home and left. She sprinted along the silent streets as fast as she could, not allowing herself to slow down, terrified that the music might stop and leave her stranded before she could find where it was coming from.

Thirty-five minutes after leaving the flat she arrived at the community centre.

*

Carl Henshawe was the twenty-fourth survivor to arrive. He'd spent much of the day hiding in the back of a builder's van, too afraid to look out. After several hours had passed and nothing had changed he had decided to try and find help. He'd driven the van around aimlessly until it had run out of fuel, spluttered and died. Rather than try and siphon diesel into it, he'd decided to simply take another vehicle. It was while he was changing cars that he heard the music.

Having quickly disposed of its dead driver, Carl arrived at the hall just before daybreak in a luxury company car.

Michael Collins had almost given up. Too afraid to go back home, or to go anywhere he recognised, he sat himself down in the freezing cold in the middle of a park. He decided that it was easier to be alone, to deny what had happened, rather than to face returning to familiar surroundings and risk seeing the bodies of people he'd known. He lay on his back on the wet grass and listened to the gentle babbling of a nearby brook. He was cold, wet, uncomfortable and scared, but the noise of the running water disguised the deathly silence of the rest of the world and, for a while, made it fractionally easier to forget.

The wind blew across the field where he was lying, rustling through the grass and bushes and causing the tops of trees to thrash about almost constantly. Soaked through and shivering, Michael eventually got up and, without any real plan or direction, he slowly walked away from the stream towards the edge of the park. As the sound of running water faded into the distance, so the unexpected strains of music drifted towards him. Marginally interested, though too numb and afraid to really care, he began to walk towards the sound.

Michael was the final survivor to reach the hall.

5

Michael Collins was the last to arrive at the centre, but he was one of the first to get his head together – or, more practically, his stomach. Just before midday, after a morning which had dragged unbearably, he decided it was time to eat. In the main storeroom he found tables, chairs and a collection of camping equipment labelled as belonging to the 4th Whitchurch Scout Group. In a large metal chest he found two gas burners and, next to the chest itself, four half-full gas bottles. In minutes he'd set the burners up on a table and started heating up catering-size tins of vegetable soup and baked beans he'd found in the small kitchen, obviously left over from the last summer's camps. The food was an unexpected and welcome discovery; more than that, actually preparing the meal was a distraction; something to take his mind off the nightmare outside the flimsy walls of the Whitchurch Community Centre.

The rest of the survivors sat in silence in the main hall, some lying curled up on the cold brown linoleum floor, others sitting on the hard plastic chairs with their heads held in their hands. No one spoke. Other than Michael, no one moved. No one even dared to make eye contact with anyone else: twenty-six people who might as well have been in twenty-six different rooms. Twenty-six people who couldn't believe what had happened to the world around them, and who couldn't bear to think about what might happen next. Each one of them had experienced a lifetime's worth of pain, confusion, fear and loss in the last day, and what made their bitter mix of emotions even more unbearable was the complete lack of reason or explanation. Each lonely, frightened person knew as little as the lonely frightened person next to them.

After a while Michael sensed that he was being watched. Out of the corner of his eye he noticed a girl sitting nearby was watching him as she rocked backwards and forwards on a blue plastic chair. Her intense stare made him feel uncomfortable. Though the silence in the hall was almost deafening, making him feel even more desperate and isolated, he didn't actually want to say anything himself. He had a million questions to ask, but he didn't know where to start, so the most sensible option was to stay silent.

The girl got up out of her chair and tentatively walked towards him. She stood there for a moment, about five feet away, before taking a step closer and clearing her throat.

'I'm Emma,' she said quietly, 'Emma Mitchell.'

He looked up at her, then looked down at the pans again without responding.

'Anything I can do?' she asked.

Michael shook his head and stared into the soup he was stirring. He watched the chunks of vegetable spinning around in the liquid and wished that she'd go away. He really didn't want to start a conversation, he decided, because a conversation would inevitably mean talking about what had happened to the rest of the world outside, and right now that was the very last thing he wanted to think about. Problem was, it was all he could think about.

'Shall I try and find some mugs?' Emma mumbled. She was damn sure she wasn't going to let him ignore her. He was the only person in the room who had done anything all morning, so logic and reason dictated that he was the person it would be most worth trying to start a conversation with. Emma was finding the silence, the lack of communication, so stifling that she'd almost got up and walked out – she'd have done it if she hadn't been so scared.

Michael looked up again. He guessed she wasn't going to go away. 'I found some mugs in the stores,' he mumbled. 'Thanks anyway.'

'No problem.'

After another long and uncomfortable pause, he said, 'I'm Michael. Look, I'm sorry but . . .' He stopped speaking because he didn't know what he was trying to say.

Emma, understanding, nodded dejectedly and was about to walk away when he suddenly realised that he wanted her to stay.

The thought of that stunted conversation ending before it had really started forced him to make an effort, to do something to keep her at the table with him. 'I'm sorry,' he said again, 'it's just with everything that's . . . I mean, I don't know why I—'

'I hate soup,' Emma grunted, deliberately interrupting and steering the conversation into safer, neutral waters. 'Especially vegetable. Christ, I can't stand bloody vegetable soup!'

'Nor me,' Michael admitted. 'Hope someone likes it though. There're four more tins of it in there.'

As quickly as it had begun, the brief dialogue ended and the silence returned. There just wasn't anything safe to say. Small talk felt inappropriate; neither of them wanted to talk about what had happened, but they knew that they couldn't avoid it.

Emma took a deep breath and tried again.

'Were you far from here when it—?'

Michael shook his head.

'A couple of miles. I spent most of yesterday just wandering around. I only live about twenty minutes away, but I've been all over town.' He stirred the soup again and then felt obliged to ask her the same question back.

'My place is just the other side of the park,' she replied. 'I spent yesterday in bed.'

'In bed?'

She nodded and leant up against the wall. 'Didn't seem to be much else to do. I just put my head under the covers and pretended that nothing had happened. Until I heard the music, that was.'

'Stroke of genius, playing that music.'

Michael ladled a generous serving of soup into a mug and handed it to Emma. She picked up a plastic spoon from the table and poked at it for a second before tentatively tasting a mouthful. She didn't feel like eating; she hadn't even thought about food since her aborted shopping trip yesterday morning.

A couple of the other survivors were looking their way. Michael didn't know whether it was the food that was attracting their attention or the fact that he and Emma were talking.

Whatever the reason, the two of them communicating had acted like a slow-release valve of sorts. As he watched, more and more of the shell-like survivors began to show signs of life.

Half an hour later, the food had been eaten and there were now two or three conversations taking place around the hall. Small groups of people huddled together while others remained alone. Some talked (with obvious relief on their faces) while others cried; the sound of sobbing could clearly be heard over the muted discussions.

Emma and Michael stayed together, talking sporadically. Michael learned that Emma was a medical student. Emma learned that Michael worked with computers. Michael, she discovered, lived alone. His parents had recently moved to Edinburgh with his two younger brothers. She told him that she'd chosen to study in Northwich, and that her family lived in a small village on the east coast. Neither of them could bring themselves to talk about their families in any detail. Neither knew if any of the people they loved were still alive.

'What did this?' Michael asked. He'd tried to ask the question a couple of times before but hadn't quite managed to force the words out. He knew that Emma couldn't answer, but it helped just to have asked.

She shrugged her shoulders.

'Don't know, some kind of virus perhaps?'

'But how could it have killed so many people? And so quickly?'

'No idea.'

'Christ, I watched thirty kids die in front of me, how could anything . . .'

She was staring at him.

He stopped talking.

'Sorry,' he mumbled.

'It's okay.'

Another awkward pause followed.

'You warm enough?' Michael eventually asked.

Emma nodded. 'I'm okay.'

'I'm freezing. Did you know there are holes in the walls of this place? I stood in one corner this morning and I pushed the bloody walls apart! It wouldn't take much to bring this place down.'

'That's reassuring, thanks.'

Michael shut up quickly, regretting his clumsy words. The last thing anyone wanted to hear was how vulnerable they were in this hall – it might be shabby, ramshackle and draughty, but today it was all they had. There were countless stronger and safer buildings nearby, but no one wanted to take a single step outside the front door, for fear of what they might find there.

Michael watched as Stuart Jeffries and another man (whose name he thought was Carl) sat in deep conversation in the far corner of the room, talking with a third person who was hidden from view. He watched them intently, sensing that frustrations were beginning to come to the surface. Their body language had changed and the volume of their voices was increasing. Less than five minutes ago they'd been mumbling quietly, privately. Now every survivor could hear every word of what was being said.

'No way! I'm not going out there yet,' Stuart said, his voice strained and tired. 'What's the point? What's outside?'

The man hidden in the shadows replied, 'So what else are we going to do? How long can we stay here? It's cold and uncomfortable in here. We've got no food and no supplies and we've got to go out if we're going to survive. Besides, we need to know what's happening out there. For all we know we could be shut away in here with help just around the corner—'

'We're not going to get any help,' Stuart argued.

'How do you know?' Carl asked. His voice was calm, but there was obvious irritation and frustration in his tone. 'How the hell can you be sure no one's going to help us? We won't know anything until we go out there and look.'

'I'm not going out.'

'Yes, we've already established that,' the hidden man sighed. 'You're going to stay in here until you starve to death—'

'Don't get smart – don't you get smart with me!'

Michael sensed that the friction in the corner might be about to turn violent. He didn't know whether to get involved or keep out of the way.

'I know what you're saying, Stuart,' Carl said cautiously,

trying to calm him down, 'but we need to do *something*. We can't just sit here and wait indefinitely.'

Stuart struggled to respond, but unable to find the words to express how he was feeling, instead he began to cry, and the fact that he couldn't contain his emotions made him even angrier. He wiped away his tears with the back of his hand, hoping that the others hadn't noticed, knowing full well that everyone had.

'I just don't want to go out there,' he cried, forcing his words out between stifled sobs. 'I don't want to see it all again. I want to stay here.'

With that he got up, shoving his chair back across the floor, and left the room. The sudden noise as the chair clattered against the radiator made everyone look up.

'The whole world's falling apart,' Michael said under his breath as he watched the little scene.

'What do you mean, "falling apart"?' Emma asked quietly. 'It's already happened. There's nothing left. This is it.'

He looked around at his miserable surroundings and the terrified people here with him and he knew she was right.

6

Dead, cold and empty inside. Carl sat alone in a dark corner of a storeroom with his head in his hands, weeping for his wife and daughter. They'd been his purpose for existing, the reason he'd gone to work every day; the reason he'd come home every evening. He'd been devoted to them in a way he'd never thought possible, and now, without any reason, warning or explanation, they were gone, taken from him in the blink of an eye, and there was nothing he could have done about it. He hadn't even been able to hold them when they'd died. When they'd needed him most, he'd been miles away.

Outside in the main hall he could hear the pitiful cries of other people who had also lost everything. He could almost taste their anger, frustration and complete bewilderment, hanging in the air like the stench of rotting flesh. In the arguing voices he could hear the raw pain that was tearing apart every one of these desperate people.

When the noise became too much to stand he dragged himself up onto his feet with the intention of leaving, but the thought of the thousands of lifeless bodies lying in the streets outside stopped him. The day was almost over and the light would soon disappear. The idea of being in the open was bad enough, but to be out there in the dark, wandering aimlessly with only the dead for company, that was too much to even consider.

Shards of brilliant orange sunlight trickled into the building above his head, dappling the wall behind him with unexpected, almost fluorescent colour. Curious about the source of the light, he looked up and saw a narrow skylight. He pulled over a small wooden table, lifted a heavy metal box on top to give him extra height, and climbed up and forced the skylight open. He stood up straight, squeezed his head, shoulders and arms through the gap, then lifted himself up and scrambled out onto a flat asphalt roof.

A bitter wind buffeted him as he stood exposed on the ten-foot-square area of roof. From the furthest edge he could see out over the main road into the dead city beyond. He followed the route of the road as it forked away to the left, heading in the general direction of Hadley, the small suburb where he had lived and where the bodies of his partner and child lay together in bed. In his mind he could still picture them both, frozen in lifelessness, their faces stained with dark, drying blood - and suddenly the icy wind seemed to blow even colder. For a while he considered driving back home. The very least they deserved was a proper burial, some dignity. The pain he felt inside was unbearable.

After a while he looked across at the rest of the city – in the far distance thick palls of dirty black smoke stretched up into the orange evening sky as unchecked fires raged. As he watched the smoke climb relentlessly, Carl's wandering mind came up with countless explanations as to how those fires could have started: fractured gas mains, perhaps, or a crashed petrol tanker, maybe even a dead body that had fallen too close to a heater. He knew that it was a pointless exercise, but thinking about such insignificancies helped him to forget about Gemma and Sarah for a while.

He was about to go back inside when one of the bodies in the road below caught his eye. He didn't know why, because it was unremarkable in the midst of the confusion and carnage. The corpse was a teenage boy who had fallen and smashed his head against a kerb stone. His neck was broken, twisted round at an unnatural angle, and his glazed eyes were still staring up into the sky. It was as if he was searching for explanations. Carl felt almost as if the boy was asking him what had happened, why he'd died. The poor kid looked so frightened and alone. Carl couldn't look into his face for more than a couple of seconds.

He went back inside, and the cold and uncomfortable community hall suddenly felt like the safest and warmest place in the world.

7

The power died. When Stuart went to turn on the lights, nothing happened. Michael pressed his face up against one of the windows and saw that the street lamps were out too. They'd expected it to happen sooner or later, but they'd all hoped it would have been later. Much later.

Carl found the others sitting in a group in one corner of the main hall, the darkness bringing them together for the first time. Some sat on chairs and benches, whilst others huddled together on the hard linoleum floor. The group was gathered around a single gas lamp, and a quick headcount revealed that he was the only absentee. Some of the poor, bewildered souls glanced up at him as he approached. Feeling suddenly self-conscious (but knowing that he had no reason to care) he sat down at the nearest edge of the group between two women. He'd been trapped in the same building as them for the best part of a day and yet he didn't even know their names. He knew very little about anyone, and they knew as little about him. As much as he might need their closeness and contact, he found the distance between the individual survivors strangely welcome.

A man called Ralph Bennett was trying to address the group. From his manner and the precise, thoughtful way he spoke, Carl assumed he'd been a barrister or a solicitor until the world had been turned upside down yesterday morning.

'What we must do,' Ralph said, clearly, carefully, and with almost ponderous consideration, 'is get ourselves into some sort of order here before we even think about exploring outside.'

'Why?' someone asked from the other side of the group. 'What do we need to get in order?'

'We need to know who and what we've got here.'

'Why?' the voice asked again. 'We can get everything we need outside. We shouldn't waste our time in here. We just need to get out and get on with it.'

Ralph's confidence was clearly a professional façade and, at the first sign of any resistance, he squirmed awkwardly. He pushed his heavy-rimmed glasses back up the bridge of his nose with the tip of his finger and took a deep breath.

'That's not a good idea. Look, I think we've got to make our personal safety and security our prime concern and then . . .'

'I agree,' the voice interrupted again, 'but why stop here? There are a thousand and one better places to go, why stay here? What makes you any safer here than if you were lying on the dotted white line in the middle of the Stanhope Road?'

Carl shuffled around so that he could see through the mass of heads and bodies to identify the speaker. It was Michael, the bloke who had cooked the soup earlier.

'We don't know what's going to happen outside—' Ralph began.

'But we've got to go out there eventually, you accept that?'

He stammered and fiddled with his glasses again. 'Yes, but . . .'

'Look, Ralph, I'm not trying to make this any more difficult than it already is, but we're not going to gain anything from just sitting here.'

Ralph couldn't answer. It was obvious to Carl that he didn't want to go out for precisely the same reason Stuart Jeffries had admitted to earlier. They were both scared.

'We could try and find somewhere else,' he said reluctantly, 'but we've got a shelter here which is secure and—'

'And cold and dirty and uncomfortable,' Carl quickly added.

'Okay, it's not ideal but—'

'But what?' pressed Michael. 'It seems to me we can have our pick of anywhere and anything we want at the moment.'

The room fell ominously silent. Ralph suddenly sat up straight and adjusted his glasses. He thought he'd found a reason to justify staying put. 'But what about the music and the fire?' he said, much more animated. 'Stuart and Jack managed to bring us all here by lighting the fire and playing music. If we did it again we might find more survivors. There may already be people on their way to us.'

'I don't think so,' said Michael. 'No one's arrived here since me. If anyone else had heard the music they'd have been here by now. I agree with what you're saying, but again, why here? Why not find somewhere better to stop, get ourselves organised there and light a bloody huge bonfire where more people will have a chance of seeing it?'

Carl agreed. 'He's right. We should get a beacon or something sorted, but let's get ourselves safe and secure first.'

'A new beacon somewhere else is going to be seen by more people, isn't it?' asked Sandra Goodwin, a fifty-year-old housewife. 'And isn't that what we want?'

'Bottom line here,' Michael said, changing his tone and raising his voice slightly so that everyone suddenly turned and gave him their full attention, 'is that we've got to look after ourselves first and foremost, and then start to think about anyone else who might still be alive.'

'But shouldn't we start looking for other survivors now?' someone else asked.

'I don't think we should,' he replied. 'I agree we should get a beacon or something going, but there's no point us wasting time actively looking for other people yet. If there are others out there, they'll have more chance of finding us than we'll have finding them.'

'Why do you say that?' Sandra asked.

'Stands to reason. Does anyone know how many people used to live in this city?'

'About a quarter of a million – two hundred thousand or something like that,' someone answered.

'And there are twenty-six of us in here.'

'So?' said Ralph, who was looking increasingly uncomfortable after losing control of the conversation.

'So what does that say to you?'

He didn't respond.

'It says to me,' Michael continued, 'that looking for anyone else would be like looking for a needle in a haystack.'

Carl picked up where Michael had left off. 'There's nothing out there,' he said, looking from left to right at the faces gathered around him. He glanced across the room and made momentary eye contact with Michael. 'The only people I've seen moving since all of this began are sitting here. We don't know how widespread this is. We might be all that's left—'

Ralph interrupted, 'Come on, stop talking like that. You're not doing anyone any good talking like that—'

Michael broke in again. 'Since this started have any of you heard a plane or helicopter pass overhead?'

No one replied.

'The airport's five miles south of here; if there were any planes flying we'd have heard them. There's a train station that links the city to the airport and the track runs along the other side of the Stanhope Road. Anyone heard any trains?'

Silence.

'If this was the only region affected,' he continued, 'logic says that help would have arrived by now.'

'What are you saying?' a man called Tim asked quietly, unsure if he really wanted to hear the answer.

Michael looked at him. 'I guess I'm saying that this is a national disaster at the very least. The lack of air traffic makes me think that it could be worse than that.'

An awkward murmur of stark realisation rippled through the group.

'Michael's right,' Emma said. 'This thing spread so quickly. There's no way of knowing what kind of area's been affected. It happened so fast I doubt whether anything could have been done to stop it spreading before it was too late.'

'But this area might be too infected to travel to,' Tim said, his voice strained and frightened. 'They might have sealed Northwich off.'

'They might have,' Michael agreed, 'but I don't think that's very likely, do you? We'd have heard something.'

Tim said nothing.

'So what do we do?' a hesitant voice asked from the middle of the group.

'I think we should get away from here,' Michael said. 'Look, I'm just thinking about myself. The rest of you should make up your own minds. I'm just not prepared to sit here and wait for help when I'm pretty sure it's never going to come. I don't want to be trapped in here for days surrounded by thousands of rotting bodies. I want out.'

8

Michael was exhausted, but he couldn't sleep. When he did finally manage to slip into unconsciousness he slept for only a few minutes before jolting awake, feeling worse than ever. He'd been lying in a draught on the floor and now every bone in his body ached. He wished he hadn't bothered.

The community centre was freezing cold this morning. He was fully clothed, and had a thick winter jacket wrapped around him, but the air was still bitter. He hated everything at the moment, but he quickly decided that he hated this time of day most of all. It was still dark, and in the shadows he thought he could see a thousand shuffling shapes where, in reality, there were none. His head was spinning. He couldn't think about anything other than what had happened to the world outside. Everything had been affected. He couldn't bear to think about his family because he didn't know if they were still alive. He couldn't think about his work and career because they didn't exist any more. He couldn't think about going out with his friends at the weekend, because those friends were most probably dead too, lying face-down on a street corner somewhere, and the places they'd have gone to were silent and empty. He couldn't think about his favourite television programmes, because there were no channels still broadcasting and no electricity to power any TVs. He couldn't even whistle his favourite songs any more. It hurt too much to remember, to feel emotions that had been gone for just a couple of days and now appeared to be lost for ever. In desperation he simply stared into the darkness and tried hard to concentrate on listening to the silence. He thought that by deliberately filling his head with nothing the pain might go away.

It didn't work. It didn't matter which direction he stared in, all he could see were other equally desperate faces staring back at him through the darkness. Everyone was suffering from the same insomnia.

The first rays of morning sunlight were beginning to edge into the room, slipping in slowly through a series of small rectangular windows along the top of the longest wall of the main hall. Each one of the windows was protected on the outside by a layer of heavy-duty wire mesh, and each window had also been covered in random layers of spray-paint by countless vandals through the years. Michael found it strange and unnerving to think that every single one of those vandals was almost certainly dead now.

He didn't want to move, but he had to: he was desperate to use the toilet. He had to summon up the courage and energy to actually get up and go there. He didn't want to wake any of the fortunate few survivors who had actually managed to get some sleep. The hall was so quiet that, no matter how careful he tried to be, every single footstep he took would probably be heard by everyone. The state of the toilets themselves didn't help. The urinals were overflowing and the group had been forced to use a small chemical toilet which someone had found amongst the Scouts' supplies instead. Even though it had been in use for less than a day it already stank: a noxious combination of strong chemical detergent and stagnating human waste.

He couldn't put it off any longer; he had to go. He tried unsuccessfully to make the short journey a little easier by convincing himself that the sooner he was up the sooner it would be done and he would be back. Strange that in the face of the enormity of the disaster outside, even the easiest everyday task suddenly became an impossible mountain to climb.

Grabbing hold of a nearby wooden bench with his outstretched right hand, he hauled himself up onto unsteady feet. For a few seconds he did nothing except stand still and try to get his balance. He shivered in the cold and then took a few stumbling steps through the half-light towards the toilets. He was only twenty-nine, for Christ's sake. Why did he feel at least fifty years older this morning?

Outside the toilet he paused and took a deep breath before opening the door. He glanced to his right. For a moment he was sure that he could see something outside through the small square window at the side of the main entrance door. He froze. Yes – he could definitely see movement.

Ignoring the dull pain in his bladder, Michael pressed his face hard against the dirty glass and peered out through the layers of spray-paint and mesh. He squinted into the light.

There it was again.

Instantly forgetting about the temperature, his aching bones and his full bladder, he unlocked the door and shoved it open. He burst out into the cold morning and sprinted the length of the car park, stopping at the edge of the road. There, on the other side of the street, he saw a man walking slowly away from the community centre.

'What's the matter?' a voice asked suddenly, startling Michael. It was Stuart Jeffries. He and another three survivors had heard him open the door and, naturally concerned, had followed him out.

'Over there,' Michael replied, pointing towards the figure in the near distance and taking a few more steps forward. 'Hey,' he shouted, hoping to attract his attention before he disappeared, 'hey you!'

No response.

Michael quickly glanced at the other four survivors before turning and running after the man. Within a few seconds he had caught up with the sluggish figure, who was dragging his feet along rather than lifting them – maybe they were injured?

'Hey, mate,' he shouted, 'didn't you hear me?'

The man continued to walk away.

Michael ran after him. 'Hey,' he said again, this time a little louder, 'are you all right? I saw you walking past and—' As he spoke he reached out and grabbed hold of the man's arm.

The moment Michael applied any force the figure stopped moving, instantly, and stood still, leaning forward and swaying unsteadily, as if he didn't even know that Michael was there. Perhaps it was shock? Maybe what had happened to the rest of the world had been too much for this poor soul to deal with?

'Leave him,' shouted one of the other survivors, 'get back inside!'

Michael wasn't listening. Instead he slowly turned the man

around so that he could look into his face. 'Fuck . . .' was all he could say as he found himself staring into the glazed and unfocused eyes of a corpse. It defied all logic, but there was absolutely no doubt in his suddenly terrified mind that the man standing in front of him was dead. His skin was pale, ashen grey with a yellow-green tinge and, like all the other cadavers he'd seen lying in the streets, he had traces of dried blood around his mouth, on his chin and throat.

Repulsed, in shock, Michael let go of the lifeless man's arm and stumbled backwards. He tripped and fell over another body, then watched from the gutter as the figure staggered off again, still moving desperately slowly, as if it had lead in its boots.

'Michael,' Stuart yelled from the entrance to the car park, 'get back inside now, we're closing the door!'

Michael scrambled to his feet and sprinted back to the others. All around him he could see more figures moving. It was obvious from their slow, unsteady gait, like the first man he'd seen, these people weren't survivors either.

By the time he'd made it back to the car park the others had already disappeared back into the community centre. He was vaguely aware of them yelling at him to come inside, but in his panic and disbelief their voices failed to register. He stopped and stood staring out towards the main road, transfixed by the impossible sight he now saw in front of him.

About a third of the bodies were moving now. Roughly one in every three of the corpses that had littered the streets around the community centre had become mobile again. Had they not been dead to start with? Had they just been in a coma, or something similar? A thousand unanswerable questions began to flood his brain . . .

'For Christ's sake, get inside!' a voice hoarse with fear yelled again from the hall.

As if to prove a point, the corpse on the ground nearest to Michael began to move. Beginning at the outermost tip of the fingers on its outstretched right hand, the body started to stretch and to tremble. As he stared at it in silent incredulity, the fingers began to claw at the ground and then, seconds later, the entire hand was moving. The movement spread steadily along one arm and then, with an almighty shudder, the body lifted itself up, falling back down several times, unable to support its own weight. It tripped and stumbled like a newborn animal as it finally raised itself up onto its unsteady feet. Once upright it simply staggered away, passing within a yard of where Michael stood. The bloody thing didn't even realise he was there. Terrified, he turned and ran back inside.

The news spread quickly to all the survivors. Carl, refusing to believe what he'd heard, clambered out onto the flat roof that he'd stood on last night.

It was true. As incredible as that was, some of the bodies were moving. He stood and surveyed the same desperate scene he'd looked out over less than twelve hours earlier and saw that many of the corpses he'd previously noticed had now disappeared. He looked down at the place on the ground where the boy with the broken neck had died.

There was nothing. The boy was gone.

9

For what felt like forever, no one dared to move. The group of survivors, shell-shocked and numb from all that they had already been through, stood together in terror and disbelief as they tried to come to terms with the morning's events. Surprisingly, it was Ralph Bennett, the man who had appeared so authoritative and keen to take control last night, who was now having the most trouble accepting what had happened. He stood in the centre of the room alongside an overweight, middle-aged estate agent called Paul Garner, pleading with Emma, Carl, Michael and Kate James (a primary school teacher in her early forties) not to open the door and go outside again.

'But we have to go back out, Ralph,' Emma said, calmly and quietly. 'We've got to try and find out what's happening to them.'

'I'm not interested,' the flustered, frightened man snapped. 'I don't care what's happening. There's no way I'm going to go out there and risk—'

'Risk what?' Michael interrupted. 'No one's asking you to go outside, are they?'

'Opening that door is enough of a bloody risk in itself,' Paul muttered anxiously. He chewed on the fingers of his left hand as he spoke. 'Keep it shut and keep them out.'

'We can't take any chances by exposing ourselves to those things . . .' Ralph protested.

'Things?' Emma snapped, her voice suddenly full of anger. 'Those things are people – bloody hell, your friends and family could be out there . . .'

'Those bodies have been lying dead on the ground for days!' he yelled, his face just inches from hers.

'How do you know they were dead?' Carl asked, perfectly seriously and calmly. 'Did you check them all? Did you check any of them for a pulse before you shut yourself away in here?'

'You know as well as I do that—'

'Did you?' he asked again.

Ralph reluctantly shook his head.

'And have you ever seen a dead body walk before?'

This time Ralph didn't answer. He turned away and leant against the nearest wall, covering his head and trying to block everything else out.

'Jesus Christ,' Paul cursed, 'of course we've never seen dead bodies walking, but . . .'

'But what?'

'But I've never seen anyone drop to the ground and not move for two days either. Face it, they were all dead.'

'I need to go out there and see if I can find out what's happening and to see if those bodies pose a threat to us,' Michael explained.

'And how will you know?' Ralph demanded, turning around to face the rest of the group again. 'Who's going to tell you if we're in danger?'

For a moment Michael struggled to answer. 'Emma's studied medicine,' he replied, thinking quickly and looking across at her. 'You'll be able to give us some idea, won't you?'

Emma shifted her weight uncomfortably from foot to foot. 'I'll try,' she mumbled. 'I don't know how much use I'll be, but—'

'Can't you see what you're doing?' Ralph protested, taking off his glasses and rubbing his eyes. 'You're putting us all in danger. If you'd just wait for a while and—'

'Wait for what?' Carl interrupted. 'Change the bloody record, will you? Seems to me we're in danger whatever we do. We're sitting here in a hall that we could knock down with our bare hands if we tried hard enough, surrounded by rotting bodies. Staying here sounds pretty risky to me.'

Knowing that the conversation was about to stray into familiar waters, with yet another pointless debate about whether to go outside or not, Michael made his feelings and intentions clear. 'I'm going out,' he said. His voice was quiet, and yet carried an undeniable force. 'Stay in here and hide if you want, but I'm going out, and I'm going out now.'

'For Christ's sake,' Ralph pleaded, 'think about it before you do anything that might—'

Michael didn't stop to hear the end of the sentence; instead he simply turned his back on the others and walked up to the main door out of the community centre. He paused for a second to compose himself. He looked back over his shoulder towards Carl, Emma and Kate. The rest of the group was silent.

'Ready?' he asked. Carl nodded and moved to stand next to him, closely followed by Emma and then Kate. Michael took a deep breath, pushed the door open and stepped out into the bright September sunlight.

It was surprisingly warm. Carl (the only one who had been outside for any length of time recently) noticed that last night's gusting wind had dropped. He shielded his eyes from the sun and watched as Michael cautiously retraced the steps he had taken earlier, walking away from their dilapidated wooden shelter and towards the road. When the first moving body staggered into view he instinctively stopped and turned back to face the others.

'What's the matter?' asked Emma, immediately concerned.

'Nothing,' he mumbled, feeling nervous and unsure.

They stood with their backs to each other in the middle of the road, each facing a different direction. Carl noticed that a crowd had gathered to watch them in the doorway of the community centre.

'So what are we going to do now?' Kate wondered. She was a quiet, roundish woman, and her usually flushed face had suddenly lost much of its colour.

Michael looked around for inspiration. 'Don't know,' he admitted. 'Anyone got any ideas?'

'We need to have a good look at one of them,' Emma whispered.

'What do you mean?' Kate asked. 'What exactly are we supposed to be looking at?'

'Let's try and see how responsive they are. We should see if they can tell us anything.'

While she'd been speaking Michael had taken a few steps further forward. 'What about her?' he asked, pointing at one of the nearest bodies. It had a slow, lopsided walk. 'What about that one?'

They stood together in silence and watched the painful progress of the pitiful creature. The dead woman's movements were tired and stilted. Her arms hung listlessly at her sides. She seemed almost to be dragging her feet behind her.

'What are we going to do with her?' Kate wondered nervously.

'Do you want to get closer and just have a look?' Carl asked.

Michael shook his head. 'No,' he said, 'let's get her inside.'

'What, back in there?' he gasped, gesturing at the building behind them. 'Are you serious?'

'Yes, in there. Is that a problem?'

'Not to me,' said Emma. 'Try convincing the others, though.'

He wasn't concerned. 'I think we should get her indoors and try and make her comfortable. We'll get more out of her if we can get her to relax.'

'Are you sure about this?' muttered Kate. Her nerves were beginning to fray.

Michael nodded. 'I'm sure,' he said, sounding far more confident than he actually was.

'Bloody hell, let's just do it. We're never going to get anywhere standing out here like this, are we?'

That was all Michael needed to hear. He strode up behind the woman, reached out and rested his hands on her shoulders. She stopped moving almost instantly, his light grip enough to restrain her.

Emma jogged the last few steps and circled the body. She looked up into her glazed eyes and saw that they were unfocused and vacant, covered with a slight, milky-white sheen. Her skin was generally pale although she could see occasional deep red veins like crawling spider legs and slowly spreading patches of yellow discolouration. She was sure that the woman couldn't see her, but Emma respectfully tried to hide her mounting revulsion. There was a deep gash on her right temple. Dark, red-black blood had flowed freely from the wound and had drenched her once-smart white blouse and grey business suit. The wound still glistened but much of the blood was dry now.

'We want to help you,' she said softly.

Still no reaction.

Michael gripped the woman's shoulders a little tighter. 'Come on,' he whispered, 'let's get you inside.'

Carl and Kate watched them with morbid fascination.

'What the hell is happening?' Kate asked, her voice becoming noticeably more unsteady each time she spoke.

'No idea,' Carl admitted. 'Bloody hell, I wish I knew.'

He took a step back and trod on the outstretched hand of another corpse, its fingers crunching under his boot. Not all of the bodies had moved. The majority still lay where they had first fallen.

'Carl,' Michael shouted, 'give us a hand, mate. Come and get hold of her legs.'

He walked over towards Emma and Michael, crouched down and grabbed the woman's strangely swollen ankles, one in each hand, and as Michael pulled back on her shoulders, he lifted her feet. She didn't react to being moved.

The two men scuttled back to the community hall, closely followed by Emma and Kate. As they approached the doorway the other survivors realised what was happening and scattered like a shoal of frightened fish that had just been invaded by the deadliest predator shark.

'What the bloody hell are you doing?' Ralph protested as Carl and Michael barged past him carrying the corpse. 'What the hell are you doing bringing that in here?'

Michael didn't answer. He was too busy directing the others. 'Group yourselves around her,' he said authoritatively. 'Try and cage her in.'

Obediently Kate and Emma drew closer, as did another two survivors whose names Michael didn't know. Carl gently lowered the woman's feet to the ground so that she was standing upright again and then took a couple of steps back so that he was level with the others. Once something resembling a circle had been formed, Michael let go of her. Without warning, the body lurched towards Kate, who screwed up her face in nervous trepidation and stretched her arms out in front of her to prevent the dead woman from getting too close. As soon as it made contact with Kate's outstretched hands the body turned and staggered away in the opposite direction, towards another survivor, and then again, repeating the action every time it reached the edge of the circle.

As the creature tripped towards Michael he allowed himself to look deep into its face for the first time. For a dangerous few seconds he was transfixed. A few days ago she might have been attractive, but today her emotionless gaze and discoloured skin immediately dissipated any beauty or serenity that her face had previously known. Her blouse was torn, and her exposed flesh appeared lumpy and bruised. Her mouth hung open – a huge, dark hole – and a thick string of gelatinous, bloody saliva trickled continually down the side of her chin. At the last possible moment he pushed her away.

The corpse turned and began to stagger towards Carl. Clearly unable to control or co-ordinate its own movements, it tripped over its own clumsy feet and half-fell, half-lurched towards him. He recoiled and pushed it down to the ground, feeling a cold sweat prickle his brow as the pathetic creature immediately scrambled back up and moved towards him again.

'Can she hear us?' Kate wondered. She hadn't really meant to ask the question; she'd just been thinking out loud.

'Don't know,' Michael answered.

'She probably can,' Emma said.

'Why do you say that?'

'It's something about the way she reacts.'

Ralph, who had until then been watching nervously from a safe distance, found himself being drawn closer and closer to the circle. 'But she doesn't react,' he said, his voice uncharacteristically light and shaky.

'I know,' Emma continued, 'that's what I mean. She's walking and moving around, but I don't think she knows why or how.'

'It's instinctive,' Carl muttered.

'That's what I'm starting to think,' Emma agreed. 'She probably can hear us, but she doesn't know what the noises we make mean any more.'

'But she reacts when you touch her,' Paul Garner jabbered anxiously.

'No, she doesn't. She doesn't react at all. She turns away because she physically can't keep moving in a certain direction. I bet she'd just keep walking in a straight line for ever if there wasn't anything in her way.'

'Christ, look at her,' Kate mumbled. 'Just look at the poor bitch. How many millions of people are wandering around out there like this?'

'Did you check her pulse?' Michael whispered to Emma who was standing next to him.

'Sort of.'

'What's that supposed to mean?'

'I couldn't find one,' she answered bluntly.

'So what are you saying?'

'I'm not saying anything.'

'So what are you thinking?'

Emma looked across at him. 'That she's dead, I suppose.'

'Get it out of here,' Paul hissed nervously from his vantage point at the far end of the room.

Michael looked around the circle and noticed that the others were all either peering at the ground or gazing at him. Guessing that it was up to him to make the next move, he took a step forward and grabbed hold of the cadaver's cold arm. He pulled it out of the hall and back towards the door, which he opened with his free hand. He pushed it out into the sunlight and watched as it listlessly staggered away from the building.

10

Time dragged unbearably slowly. An hour now felt like five, and five hours more like fifty. As the sun began to sink back below the horizon Carl clambered out of the community centre once again and stood alone on the small area of flat roof he'd discovered the previous evening.

For a moment the air was pure and refreshing, and he took several deep, calming breaths before the now-familiar stench of death and burning buildings quickly returned, blown towards him on a cool, gusty wind. There was a sudden unexpected noise behind him and he turned around to see Michael struggling to climb up through the tiny skylight, hauling himself up on his elbows.

'Did I make you jump?' he asked as he pushed himself out onto the roof. 'Sorry, mate, I didn't mean to. I was looking for you and I saw you disappear up here and . . .'

Carl shook his head and looked away, disappointed that his little sanctuary had been discovered. In the community centre private space was at a premium. They were limited to just a few square feet each. Almost every move that anyone made indoors could be seen by everyone else.

Carl hated it. He'd been looking forward to getting out here and spending some time alone. This small square roof had become the only place so far where he'd been able to stretch, scratch, stamp, scream, punch and cry without having to give a damn about anyone else. Stupid that almost everyone else was dead and yet he still instinctively found himself considering what the last few remaining people left might think of him. The effects of years and years of conditioning by society were going to take more than a few days to fade away.

'You're okay,' he sighed as the other man approached. 'I just came out here to get away for a while.'

'Do you want me to go back inside?' Michael asked anxiously, sensing that he wasn't wanted. 'If you want me to go then I'll . . .'

Carl repeated, 'No, it's okay.'

Glad to know that he wasn't intruding (although not entirely convinced that he really was welcome) Michael walked across to stand next to Carl at the edge of the roof. 'What the bloody hell's happening, mate?' he asked.

'Don't know.'

'Christ, it's just the speed of it all. A few days ago everything was normal, but now . . .'

'I know,' Carl sighed. 'I know.'

The two men stood in silence and surveyed the devastation around them. How could any of this be happening?

'Almost makes you envy them, doesn't it?' Carl said quietly.

'Who?'

'The bodies still lying on the ground. The ones that didn't get up. I can't help thinking how much easier it would have been to be . . .'

'That's a stupid way to talk, isn't it?'

'Is it?'

In the heavy silence that followed Carl thought about his words and Michael's rebuke. Bloody hell, how uncharacteristically defeatist he suddenly sounded. But why not, he thought? Why shouldn't he be? His life had been turned upside down and inside out, and he'd lost everything: not just his possessions and his property, he'd lost *absolutely everything* – and when he thought about poor Sarah and Gemma, lying dead together in their bed at home, the pain he felt became immeasurably worse. But were they still there? Or had they too been affected by this new change? The thought of his beautiful little girl's shell-like corpse walking aimlessly through the dark streets alone was too much to bear. He tried unsuccessfully to hide the tears which streamed freely down his tired face.

'Come on, mate.'

'I'm okay,' Carl replied, again. It was obvious that he wasn't.

'Sure?'

Carl looked into his face. He was about to reply with a standard 'I'm fine,' but he stopped himself. There was no point hiding the truth any more. 'No,' he admitted. 'No, mate, I'm not all right . . .' Suddenly unable to say another word, he found himself sobbing helplessly.

'Me neither,' Michael admitted, wiping tears of desperation and pain from his own eyes.

The two men sat down on the edge of the roof, their feet dangling freely over the side of the building. Michael ran his fingers through his matted hair. He felt dirty. He'd have paid any price to have been able to relax in a hot bath or shower and follow it up with a night spent in a comfortable bed. Or even an uncomfortable bed. Just something better than a hard wooden bench or the cold floor of this ramshackle building.

'You know what we need?' he asked.

'I can think of about a million things that I need,' Carl answered.

'Forget about all the practical and obvious stuff for a minute; do you know what I need more than anything?'

'No, what?'

Michael paused, lay back on the asphalt and put his hands behind his head. 'Booze. I need to get absolutely fucking plastered. I need to drink so much that I can't remember my own name, never mind anything else.'

'There's an off-licence over there,' Carl said, half-smiling and pointing across the main road. 'Fancy a walk?' He glanced down at Michael.

He shook his head. 'No.'

'Christ, look at him,' Carl said suddenly.

Michael sat up.

'Who?'

'That one over there,' he replied, gesturing in the direction of a solitary figure which tripped and stumbled along the edge of the main road. The shadowy shell had once been a man, perhaps six feet tall and probably aged between twenty-five and thirty. It was walking awkwardly, with one foot on the kerb and the other dragging behind in the gutter. It walked into the back of a crashed car.

'What about him?'

Carl shrugged his shoulders.

'Just look at the state of him. That could be you or me, that could.'

'Yes but it isn't.' Michael yawned, about to lie back down again.

'And there's another. See that one in the newsagent's?'

Michael squinted to see.

'Where?'

'The newsagent's with the red sign. Between the pub and the garage . . .'

'Oh yeah, I see it.'

The two men stared at the body in the building. It was trapped in the shop. A display rack had fallen behind it, blocking any backwards movement, and a corpse prevented the door from opening outwards. The body moved incessantly, edging forward then back, edging forward again then stumbling back, repeatedly covering the same small square of space.

'It hasn't got a clue what's happening, has it? You'd think it would just give up.'

'It's moving for the sake of it. It doesn't know how or why it does it.'

'And how long will they keep moving? Bloody hell, when will they stop?'

'Maybe they won't. There isn't any reason to stop, is there? Nothing registers with them any more. Look, watch this.'

Michael stood up and looked around. He walked over to where the slanted roof of the main part of the building met the flat roof of the extension and pulled off a single slate.

Carl watched, bemused, as he walked back to the edge.

'What the hell are you doing?'

'Watch,' Michael said quietly. He waited for a few seconds until one of the wandering bodies came into range. Then, after taking careful aim, he threw the tile at the staggering corpse like a Frisbee. With surprising accuracy he hit the body in the small of the back. It faltered momentarily, but carried on regardless.

'Why did you do that?' Carl asked.

Michael shrugged. 'Just proving a point, I suppose.'

'What point? That you've got good aim?'

'That they don't react. They don't function like you and me; they just exist.'

'So do you think it was a virus that did this to them?' Carl asked. 'Emma seems to think so. Or do you think it was—?'

'Don't know and I don't care.'

'What do you mean, you don't care?'

'What difference does it make? What's happened has happened. It's the old cliché, isn't it? If you get knocked down by a car, does it matter what colour it is?'

'Suppose.'

'It doesn't matter what caused any of this. What's done is done and I can't see the point in wasting time coming up with bullshit theories and explanations when none of it will make the slightest bit of difference. The only thing that any of us have any influence and control over now is what we do tomorrow.'

'So what are we going to do tomorrow?'

'Haven't got a clue!' Michael laughed.

It started to rain. A few isolated spots fell at first, becoming a downpour of almost monsoon proportions in less than a minute. Carl and Michael quickly squeezed back through the skylight and lowered themselves down.

'Does you good to get out now and then, doesn't it?' Carl said sarcastically.

'There's a lot of truth in that, mate,' Michael replied, struggling to make himself heard over the noise of the rain lashing down on the flat roof.

'What?'

'You're right. I think it would do us good to get out. Have you stopped to think about the bodies yet?'

'Christ, I haven't thought about much else . . .'

'No,' Michael said, 'I mean, have you stopped to think about what's going to happen when they really start to rot? Jesus, the air's going to be filled with all kinds of germs.'

'There's not a lot we can do about that, is there?'

'There's fuck-all we can do about it, but we could get out of here.'

'Where to? It's going to be like this everywhere, isn't it?'

'Maybe. Maybe not.'

It became immediately obvious to Carl that Michael had been doing more logical thinking about their position than the rest of the group put together. 'So what would we gain from leaving?'

'Think about it. We're on the edge of a city here. There are hundreds of thousands of bodies around.'

'And . . . ?'

'And I think we should head for the countryside. Fewer bodies means less chance of disease. We're probably not going to be completely safe anywhere, but I think we should try and give ourselves the best possible chance. We should pack up and leave here as soon as we can.'

'You really thinking of going?'

'I'd go tonight if I was ready.'

11

Each member of the fragmented group had reached new depths of emotional and mental exhaustion, but still hardly anyone could sleep. Their increasing fatigue caused the frightened and desperate people to become even more frightened and desperate with each passing minute. The hall was lit only by a few dim gas lamps and the odd torch, and the lack of light compounded the disorientation and fear felt by everyone. By midnight the tensions and frustrations of even the most placid members of the group were running dangerously high.

Jenny Hall, who had held her three-month-old baby boy in her arms as he died on Tuesday morning, had said something which had upset the usually quiet and reserved Stuart Jeffries.

'You stupid fucking bitch,' he screamed, his face an inch from hers, 'what gives you the right to criticise? You're not the only one who's had it hard. Christ, we're all in the same fucking boat here . . .'

Jenny wiped streaming tears from her face with trembling hands. She was shaking with fear. 'I didn't mean to . . .' she stammered. 'I was only trying to—'

'Shut your fucking mouth!' Stuart shouted, grabbing hold of her arms and slamming her back against the wall. 'Just shut your fucking mouth!'

For a second Michael stood and watched, numb, almost unable to comprehend what he was seeing, until a yelp of fear and pain from Jenny forced him into action.

He grabbed hold of Stuart and yanked him away from her, leaving her to slide down the wall and collapse in a sobbing heap. 'What the hell's going on?'

Stuart didn't respond. He stared at the floor, his face flushed red. His fists were clenched tight, his body shaking with anger.

'What's the problem?' Michael asked again.

Stuart still didn't move. 'Not good enough for her, are we?' he eventually said.

'What?'

'That little bitch . . . she thinks she's something special, doesn't she? Thinks she's a cut above the rest of us.' He looked up and pointed at Jenny. 'Thinks she's the only one who's lost everything!'

'You're not making any sense,' Michael said. 'What are you talking about?'

Stuart couldn't – or wouldn't – answer. Tears of frustration welled in his tired eyes. Rather than let Michael see the extent of his fraught emotion he got up and stormed out of the room, slamming the door shut behind him.

'What was all that about?' Emma asked as she walked past Michael and made her way over to where Jenny lay curled in a ball on the ground. She crouched down and put her arm around her shoulders. 'Come on,' she whispered, gently kissing the top of her head, 'it's all right.'

'All right?' she sobbed. 'How can you say it's all right? After everything that's happened, how can it be all right?'

Kate James sat down next to them. Cradling Jenny in her arms, Emma turned to face her.

'Did you see what happened?' she asked.

'Not really,' Kate replied. 'They were just talking. I only realised that something was wrong when Stuart started shouting. He was fine one minute, talking normally, then he just exploded at her.'

'Why?'

Kate raised her eyes to the ceiling. 'Apparently she told him that she didn't like the soup.'

'What?' asked Emma, incredulous.

'She didn't like the soup he'd made,' Kate repeated. 'I'm sure that's all it was.'

'Bloody hell,' she sighed, shaking her head in resignation.

Carl walked into the room with Jack Baynham. He'd taken no more than two or three steps when he stopped, realising that something was wrong.

'What's the matter?' he asked cautiously, almost too afraid to hear the answer. Something terrible must have happened.

Michael shook his head. 'It's nothing,' he said. 'It's sorted now.'

Carl looked down at Emma on the floor, holding Jenny in her arms. Something had obviously happened, but as whatever it was seemed to have been confined to inside the hall and now looked as if it had been resolved, he decided not to ask any more questions. He didn't want to get involved. Selfish and insensitive maybe, but he just didn't want to know. He had enough problems of his own to deal with without getting wrapped up in other people's worries.

Michael felt the same, but he couldn't switch off as easily as Carl. When he heard more crying coming from another corner of the room he went to investigate. Annie Nelson and Jessica Short, two of the eldest survivors, were wrapped under a single blanket, holding each other tightly and doing their best to stop sobbing, to stop drawing attention to themselves.

Michael sat down next to them. 'You two okay?' he asked. A pointless question, maybe, but he couldn't think of anything else to say.

Annie smiled for the briefest of moments, trying hard to put on a brave face. She nonchalantly wiped away a single tear which trickled quickly down her wrinkled cheek. 'We're all right, thank you,' she replied, her voice wobbling a little.

'Can I get you anything?'

Annie shook her head. 'No, we're fine,' she said. 'I think we'll try and get some sleep now.'

Michael smiled and rested his hand on hers. He tried not to let his worry show, but she felt disconcertingly cold and fragile. He felt so sorry for these two. They had been inseparable since arriving at the hall. Jessica was a well-to-do widow who had lived in a large house in one of the most exclusive suburbs of Northwich. Annie, on the other hand, had told him yesterday that she'd lived in the same two-bedroom Victorian terraced house all her life. She'd been born there and, as she'd wasted no time in telling him, she intended to see out the rest of her days there too. When things settled down again, she had naïvely explained, she was going to go straight back home. She had even invited Jessica over for tea one afternoon. She thought it would be nice if they kept in touch after everything was sorted out.

Michael patted the old lady's hand again before he stood up and walked away. He glanced back over his shoulder and watched as the two pensioners huddled closer together, talking in hushed, frightened whispers. Clearly from opposite ends of the social spectrum, they were drawn to each other for no other reason than their similar ages and the fact they were still alive. Money, status, possessions, friends and connections didn't count for anything any more.

Emma was still sitting on the floor two hours later. As half-past two approached she cursed herself for being so bloody selfless. There she was, cold and uncomfortable, still cradling Jenny Hall in her arms. What made matters worse was that Jenny herself had been asleep for the best part of an hour. The building was silent, but for a muffled conversation taking place in one of the dark rooms off the main hall. She carefully eased herself out from underneath Jenny, laid her down on the floor and covered her with the sheet someone had draped over them. In the stillness every sound she made, no matter how slight, seemed deafening. She listened carefully and tried to locate the precise source of the conversation, desperate for some calm and rational adult company.

The voices sounded as if they were coming from a little room that she hadn't been into before. She cautiously pushed the door open and peered inside. It was pitch-black, and the talking stopped immediately.

'Who's that?'

'Emma,' she whispered. 'Emma Mitchell.'

As her eyes slowly became accustomed to the darkness of the room, she saw that there were two men sitting with their backs against the far wall. It was Michael and Carl. They were drinking water from a plastic bottle which they passed between themselves.

'You okay?' Michael asked.

'I'm fine,' Emma replied. 'Mind if I come in?'

'Not at all,' said Carl. 'Everything calmed down out there?'

She stepped into the room, tripping over his outstretched legs and feeling for the wall. She sat down carefully. 'It's all quiet,' she said. 'I just had to get away, know what I mean?'

'Why do you think we're sitting in here?' Michael asked rhetorically.

After a brief silence Emma spoke again. 'I'm sorry,' she said apologetically, sensing that she was in the way, 'have I interrupted something? Did you two want me to go so you can . . . ?'

'Stay here as long as you like,' Michael answered.

'I think everyone's asleep out there now. At least if they're not asleep they're quiet. I guess they're all thinking about what happened today. I've just sat and listened to Jenny going on about . . .' Emma realised she was talking for the sake of talking and let her words trail away into nothing.

Both Michael and Carl were staring at her. 'What's the matter?' she asked, suddenly self-conscious. 'What's wrong?'

Michael gave a wry grimace. 'Bloody hell, have you been out there with Jenny all this time?'

She nodded. 'Yes, why?'

'Nothing – I just don't know why you bother, that's all.'

'Someone's got to do it, haven't they?' she replied dismissively as she took the bottle of water from Carl.

'So why does it have to be you? Christ, who's going to sit up with you for hours when you're . . .'

'Like I said,' she snapped, 'someone's got to do it. If we all shut ourselves away in rooms like this when things aren't going well then we haven't got much of a future here, have we?'

'So do you think we've got a future here then?' Carl asked.

Now Emma really was beginning to feel uncomfortable. She hadn't come in here to be interrogated. 'Of course we've got a future.'

'We've got millions of people lying dead in the streets around us and we've got people threatening to kill each other because someone doesn't like soup. Doesn't bode well really, does it?' Michael mused.

'So what do you think?' Emma asked. 'You seem to have an opinion on everything. Do you reckon we've got any chance here, or do you think we should just curl up in the corner and give up?'

'I think we've got a damn good chance, but not here.'

'Where then?'

'What exactly have we got here?'

Emma began to answer before Michael interrupted, 'I'll tell you: we've got shelter, we've got limited supplies and we've got access to what's left of the city. We've also got an unlimited supply of dead bodies, some of them mobile, all of them rotting. You agree?'

She thought for a moment, then nodded.

'And I suppose,' he continued, 'there's also the flipside of the coin. As good a shelter as this is, it's fast becoming a prison. We've got no idea what's around us. We don't even know what's in the buildings on the other side of the street. We've lost the power now, and that's only going to make things worse.'

'But isn't it going to be the same wherever we go?'

'Possibly. Carl and I were talking earlier about heading out into the country, and the more I think about it the more it seems to make sense.'

'Why?'

Carl explained the conversation he'd had with Michael. 'The population was concentrated in cities, wasn't it? There will be fewer bodies out in the sticks. And fewer bodies equals fewer problems . . .'

'Hopefully,' Michael added cautiously.

'So what's stopping us?' Emma asked.

'Nothing.'

'So are you going?'

'Looks like it.'

'And what if no one else wants to leave?'

'Then I'll go on my own.'

'When?'

'As soon as I can.'

Emma had to admit that as arrogant and infuriatingly superior as he sounded, Michael's reasoning made sense. The more she thought about his proposals, the more she realised he was right.

12

Ralph heard it first: a sudden loud banging on the entrance door, the relentless thump, thump, thump of someone or something trying to get inside. It shattered the early morning silence. He jumped up from where he'd been trying unsuccessfully to sleep in the corner of the community centre kitchen and ran the full length of the building away from the noise, putting as much distance as possible between himself and whatever it was outside. In the miserable grey half-light he fell over Jack Baynham's sleeping bulk and skidded across the cluttered floor, landing on top of someone else who yelped with pain.

'What the hell are you doing?' Jack shouted. 'You fucking idiot, you could have—'

He stopped speaking when he heard the hammering on the door. By now others had heard it too, and those who hadn't had been awakened by the shouting. Carl, Michael and Emma cautiously emerged from the storeroom where they'd spent the night.

'Listen . . .' Carl said, and he began to move forward, following Jack who was creeping towards the door.

Emma held back. She looked over her shoulder at Michael who stood in the doorway, his face half-hidden by shadows. 'What is it?'

'How am I supposed to know?'

'Do you think it's one of them?'

'Emma, I don't know . . .'

'But it could be, couldn't it? What if they've found us? What if they know where we are?'

He looked at her and lifted his finger to his lips. Suddenly self-conscious, she realised that other people around them were also starting to react. They were already frightened by the raised voices and the noise at the other end of the building, and she knew it wouldn't take much to tip them over the edge and start a full-scale panic. People were at breaking point; she'd seen that for herself last night.

Michael gently pushed past her, pausing only to whisper in her ear. 'There's only one way to find out . . .'

By the time he'd reached the door, Carl and Jack were already there. Kate James stood a short distance back and watched as Jack stood to one side and cautiously pressed his face against the narrow window at the side of the door.

'See anything?'

'There's only one of them.'

'You sure?'

'Think so. I think there's—' He jumped back in surprise when the figure outside saw him and reacted. Before he could get out of the way it moved across to the window and began hitting the glass. Carl crept closer as Jack moved away, and then the noise stopped. The figure outside stood still and leant against the window, covering its eyes to try and see inside.

Then it spoke. 'Help me.'

The words, muffled by the door, were only just loud enough to be heard. Carl and Kate looked at each other in disbelief. Carl couldn't make sense of what was happening.

'They can talk?'

Kate barged him out of the way and unlocked the door.

'Careful!' Paul Garner hissed, peering out from the other end of the entrance corridor.

'You bloody idiots,' she said as she struggled with the lock, 'she's not one of them, she's like us. She's still alive!'

She threw the door open and stood back as a teenage girl stumbled into the community centre. Kate caught her and sat her down as her legs buckled beneath her. She was freezing cold, and her dirty clothes were soaked with rain. Her face was ghostly pale and her wide eyes darted around the many faces which were suddenly staring back. Carl slammed the door shut, pausing only to do a double-take as another figure appeared at the mouth of the car park. It walked slowly and awkwardly, and was out of sight again in a matter of seconds, oblivious to the watchers in the hall.

'What's your name, sweetheart?' Kate asked, crouching down in front of the girl.

'Ronnie— Ver— Veronica . . .'

Someone passed her a blanket, which she wrapped around the girl's shoulders.

'How long have you been out there?'

'Not long,' she replied, still shivering with the cold, but beginning to regain her composure slightly. She took a drink from Emma and tried to sip it, but her hands were shaking too much.

Kate held it steady for her.

'And are you on your own?'

Veronica nodded. 'I was with my sister, but she died when everyone else did. I left her outside the flat, but she's gone now . . .'

'So how did you know we were here?' Jack asked, sounding distinctly less sympathetic than Kate.

'Been watching you.'

'Watching us? How?'

'Over the road. I live in one of the flats above the shops over the road. I heard your music and saw you come in here, then I saw what happened outside yesterday when they started to get up . . .'

'Why didn't you come sooner?' asked Kate. 'Why wait over there on your own?'

'I was too scared. Didn't want to go outside.'

'So why are you here now?' Jack demanded. 'What's changed?'

For a few seconds Veronica didn't answer, staring instead at the floor between her feet. Then she slowly lifted her head and looked straight at him. 'They're coming.'

'What?'

'Loads of them . . . hundreds, maybe . . . they're coming . . .'

Jack's reaction was lost in the sudden wave of hysteria which swept through the building. Veronica's unexpected arrival had woken almost all of the group and most of them had gathered close to the entrance corridor to find out what was happening. Just about everyone had heard what she'd said.

'Who's coming?' Carl asked anxiously, fighting to make himself heard.

'Those people. The sick people. The ones that got up . . .'

'Where?'

'Out on the road. You can't go out there . . . there's hundreds of them.'

'Oh Christ,' Ralph wailed, 'that's it, we're finished now. Once they find out we're here we'll be surrounded.'

'Don't talk crap,' Michael said angrily.

'They probably already know,' Stuart shouted. 'That stupid little cow has led them straight to us!'

'You shouldn't have come here,' Paul Garner yelled.

Veronica stared unblinking at the wall in front of her. Michael, furious, watched the situation deteriorate with incredible speed. Even Kate had backed away from the girl.

'She hasn't done anything wrong,' Emma said. 'This isn't fair. She was on her own; what else was she supposed to do?'

Michael shook his head. 'Don't waste your breath. They're not going to listen.'

'But it's not fair . . .'

'Leave it.'

'Kick her out!' another voice hissed from the shadows.

Veronica looked up at Kate, terrified. 'Don't . . .' she began to say.

'She's not going anywhere,' Emma said, her voice almost completely drowned out by noise.

Carl walked back towards the door. Everyone was so preoccupied with their pointless arguments and finger-pointing that no one noticed when he checked the window, turned the key in the lock and threw the door open. The car park was empty. The noise was suddenly silenced.

'See? There's *nothing* there. No one's following anyone. You're a bunch of fucking idiots, scared of your own shadows.'

'They're not here,' Veronica said quietly, 'they're out on the road . . .'

'Shut the door,' Ralph shouted. 'Shut the bloody door before someone sees us . . .'

Ignoring him, Carl turned and looked at Michael and Jack, who were both standing nearby. 'What do you reckon?'

Michael swallowed, his mouth suddenly dry. 'We should go and see what she's talking about. We can outrun them. If there's a problem we'll just turn around and leg it back here.'

‘Think she’s telling the truth?’ Jack asked.

‘She’s got no reason to lie, has she? Christ, anything’s possible at the moment.’

‘But yesterday they couldn’t even *see* us . . . they didn’t even know we were there . . .’

‘The day before that they were lying dead on the ground,’ Jack added unhelpfully.

‘Tell us again,’ Michael said to Veronica, ‘what exactly did you see outside?’

Tears of fear rolled down her cheeks and she started sobbing. She shook as she tried to explain.

The frightened crowd still hovered around her, some trying to move away, others coming closer to hear more. Emma pushed the nearest of them back, giving the girl space to breathe.

‘I noticed them last night,’ she began, sniffing as she spoke, still not taking her eyes off the open door. ‘There was a crowd of them out in the road but I didn’t think anything of it. I woke up and went to the window about an hour ago and there was loads of them there – hundreds—’

‘Doing what?’

She stopped, surprised by Michael’s question, not knowing exactly how to answer, then started, ‘Nothing . . . just standing there . . . just waiting . . . I think they know we’re around here—’

The noise from the frightened group increased in volume again as the girl’s words were passed from person to person in nervous whispers.

‘I’m going to have a look,’ Michael said. He moved towards the door. Veronica got up and backed away, and several others scurried for cover.

‘Don’t be fucking stupid,’ Stuart Jeffries shouted from the main hall. ‘Don’t go out there.’

‘I saw one of them when the door was first open,’ Carl said, his voice quiet enough to be heard only by Michael and Jack, ‘and it looked the same as yesterday. If they were out to get us, it would have reacted, wouldn’t it?’

‘You’d have thought so,’ Michael replied.

‘Go out there and I’ll lock the bloody door behind you,’ Stuart threatened, barging his way along the corridor. 'You're not coming back in here once it's shut.'

'Grow up and get a grip, Stuart,' Carl said. Michael took a few steps outside, then stopped. Stuart shoved Carl out after him then slammed the door and locked it.

'Stuart!' Emma protested, 'You can't—'

'What happens to them is their fucking problem. No one asked them to go out. If they want to risk their own necks then that's their problem. I'm not taking any chances.'

'Fucking hell,' Carl cursed as they left the car park and neared the junction with the Stanhope Road. 'Would you just look at that . . . ?'

Michael stopped and stood transfixed in the middle of the road, his heart pounding. Up ahead of them, a couple of hundred yards away at most, was a huge crowd of bodies, just as the girl had said. The early morning gloom made it difficult to estimate how many of them were there. They stood their ground: a tightly packed, incalculable number of figures which looked in the low light to have become a single solid dark shape.

'Jesus Christ,' Carl said, 'there're hundreds of them.'

'Yes, but why? What do they want?'

'I don't care,' he replied, slowly retreating. 'I'm going back.'

He started to walk backwards, not daring to take his eyes off the mass of dark figures in the middle of the road. He collided with something and quickly spun around. It was another body, and the force of the impact had knocked it over, but it was already dragging itself back up. He stared into its vacant, emotionless face as it lumbered towards him again, finding himself unable to look away from its discoloured skin, the dry blood caked around its mouth, its dull, unfocused eyes . . .

He charged forward, hitting it square in the chest with his shoulder and sending it tumbling back down to the tarmac.

'Fucking things are going for us,' he said breathlessly, getting ready to defend himself again.

'No, they're not.'

Carl turned back again to see another corpse, staggering towards Michael. Michael walked forward to meet it and roughly grabbed its arm. It continued to try and move, but its strength was virtually non-existent and he held it steady. He let go of it and it immediately began to walk away again, apparently unaware of the change of direction it had just been forced to make.

'They're not interested in us, Carl. Christ, they can't even bloody see us.'

'So what about that lot then?' he said, pointing towards the huge crowd. 'What's that all about? Why are they here if they can't see us?'

Michael couldn't answer that. Despite the fact that he'd just casually manhandled one of the corpses, the presence of so many others so close still worried him. The rest of the world appeared to be dead. What else was drawing them here if it wasn't the survivors sheltering nearby?

'There's got to be an explanation.' With mounting trepidation, he crept forward towards the crowd.

'What the hell are you doing?' Carl shouted as he began to move back to the community centre again. 'Come on, mate, maybe this was a mistake . . .'

None of the bodies were reacting to his presence. Some, he noticed, even had their backs to him, while further ahead, others faced forward. Were they gravitating to something in particular? Perturbed, he edged closer still, then climbed up onto the roof of a car, trying to ignore its dead driver hanging out of the open door directly below his feet. When the crowd still didn't react he stamped his boot down on the roof, and the dull metallic thud echoed along the entire length of the Stanhope Road. Still no reaction.

'Over here!' he shouted. 'Hey, can any of you hear me?'

No reaction.

'Michael, come on . . .'

Ignoring Carl, Michael crouched down on the roof of the car to try and get a better view of the crowd. There was a gap and in the middle of them he could see something large and indistinct, which appeared to be stopping them from moving down the road. That was it, he thought to himself, the bloody things are stuck! Without explaining, he jumped down and ran towards the crowd, pausing momentarily once he was near enough to touch them.

With his heart still racing he took a deep breath, then disappeared deep into the throng.

Carl, watching helplessly from a distance, lost sight of Michael in the gloom. He waited anxiously for him to reappear. He was contemplating going back and trying to get help when he saw him again, scrambling up onto the top of something.

'You still there, Carl?' he called.

'I'm here,' he answered, creeping forward again, side-stepping another corpse. 'What the hell are you doing?'

'It's a truck.'

'What?'

'I'm on a truck. It's on its side, and there's another car wedged in front of it. Between them they've virtually blocked the width of the road.'

'So?'

'So these dumb fuckers can't get past. They're stuck. And the longer they've been stuck, so more have got themselves trapped. They've come from both directions and none of them can get through.'

Carl was relieved. He still didn't fully understand, but the fact Michael had found an explanation at all helped: all he needed to know was that the dead were still as dumb and useless as they'd been when they first started picking themselves off the ground yesterday morning.

'So can we go back inside now?'

'I'm going to try and shift the car . . . see if I can get them to disperse.'

'Are you sure about this? Don't do anything that . . .'

There was no point finishing his sentence because Michael had disappeared again.

Michael jumped down off the side of the truck and squeezed his way through the foul-smelling crowd, shoving bodies out of the way to get to the car. He pulled the passenger door open and got inside, to find the dead driver sitting motionless next to him, slumped over the steering wheel. He undid his belt, leant across the corpse and opened the door as far as it would go, then manoeuvred himself around until he could get his feet onto the driver's torso. He pushed and kicked the body until he'd managed to force the dead driver out of his car.

Michael slid across into the empty seat and started the engine. He reversed slowly at first, gently pushing throngs of cadavers out of the way, then accelerated once he was clear of the crowd. He drove back to Carl and gestured for him to get into the passenger seat. They watched as the dead masses slowly continued their clumsy advance. Many of those who had been nearest to the car had gone down, forced forward too quickly for their clumsy feet by the pressure of the inexorable masses behind them, pushing into the suddenly empty space ahead. Even more of the senseless creatures tripped over those that had already fallen, and for a moment it was looking like so many had lost their footing that the road might be blocked again, this time by corpses . . . but then, painfully slowly, the first few managed to drag themselves free and gradually more and more of them were able to stagger unsteadily off down the road, disappearing in various directions. Michael thought they looked like a crowd of football fans, heads down, drifting miserably away from the ground after their team had lost.

'We seriously need to get out of this place,' Carl said as they drove the short distance back to the community centre.

'Tell me about it. You know what bothers me most of all?'

'What?'

'It's not what was going on out here; it's how Ralph and that lot reacted. They panicked, and there wasn't even anything worth panicking about. What's going to happen if the shit really hits the fan? Don't know about you, mate, but I don't think I want to be around to find out.'

13

Stuart Jeffries, Paul Garner and Ralph Bennett refused to let them back inside. Rather than waste time arguing, Michael decided that his hand had been forced; it was time to leave. He managed a brief, shouted conversation with Emma through a window, and told her he and Carl were heading out into the city to look for transport and supplies.

The thought of being outside in an unfamiliar part of town proved to be worse than the reality. The two men were able to move around freely, going wherever they wanted and taking whatever they thought they might need. It was like shopping with a credit card without a limit. Apart from the bodies still lying on the ground, the world was disturbingly familiar. The corpses which dragged themselves along the streets this morning bore more than a passing resemblance to the hordes of aimless consumers who had trampled the same path in search of retail therapy less than a week earlier.

They dumped the car and found a large silver people carrier with seven seats which they loaded with food, clothes, camping gear, and anything else they thought they might need. For a short time Michael considered going back home to get some of his own things, but he decided against it. His possessions could easily be replaced now, and he didn't want to risk stirring up the memories and emotions which, for the moment at least, he was just about managing to keep in check.

Emma breathed a sigh of relief just before eleven when Carl and Michael returned. She'd been waiting by the door, and she managed to get it open before Stuart or any of his cronies realised what she was doing. She'd packed her belongings into two carrier bags and a cardboard box, and had done the same with Michael and Carl's things. Between the three of them the entire remains of their lives had been condensed into five carrier bags and three boxes.

Hardly anyone had spoken to her once the two men left the community centre – almost as if she'd suddenly ceased to exist. They seemed to think that they were abandoning them, and Emma had real difficulty trying to understand why they felt that way. Michael and Carl's invitation was open, and even after Ralph and Stuart and Paul's needless behaviour, it still stood: any of them – *all* of them, if they wanted – could leave with Michael and Carl, like she was. She guessed uncertainty and their personal – and irrational – fears of stepping outside the creaky wooden building were the only things stopping them from taking any action.

While she'd been waiting for them to come back she'd made countless attempts to look up and make eye contact with other people, but they wouldn't, quickly looking away from her, *just in case.*

'Everything all right?' she asked as Michael parked the vehicle in front of the building and got out and stretched.

'Fine,' he replied quietly. 'You okay?'

She nodded as Carl walked around from the other side of the people carrier.

'We got everything we need,' he said. 'What do you think of the transport?'

She slowly circled the large family-sized car. There were seven seats inside, two at the front, two at the back and three in the middle. The front two seats and the seat behind the driver's were empty. The others were piled high with supplies.

'Have any trouble while you were out there?' she asked.

'Trouble?' Carl replied, sounding surprised. 'What kind of trouble?'

'I don't know. Christ, you spent the morning in the middle of a city full of walking corpses. I don't know what you saw or what—'

Michael interrupted.

'Nothing happened,' he said abruptly. 'There were plenty of bodies walking around, but nothing happened. These people are idiots. It's nowhere near as bad as they think it is.'

He headed back inside to collect their few belongings. The silence which greeted him as he walked into the hall was ominous. The rest of the survivors – almost all of the two dozen increasingly frightened individuals – stopped and stared at them. Some of those people hadn't even acknowledged him in all the time they'd been at the community centre. There were others who hadn't spoken a word to *anyone* since they'd got there. And yet, suddenly and unexpectedly, he felt real animosity and anger in the room, as if it was the three of them against the rest. A wave of hostility stopped him in his tracks, and he turned around to face Emma and Carl, feeling suddenly exposed.

'It's been like this since you went outside,' Emma replied. 'They're bloody terrified.'

'Fucking idiots,' Carl sneered. 'There's no bloody need for this. We should tell them that . . .'

'We'll tell them nothing,' Michael ordered. The surprising authority in his voice silenced Carl. 'Let's just go.'

'What, right now?' Emma said, surprised. 'Are we ready? Do we need to . . . ?'

Michael glanced at her. The expression on his face left her in no doubt as to his intentions.

'What are we going to gain from waiting?' he hissed. 'By the looks of things it's going to be far riskier staying here than being outside. We're better off travelling in daylight, so let's make the most of it.'

'Are you sure . . . ?'

'You sound like you're having doubts – you can both stay here with this lot if you want to . . .'

Carl looked away, feeling intimidated and pressurised.

'Oh bollocks to it,' Emma said, her voice now a fraction louder, 'you're right. Let's just get out of here.'

Michael turned back to face the rest of the survivors again. He cleared his throat, not quite knowing what he was going to say, or why he was even bothering.

'We're leaving,' he began, his words echoing around the cold wooden room. 'If any of you want to—'

Stuart Jeffries got up from his chair and strode purposefully towards Michael until he was standing face-to-face with him.

'Just get in your damn car and fuck off now. We don't need people who are going to take senseless chances like you did this morning. You put the rest of us at risk. Every second you stay here is a second too long,' Stuart shouted.

Michael looked at him for what felt like an eternity. There were countless things he could have said, countless reasons why he thought they should follow him, not stay locked in the community centre, reasons why he was right and they were wrong, but the anger in the other man's eyes left him in no doubt that to say anything at all would be pointless.

'Come on,' Emma said, grabbing his arm and pulling him away.

Michael looked around the room one last time before turning his back on them and walking to the door.

Emma passed Kate in the corridor. Her eyes full of tears, she tried to speak to Emma, but she couldn't.

'Come with us,' Emma said softly.

Kate chewed on her lip and looked away.

'Can't.'

'You can. Look, there's no reason why you—'

'Can't,' she said again, shaking her head furiously, 'just can't go out there . . .'

Carl gently shoved Emma forward. Michael was already outside, waiting impatiently. As they followed him, the community centre door was quickly slammed and loudly locked behind them. Knowing now that there was no turning back (and suddenly feeling undeniably nervous and unsure) they exchanged quick, anxious glances, then got into the van. Michael started the engine and drove out towards the main road, pausing only to let a single willowy-framed, greasy-skinned body stagger past.

14

Less than an hour into the journey and Carl, Michael and Emma found themselves racked with fear and scepticism. Leaving the shelter had felt like the only option before, but now they had actually left the building – and the other survivors – behind, uncertainty had begun to set in. Doubt bordering on paranoia plagued Michael as he fought to concentrate and keep the van moving forward. Problem was, he decided, they didn't actually know where it was they were going. Finding somewhere safe and secure to shelter had sounded easy at first, but now that they were outside and they could see for themselves the full extent of the endless death and devastation, it was beginning to look like an impossible task. The whole world was theirs for the taking, but they couldn't actually find any part of it they wanted. They stopped outside many buildings, but always managed to convince themselves there might be somewhere better around the next corner . . .

Emma sat bolt upright in the seat next to Michael, staring out of the windows around her, looking from side to side, too afraid to sit back and relax. Before she'd seen it for herself, she had thought it logical to assume that only the helpless population had been affected by the inexplicable tragedy. The reality was that the land too had been battered, ravaged beyond all recognition. Countless buildings – sometimes entire streets – had been razed to the ground by unchecked fires, some of which still smouldered even now. Almost every car which had been moving when the disaster had struck had veered out of control and crashed. She counted herself lucky that she had been indoors and relatively safe when the nightmare had begun. She wondered how many other people that had died in a car crash or some other sudden accident might actually have gone on to survive had fate not dealt them such a bitter hand? How many people who shared her apparent immunity to the disease, virus or whatever it was that had caused all of this, had been wiped out because of misfortune and bad luck? Something caught her eye in a field at the side of the road. The wreckage of a light aircraft was strewn over the boggy and uneven ground at one end of a long, deep furrow. All around the wreck lay twisted chunks of metal and the bloody remains of passengers. She wondered what might have happened to those people had they survived their flight. It was pointless thinking about such things, but in a strange way it was almost therapeutic; it helped to keep her mind occupied.

With unnerving speed the three survivors found themselves becoming impervious to the carnage, death and destruction all around them. But even though the sight of thousands of battered and bloodied bodies and the aftermath of hundreds of horrific accidents were now commonplace, from time to time each of them witnessed things so terrible and grotesque that it was almost impossible for them to comprehend what they saw. As much as he wanted to look away, Carl found himself staring as they passed a long red and white coach. The huge vehicle had collided with the side of a redbrick house. The bodies of some thirty or so children remained trapped in their seats. Even though they were held tight by their seat belts, he could see at least seven of the poor youngsters trying to move. Their withered arms flailed and their empty, pallid faces made him remember Gemma, the perfect little girl he had left behind. The realisation that he would never see or hold her again was a pain that was almost too much to bear. It had been hard enough to try and come to terms with his loss while he had been in the community centre but now, strangely, every single mile they drove further away made the agony harder to stand. Sarah and Gemma had been dead for almost a week but he still felt responsible for them. They were still his family.

Conversation had been sparse and forced since the journey began and the silence was beginning to deafen Emma. She could see that Michael was having to concentrate hard on his driving (the roads were littered with debris) and Carl was preoccupied, but she needed to talk. The ominous quiet in the van was giving her far too much time to think.

'Have either of you two actually thought about where we might be going?' she asked.

No reply. All three of them had been intermittently thinking about that question individually, but the constant distractions of the scarred landscape had made it impossible for any of them to come to any conclusions.

'Well we've got to decide something soon,' Emma said. 'We need some kind of plan, don't we?'

Michael shrugged his shoulders. 'I thought we'd got one. Just keep driving until we find somewhere safe then stop.'

'But what does safe mean? Is anywhere safe?'

'I don't know.'

'What about disease?' she continued. 'They're starting to rot.'

'I know.'

'So what are we going to do?'

He shrugged again. 'There's not a lot we can do, is there? We can't see the germs, so we'll just have to take our chances.'

'So what you're saying is we could stop anywhere?'

He thought for a second. 'Yes.'

'So why haven't we? Why do we just keep driving and—'

'Because—' he snapped.

'Because we're too bloody frightened,' she interrupted, answering her own question. 'Because nowhere is safe, is it? Everywhere might well be empty and we might well be able to pick and choose, but that doesn't matter. Truth is I'm too frightened to get out of this van and so are both of you.'

Her unexpected and accurate admission brought the conversation to a swift and sudden end.

15

Nearly half past four. The long, laborious afternoon was drawing to a close and Carl knew they only had a few hours left before the light faded. When he'd handed the driving duties over to Carl, Michael (who was now curled up on the empty seat in the back of the van, sleeping fitfully) had estimated that they should have reached the west coast in an hour or so. It had now been two and a half hours since they'd swapped places and still there was nothing ahead of them but endless road and aimless travelling.

It was a cool but bright afternoon. The brilliant sun shone down from its slowly sinking position in a sky which was mostly blue but which was increasingly dotted with bulbous grey and white clouds. The road glistened with the moisture which remained from a brief shower of rain they'd passed through a few minutes earlier.

Emma remained wide awake, concentrating intently on the dead world, hoping she'd find somewhere safe to shelter.

'You all right?' Carl asked suddenly, making her catch her breath with surprise.

'What?'

'I asked if you were all right,' he repeated.

'I'm fine.'

'Is he asleep?' he asked, gesturing over his shoulder at Michael.

Emma glanced back. 'Don't know.'

Michael stirred. 'What's the matter?' he groaned, sounding groggy and confused.

No one answered.

There was a hand-painted sign at the side of the road. It had been battered and worn by the weather and was only partially visible, but as they passed it Carl managed to make out the words 'café', 'turn' and '2 miles'. He hadn't had much of an appetite all day (all week, if the truth be told) but the thought of food made him suddenly hungry. They did have some supplies with them in the van, but in their rush to leave the city they'd loaded the various bags and boxes haphazardly and the supplies had been buried somewhere deep.

'Either of you two want anything to eat?' he asked.

Emma just grunted, but Michael sat up immediately.

'I do,' he said, rubbing his eyes.

'I saw a sign for a café up ahead. We should stop for a bit.'

There were empty grassy fields on either side of the uninterrupted road. There were no cars, buildings or wandering bodies anywhere to be seen. On balance Carl thought it was worth taking a chance. He needed a break from driving and they all needed to stop for a while, to discuss what it was they were actually trying to achieve.

Suddenly interested in the day again, Michael stretched and looked around. He too noticed the lack of any obvious signs of human life. He could see a flock of sheep grazing up ahead. Until then he hadn't stopped to think about the significance of seeing animals. In the city they'd seen the odd dog, and there had always been birds flying overhead, but the relevance of their survival had been lost on him because he'd always had a million other confused thoughts running through his mind. Seeing the sheep in their ignorant isolation today forced him to think about it further. It must only have been humans that had been wiped out. Whatever it was that had happened looked to have left other species untouched.

Their arrival at the café interrupted his train of thought.

The tall white building appeared from out of nowhere: a large, lonely house that looked completely out of place in its lush green surroundings, it had been hidden from the road by a row of bushy pine trees. Carl slowed the van down and pulled into a large gravel car park, stopping close to a side door. He turned off the engine, closed his tired eyes and relaxed. After hours of driving the sudden silence was a welcome relief.

Despite having been virtually asleep only minutes earlier, Michael was immediately wide awake and alert. Before Carl had even taken the keys out of the ignition he was already out of the van and jogging over to the café door.

'Careful,' Emma instinctively warned. He looked back over his shoulder and flashed her a brief but reassuring smile as he reached out and tried the door. It wasn't locked but it wouldn't open. He pushed against it with his shoulder.

'What's up?' asked Carl.

'Something's blocking it,' he replied, still pushing and shoving. 'There's something in the way.'

'Be careful,' Emma said again. It was clear from the trepidation in her voice that she was nowhere near comfortable with the situation.

Michael shoved at the door again, and this time it opened inwards another couple of inches. He took a few steps back out into the car park and then ran at the door once more, charging it with his shoulder. This time it opened just wide enough for him to be able to force his way inside. He glanced back at the others momentarily before disappearing.

'I really don't like this,' Emma mumbled to herself, looking around anxiously. The icy wind blew her hair across her face and made her eyes water. She stared intently at the café door, waiting for Michael to reappear.

Inside the building he found that the blockage preventing him from opening the door fully was the stiff, unmoving body of a teenage girl. She'd fallen on her back when she'd died and his brutal shoving had forced her up and over onto her side, giving him those few vital extra inches to squeeze through. He gingerly took hold of her left arm and pulled her out of the way. 'It's okay,' he shouted back to Carl and Emma, 'it was just a body. I just—'

He stopped speaking suddenly. He could hear sounds of movement inside the building behind him.

'What's the matter?' Emma asked frantically as Michael half-ran and half-tripped back outside.

'In there,' he gasped, 'there's something in there . . .'

The three survivors stood in silence as a lone figure appeared in the shadows of the doorway. Its progress blocked by the lifeless body on the ground that Michael had moved, it turned awkwardly and stumbled out into the car park.

'Is it . . . ?' Carl began.

'Dead?' Michael interrupted, finishing his sentence for him.

'It could be a survivor,' Emma mumbled hopefully although in reality she held out little hope of that being the case. From its stilted, uncoordinated movements Michael instantly knew that the figure which slowly emerged into the light was just another corpse. As it lurched closer Michael saw that it had been a woman, perhaps in her late fifties or early sixties, and it was wearing a loose-fitting gaudy green and yellow waitress uniform. A layer of heavy make-up was smudged across its wrinkled face, partially camouflaging the discolouration of its skin.

'Can you hear me?' Emma asked. She knew it was pointless, but she felt that she had to try and force a response from the desperate figure. 'Is there anything we can do to . . . ?'

She let her words trail away into silence as the body approached. The world was silent save for the gusting wind and the relentless dragging *clump, clump* of the creature's uncoordinated feet on the gravel as it took step after painfully slow step towards the survivors. It tripped on an edging stone and lurched towards Carl, who instinctively jumped back out of the way. Regaining its balance, the body walked slowly between the three of them, completely oblivious to their presence. The road behind them curved gently to the right but the dead waitress's course remained relatively straight until it had crossed the tarmac and become entangled in a patch of wiry undergrowth on the other side.

Michael watched the pathetic creature for a little longer. He couldn't help but think about what might happen to it. In his mind he pictured it staggering on through the dark night, through wind and rain, and he felt a sudden and surprising sadness. It had once been a defenceless old woman – a mother, wife and grandmother perhaps – who'd left for work last Tuesday just as she had done on any other day. Now she was destined to spend an eternity wandering without direction or shelter. He had built up a resistance to such thoughts and feelings in the city, perhaps because there were so many bodies there that they just combined to form a single, unidentifiable mass. It felt different out here.

Carl had disappeared. Emma could see him moving around inside and she gestured to Michael to follow her into the café.

A short passageway led them into a large, dark and musty room. There were various bodies scattered around numerous tables and slumped awkwardly in comfortable chairs. Michael smiled morbidly to himself as he walked past the corpses of an elderly couple. They'd been sitting opposite each other when they'd died. Alice Jenkins (that was the name on the credit card on the table beside her) was sitting back in her seat with her head lolling heavily on her shoulders, her dry eyes fixed unblinking on the ceiling above. Her partner was slouched forward with his face buried in the remains of a mouldy three-day-old full English breakfast.

There was a noise from the kitchen area and Carl appeared carrying a large plastic tray.

'Found some food,' he said as he threaded his way over to the others through the confusion of corpses. 'Most of the stuff in there has gone bad. I managed to find some crisps and biscuits and something to drink though.'

Without responding Emma walked past the two men and made her way towards a large glass door at the end of the room. She pushed the door open and went back outside.

'Where the hell's she going?' Carl muttered.

Emma wasn't out of earshot. 'I'm not eating in there,' she shouted back into the building. 'You two can if you want.'

Michael looked around at the gruesome surroundings and followed her out into a grassy area beyond the car park. Carl also followed, a little slower than Michael, as he was carrying the food and was having difficulty seeing his feet and avoiding tripping over outstretched dead limbs. Two bodies sitting in a bay seat by the window caught his eye. A woman and a man, both of whom looked like they'd been about his age, had been sitting next to each other when they'd died. Spread out over the table in front of them was a tourist map that was marked with spots and dribbles of dark dried blood. On the ground, twisted around his parents' feet, was a young boy. His face was frozen with panic and pain. Carl remembered the terrified, agonised faces of his own wife and child, and the sudden recollection of all that he had lost was almost too much to bear. With tears streaming down his cheeks he carried on out to the others, hoping that the gusting wind would hide his weeping from them.

Michael and Emma had sat down next to each other at a large wooden picnic table. Carl sat opposite.

'You okay?' asked Michael.

'Does anyone want a can of Coke?' Carl said, deliberately ignoring his question. 'There are some other cans inside if you'd prefer. I think I saw some bottled water back there . . .'

'Are you okay?' Michael asked again.

This time Carl didn't answer. He just nodded, bit his lip and wiped his eyes with the back of his sleeve. He began to busy himself by opening the food he'd brought outside.

'You look tired,' Emma said gently, reaching out and giving his hand a quick and reassuring squeeze. 'Maybe we should stay here tonight. I know it's not ideal but . . .'

Her unexpected touch triggered a change in Carl. Suddenly, and without any warning, his defences crumbled. 'Either of you two got kids?' he asked, his voice wavering and unsteady.

Both Emma and Michael looked at each other momentarily and then shook their heads.

'I did. I had a daughter. The most beautiful little girl you've ever seen. She's got . . . I mean she had—'

'It hurts so much, doesn't it?' Emma said, sensing Carl's pain. 'My sister had two boys. Great lads, I saw them a couple of weeks ago and now—'

'Christ,' he continued, not listening, 'they do something to you, kids. When we found out we were expecting Gemma, we were gutted – I mean absolutely fucking devastated. Sarah didn't talk to me for days and . . . and—'

'And what?' Michael pressed gently.

'And then she was born and everything changed. I tell you, mate, you can't understand what it's like until you've been there yourself. Maybe you'll find out some day. I watched that little girl being born and that was it. You don't know what life's about until you've been there. And now she's gone I . . . I can't believe it. I feel so fucking empty and I just want to go back home and see her. I know she's gone but I want to see her again and just . . .'

'Shh . . .' Emma whispered. She tried desperately to think of something to say, but she knew she could never fully appreciate the extent of Carl's pain; nothing she could say or do would make any of that pain disappear.

'I'm starving,' he sobbed, forcing the conversation to change direction. He grabbed a packet of biscuits and tore them open. A gust of wind picked up the empty cellophane wrapper and whisked it away.

Michael, Carl and Emma sat eating for almost half an hour in virtual silence. From where they were sitting they could see right the way down the side of the café to their well-loaded van. The thought of getting back behind the wheel again and driving without any idea of their eventual destination was depressing, but they knew they had little option. At least the fresh air and open space was better than the uncomfortable and stifling confines of the community centre.

Emma was the first to speak. 'How are you two feeling?' she asked.

Neither man responded. Michael was deep in thought, playing with a broken ring-pull, and Carl was neatly folding up an empty crisp packet as small as he could make it. Both of them waited for the other to answer.

'Do you still think we've done the right thing?'

Michael looked up at her, concerned. 'Of course we have. Why, are you having doubts?'

'Not at all,' she answered quickly. 'It's just that we're sitting out here and we don't seem to be making much progress. It'll be dark soon and—'

'Look, if push comes to shove we can sleep in the van,' Michael said. 'It won't be a problem. I know it won't be comfortable but—'

'I'm not worried,' she snapped, interrupting to justify her comments. 'I just think we should be on our way. The sooner we find somewhere to stop, the sooner we can get ourselves settled and sorted out.'

'I know, I know,' Michael mumbled, getting up from his seat and stretching. 'We'll get moving in a little while.'

With that he began to wander back down the side of the café towards the van. Emma stared after him. She found him a very strange man; inspiring and irritating in equal measure. Most of the time he seemed cool, collected and level-headed, but there were occasions like this when he didn't appear to give a damn, and when he was like that his apathy was infuriating. Not for the first time in the last week their safety was on the line, but Michael didn't seem the slightest bit bothered. She assumed it was because they hadn't yet found anywhere obvious to stop. If things weren't going Michael's way, she'd noticed, he didn't want to know.

Michael stopped walking when he reached the edge of the road in front of the café. He looked out across a lush green valley landscape and drew in several long, slow breaths of the cool, refreshing air. He slowly scanned the horizon from left to right and then stopped and turned around with a broad grin plastered across his tired face. He beckoned the others to come over to where he stood. Intrigued and concerned in equal measure, Carl and Emma quickly jumped up.

'What's the matter?' Carl asked, his heart beating anxiously in his chest.

'Over there,' he replied, pointing out into the distance. 'Just look at that. It's bloody perfect!'

Emma struggled to see what it was that he had found. 'What's perfect?'

'Can't you see it?' he babbled excitedly.

'See what?' Carl snapped.

Michael moved around so that he was standing between the other two. He lifted his arm and pointed right across the valley.

'See that clearing over there?'

After a couple of seconds Emma spotted it. 'I see it,' she said.

'Now look slightly to the right.'

She did as instructed. 'All I can see is a house,' she said, dejectedly.

'Exactly. It's perfect.'

'So you found a house in the woods,' sighed Carl. 'Is that all? Bloody hell, we've passed a thousand houses already today. What's so special about this one?'

'Well, you two had trouble seeing it, didn't you?'

'So?'

'So what does that tell you? What does the location of a house like that tell you?'

Emma and Carl looked at each other, puzzled, sure that they were missing the point (if there was a point to be missed).

'No idea,' Emma grumbled.

'It's isolated, isn't it? It's not easy to find. It's going to be right off the beaten track.'

'So? We're not trying to hide are we? There's no one left to hide from . . .'

Emma still couldn't understand what the big deal was. Carl on the other hand was beginning to get the idea.

'It's not about hiding, is it, Mike?' he said, grinning suddenly. 'It's the isolation. People who lived in houses like that must have been pretty self-sufficient.'

'Exactly. Imagine this place in winter. Christ, a couple of inches of snow and you're cut off from everything. And these people were farmers; they couldn't afford to be without heat and light, could they? My guess is that whoever lived in that house would have been used to being out on a limb and would have been ready for just about anything. I'll bet they've got their own power and everything.'

Emma watched as the two men became much more animated than they had been at any other time in the last week.

'It's going to be hard enough for us to get there,' Carl continued, 'and you've seen the state of the poor bastards left wandering the streets. They'll never find us.'

'It's perfect,' Michael beamed.

16

Michael had been right about the isolation of the house in the woods. It had proved impossible to find. They'd been on the road again for over an hour, and it had taken most of that time just to get over to the other side of the valley. Their brief euphoria at finally having made some progress quickly gave way to desperation and melancholy again. Now they were hopelessly lost, and disorientated. The sides of the twisting, seemingly endless roads along which they travelled were lined with tall trees which made it virtually impossible to see very far into the distance in any direction. The nervous irritation inside the van was increasing.

'This is bloody ridiculous,' Michael sighed. 'There must be something around here somewhere.'

He was driving again, with Emma sitting directly behind. She leant forward and put a reassuring hand on his shoulder. He instinctively pulled away, annoyed and frustrated.

'Calm down,' she sighed, trying hard to soothe his nerves despite the fact that her own were tattered and torn. 'Don't worry, we'll get there.'

'Get *where*? Christ, all I can see are fucking trees. I haven't got a clue where we are. We're probably driving in completely the wrong direction . . .'

A lethargic, staggering body appeared from the side of the road (only the fifth they'd seen since leaving the café) and wandered into the path of the van. Michael yanked the steering wheel to the left and swerved around the miserable creature, scraping the van against the hedge on the other side of the road as he missed it by inches. For a fraction of a second he watched in the rear-view mirror as the corpse continued to stumble across, completely oblivious to the vehicle which had just thundered past.

'Got it!' Carl shouted.

'Got what?'

Carl had been poring over the pages of a road atlas. 'I think I've found where we are on the map.'

'Well done,' Michael said sarcastically. 'Now can you find that bloody house?'

'I'm trying,' he replied. 'It's not easy. I can't see any landmarks or anything to check against.'

'So can you see any buildings at all around here?'

'Hold on . . .' Carl struggled to focus his eyes on the map. He was being thrown from side to side as Michael followed the winding route of the narrow road.

'Anything?'

'I don't think so,' Carl eventually answered. 'Can you slow down a bit, mate? I'm having trouble . . .'

'Look, if you can't find anything on this road,' Michael interrupted angrily, 'do you think you could tell us how to get to another road that might actually lead somewhere?'

Another pause as Carl again studied the map. 'There's not very much round here at all . . .'

'Christ, there must be something . . .'

'Will you calm down,' Emma said from the back. 'We'll get there.'

Michael thumped the steering wheel in frustration then swung the van around a sharp bend in the road. He had to fight to keep control of the vehicle and was forced to steer hard in the other direction to avoid hitting the back end of a car which had crashed nose-first into the hedge.

'If I've got this right then we should reach another bend in the road soon,' Carl said, trying hard to provide some definite directions. 'Immediately after the bend there's a junction. Take a right there and we'll be on a main road in a couple of miles.'

'What good's a main road? We're looking for somewhere *away* from main roads.'

'And I'm trying to find you somewhere,' Carl shouted. 'Do you want to swap places 'cause all you've done is criticise everything I've tried to do for the last—'

'Bend coming,' Emma said, cutting right through their argument.

Without slowing down at all Michael threw the van around the turning. 'Okay, here's the junction. Was it right or left?'

'Right . . .' Carl replied. He wasn't completely sure, but he didn't dare admit it. He turned the map around in his hands, and then turned it back again.

'You're positive?'

'Of course I'm positive,' he yelled, 'just bloody well turn right.'

Seething with anger and not thinking straight, in the heat of the moment Michael screwed up and turned left.

'Shit!'

'You idiot, what the hell did you do that for? Christ, you ask me which way to go, I tell you, and then you go in the opposite bloody direction. Why bother asking? Why don't I just throw this fucking book out of the window?'

'I'll throw you out of the fucking window,' Michael threatened. He became quiet as the road climbed and narrowed dramatically.

'Keep going,' suggested Emma. 'There's no way you're going to be able to turn the van around here.'

The width of the road reduced to a single-lane track and the surface beneath their wheels became increasingly potholed and uneven.

'What the hell is this?' Carl demanded, still livid. 'You're driving us down a fucking dirt track!'

Michael didn't answer; he just slammed his foot down harder on the accelerator, forcing the van up another sudden steep rise. The front right wheel clattered through a deep pothole filled with dirty rain water which splashed up, showering the front of the van. He switched on the wipers to clear the muddy windscreen but rather than clear the glass, they instead smeared greasy mud right across his field of vision, reducing his already limited visibility even more.

'There,' he said, squinting into the distance and looking further ahead. 'There's a clearing up there. I'll try and turn around.'

It wasn't so much a clearing, rather just a slightly wider section of track at the entrance to a field. Michael slowed the van to almost a dead stop.

'Wait!' Carl shouted, 'Down there!' He pointed through a gap in the trees on the other side of the road.

Michael again used the wipers to clear the windscreen. 'What?'

'I can see it,' Emma said. 'There's a house.'

Michael's tired eyes finally settled on the isolated building. He turned and looked at both Carl and Emma.

'What do you think?' Carl asked.

Michael accelerated again and sent the van flying down the track, giving it a final burst of speed like a runner in sight of the finishing line. Once over another slight rise they had a clear view of the building in the near distance. The track they were following led directly to the front door of the large house.

'Looks perfect,' Emma said quietly.

The uneven road became less defined with each passing yard. It swooped down through a section of dense forest in a gentle arc and then crossed a little humped-back stone bridge. The bridge itself spanned the width of a gentle stream which meandered down the hillside.

'It's a farm,' Carl said, stating the obvious as they passed an abandoned tractor and plough.

'No animals, though.'

Michael wound down the window and sniffed the air. Emma was right – he couldn't see or smell a single cow, pig, sheep, chicken, duck, horse, or anything else for that matter, but the air smelled refreshingly clean. He stopped the van in the centre of a large gravel yard, right in front of the house, then climbed out of his seat and stretched, glad to have finally stopped.

The apparent tranquillity of their isolated location belied the turmoil and devastation they had left behind them. Emma, Carl and Michael stood together in subdued silence as they took stock of their surroundings. They were standing in a yard. It was about twenty yards square, boxed in by the stream, the farm buildings and the forest. Farm machinery was scattered about in varying degrees of repair; some tools looked to have recently been in use, others lay broken, forgotten and rusted. On the furthest side of the yard (opposite to where the track crossed the bridge) were two dilapidated wooden barns. The farmhouse itself was a large, traditional brick-built building with a sloping grey roof dotted with green and yellow lichen. Three stone steps led up to a wooden porch and tacked to the side of the building was an out-of-place-looking concrete garage with a blue metal door. Twisting ivy covered between a half and a third of the front of the house and its unchecked tendrils had begun to reach across to the roof of the garage.

'This looks ideal,' Emma said. 'What do you two think?'

As he was nearest she looked towards Michael for a response. Not for the first time today he seemed to be miles away, wrapped up in his own private thoughts.

'What?' he mumbled, sounding annoyed that he had been disturbed.

'I said it looks perfect,' she repeated. 'What do you think, Carl?'

'Not bad,' he said nonchalantly, deliberately trying to hide the fact that standing out in the open like this scared him. He didn't know who (or what) was watching. 'It'll certainly do for tonight.'

Michael, too tired to be nervous, climbed the steps to the front of the house, opened the porch and stepped inside while the other two watched from a cautious distance. He banged on the door with his fist.

'Hello,' he yelled, 'hello, is anyone there?'

Carl found the volume of his voice unsettling. He looked around anxiously.

When, after a few seconds, there was no response, Michael tried the door. It was open and he disappeared inside. Emma and Carl looked at each other for a moment before following him. By the time they'd made it into the hallway he'd already checked every room downstairs and was already working his way through the second floor. He reappeared at the top of the staircase.

'Well?' asked Emma.

'It looks okay,' he replied breathlessly as he walked back down.

'Anyone here?'

He nodded and pointed to the right. Emma peered through a door into a large, comfortable sitting room. A single corpse – an overweight, white-haired man wearing an open dressing gown, trousers and slippers, his gut bloated with the first signs of decay –

lay on the ground in front of an open fireplace. Feeling a little safer now he knew that this was the only body, Carl went into the sitting room. There was an unopened letter on the ground next to the man's lifeless hand. He crouched down and picked it up.

'This must be Mr Jones,' he mumbled, reading from the address on the envelope. 'Mr Arthur Jones, Penn Farm. Nice place you had here, Mr Jones.'

'No sign of Mrs Jones?' wondered Emma.

'Couldn't find anyone else,' Michael replied, shaking his head. 'And he looks too old for there to be any little Joneses here.'

Emma noticed that Carl was still crouched down next to the body, staring into its face.

'What's the matter?' she asked. No response. 'Carl, what's the matter?'

He looked up at her and smiled. 'Nothing. Sorry, I was miles away.' He looked away quickly, hoping that the other two hadn't picked up on the sudden anxiety and unease he was feeling. Christ, he thought, he'd seen literally thousands of dead bodies over the last few days, so why did this one in particular bother him? Was it because this was one of the first bodies he'd actually looked at closely, or was it because this was the first body he'd seen with a known identity? He knew the man's name and what he'd done for a living and he had broken into his home. It made him feel uncomfortable.

Michael sat down in an armchair and shielded his eyes from the early evening sunlight which seeped into the room.

'So will this do?' he asked. 'Think we should stop here?'

'There's plenty of room,' Emma replied, 'and there's the stream outside for water.'

'And it's not easy to get to,' Carl added, forcing himself to look away from Mr Jones. 'Christ, we had enough trouble finding it.'

'And it's a farm,' Michael said, 'so there's bound to be more to this place than just this house.'

'Like what?' Emma wondered.

'Don't know,' said Michael. 'Let's find out, shall we?'

He jumped up from his seat again. Carl and Emma followed him down a hallway which led right the way through the building. On their left were the stairs and doors into the kitchen and a small office, on their right the living room and dining room. Michael stopped by the back door and tapped on the window.

'There you go,' he said, turning around and grinning again, 'told you. That should help.'

Intrigued, Carl and Emma peered past him. On the lawn at the back of the house was a decent-sized gas cylinder mounted on a strong, rectangular concrete base. Carl looked further down the garden. There was a large shed in the bottom left-hand corner.

'Wonder what's in there? Bit big for a potting shed.' He opened the door, jogged the length of the garden and disappeared inside.

'What is it?' Michael asked, watching him with interest.

Carl quickly reappeared. 'You won't believe this! It's only a bloody generator!'

'What, for making electricity?' Emma said stupidly.

'That's what they're usually for,' Michael sighed.

'Will it work?' she then asked, equally stupidly.

'Don't know,' Carl replied, following them back indoors. 'I'll try and get it going later.'

'There's no desperate rush,' Michael said. 'We might as well stop here. We're not going to find anywhere better tonight.'

17

Michael was asleep by eight o'clock. Curled up on a sofa in the sitting room of the rustic farmhouse, it was an unexpectedly deep and refreshing sleep. The house was silent save for his gentle snoring and the muffled sounds of Emma and Carl's gentle conversation. Although they were easily as tired as Michael, neither was relaxed enough to be able to close their eyes and switch off. No matter how comfortable, how peaceful their surroundings had unexpectedly become, they knew that the world outside remained as inhospitable and fucked-up as it had been since the first minutes of the tragedy last week.

'I could have tried to get it going tonight,' Carl said, still talking about the generator in the shed behind the house, 'I just couldn't be bothered though. We've got plenty of time. I'll work on it in the morning.' He'd repaired machines for a living and was looking forward to getting on with the job tomorrow. He secretly hoped, for a short time at least, that the grease and graft would allow him to imagine he was back at work. For a while he'd be able to pretend that the last few days had never happened.

Emma and Carl sat on either side of the fireplace, wrapped up in their coats because the room was cold. Michael had prepared a fire earlier but they had decided against lighting it for fear of the smoke drawing attention to their location. Their fear was irrational, but undeniable. Chances were they were the only living people for miles around but they didn't want to take any risks, no matter how slight. Anonymity seemed to add to their security.

The large room was comfortably dark. Dancing orange light came from three candles which cast strange, over-sized, flickering shadows on the walls. After a long silence Emma spoke. 'Do you think we're going to be all right here?' she asked cautiously.

'We should be okay for a while,' Carl replied, his voice quiet and hushed.

'I like it.'

'It's okay. Listen, Emma, you don't think . . .' He stopped before he'd finished his question, obviously unsure of himself.

'Think what?'

He cleared his throat and shuffled awkwardly in his seat. With some reluctance he began again. 'You don't think the farmer will come back, do you?' As soon as he'd spoken he regretted what he'd said. It sounded so bloody ridiculous when he said it out loud but, nonetheless, the body of the farmer had been playing on his mind all evening. These days death didn't have the same finality it had previously had, and he wondered if the old man might somehow find his way back to his home and try to reclaim what was rightfully his. He knew that they could get rid of him again if they needed to, and that in a dumb, reanimated state he would pose little threat, but it was just the thought of the body returning which unnerved him. He knew his fear was irrational but even so, the hairs on the back of his neck were suddenly tingling and prickling with nerves.

'I'm sorry. That was a stupid thing to say.'

'Don't worry about it. It's okay.' She watched a ghostly whisper of grey smoke snake away from the top of the candle nearest to her as it dissolved into the air. She sensed that Carl was watching her and, for a moment, that made her feel uneasy. She wondered if he could sense what she was thinking. She wondered if he knew that she shared his own deep, dark and unfounded fears about the body of the farmer. Logic told her that they would be all right and that he would stay down – after all, the bodies seemed to have risen *en masse* last week: they'd either dragged themselves up on that one day, or had stayed where they'd fallen and died. And even if Mr Jones did somehow get up and start to walk again, his movements would be as random, awkward and uncoordinated as the rest of the wandering corpses. Pure chance was the only thing that would ever bring him back home. She knew that nothing was going to happen and that they were wasting their time thinking about the dead man, but she still couldn't help herself.

'You okay?' Carl asked.

She nodded and smiled, then stared into the flickering candle flame again. She thought back to a couple of hours earlier, when the three of them had shifted the bodies of the farmer and a farmhand they'd found face-down on the banks of the stream. Mr Jones had been the most difficult corpse to get rid of. Before he'd died he'd been a burly, well-built man who, she imagined, had worked every available hour of every day to ensure that his farm ran smoothly and profitably. Large in life, he was even larger in death, his body inflated by the gases and liquids it produced as it decayed. She had watched with horror and disgust as Michael had taken hold of his shoulders and Carl his legs and, with a total lack of respect, dragged him unceremoniously through what used to be his home. She recalled the look of irritation so clear on Michael's face when they hadn't been able to manoeuvre the farmer's heavy bulk through the front door. He'd angrily kicked and shoved the cadaver like it was a sack of potatoes.

They'd carried the bodies deep into the pine forest which bordered the farm and laid them side by side. Michael and Carl had shared the weight of the dead, making two trips, and she had carried three shovels from the house.

She remembered what happened next with an icy clarity. Michael had turned to walk back towards the house when she and Carl had instinctively picked up a shovel each and started to dig.

'What the hell are you doing?' Michael had asked.

'Digging,' Carl replied. Although factually correct, he'd completely missed the other man's point.

'Digging what?'

Thinking for a moment that he'd been asked a trick question, Carl paused before answering, 'Graves of course,' before adding a cautious, 'Why?'

'That was what I was going to ask you.'

'What do you mean?'

Emma had been standing between the two men, watching the conversation develop.

'Why bother? What's the point?'

'What?'

'Why bother digging graves?'

'To put the bloody bodies in,' Carl snapped. 'Is there a problem?'

Instead of answering, Michael just asked another question. 'So when are you going to do the rest? If you're going to bury these two, then you might as well finish the job off and bury the thousands of other corpses lying round the country. For Christ's sake, just look around you! There are millions of bodies and none of them have been buried. More to the point, none of them *need* to be buried.'

'Listen, we've taken this man's home from him. Don't you think that at the very least we owe him . . . ?'

'No,' Michael interrupted, his voice infuriatingly calm and level. 'We don't owe him anything. He's dead. It doesn't matter.'

And he'd turned and walked back towards the farmhouse. The light had faded and he'd almost been out of view when he'd shouted back to the others, 'I'm going back inside. I'm cold and I'm tired and I'm not wasting any more time out here. There are all kind of things wandering round out here and I—'

'All we're doing is—' Carl said.

Michael stopped and turned back around. 'All you're doing is wasting time. The two of you are standing out here risking your necks trying to do something that doesn't need to be done. I'm going in. I'll see you later.'

With that he was gone, and Carl and Emma were left alone with the two bodies at their feet. Emma had been annoyed by Michael's attitude and manner, but what upset her most of all was the fact that he was right. He was cold, heartless and unfeeling, but he was right. Burying the bodies would have served no real purpose other than to make the two of them feel a little better, less guilty about what they were doing. But they were simply trying to survive. The farmhouse and everything in it was of no use to Mr Jones any more . . .

'What are you thinking?' Carl asked, suddenly distracting Emma and bringing her crashing back into the cold reality of the living room.

'Nothing.'

Carl stretched out in the chair and yawned. 'What do we do next then?'

She looked at him. 'Don't know. If you're talking about tonight, I think we should try and get some sleep. If you mean in the morning, I'm not sure. We need to decide if we're going to stay here first of all.'

'So what do you think? Should we stay here or . . . ?'

'I think we'd be stupid to leave right now,' said Michael. He had been sound asleep just a few moments earlier and his sudden interruption startled Carl and Emma.

'How long have you been awake?' Carl asked.

'Not long. Anyway, in answer to your question, I think we should stay here for a while and see what happens.'

'Nothing's going to happen,' Emma grumbled.

'I hope you're right,' he said, yawning. 'I think we should spend tomorrow trying to find out exactly what we've got here. If we're safe, sheltered and secure, then I think we should stay.'

'I agree,' said Carl. He wasn't particularly keen to stay in the farmhouse; he just didn't want to go anywhere else. In the journey here from the city he'd seen more death and destruction than he'd ever thought possible. The walls of this strong old house were protecting him from the rest of the world.

'I'm going to bed,' Michael said, standing up and stretching. 'I could sleep for a week.'

18

Emma was the first to wake up next morning. It was Saturday (not that it mattered any more), and judging by the amount of low light which seeped in through the crack between the curtains, she decided it was early morning, probably no later than five o'clock.

After a few seconds of disorientation she remembered where she was and how she'd got there. She gazed up at the ceiling and stared at the numerous bumps and cracks. Her eyes drifted down to the walls where, in the semi-darkness, she began to count patterns on the wallpaper. The design was made up of five different pastel-pink flowers (which looked grey in the half-light), printed on a creamy white background. The flowers were printed in a strict and repetitive rotational sequence and she had counted twenty-three rotations before she stopped to question what it was she was doing. She realised that, subconsciously, she had been filling her mind with rubbish. It was easier to think about patterns on walls, cracks on the ceiling and other such crap than it was to have to remember what had happened to the world outside Penn Farm.

There was a sudden groaning noise from the side of the bed and she froze, rigid with fear. Lying perfectly still she listened intently. There was something in the bedroom with her, moving around on the floor next to the bed. Her heart pounded in her chest with an anxious ferocity and she held her breath, petrified that whatever it was that was in there with her might sense her presence.

When nothing happened she managed to pluck up enough courage to lean over the side of the bed and look down. A wave of relief washed over her when she saw that it was just Michael, asleep on the floor, curled up tightly in a sleeping bag. She lay back on the bed again and relaxed.

She was certain that Michael had begun the night sleeping

somewhere else. They had talked together on the landing outside her room for a few minutes after Carl had gone to find a bed. There were four bedrooms in the house – three on the second floor and one in the attic – and she could clearly remember Michael going into one of the other rooms adjacent to hers. So why was he sleeping on the floor next to her bed now? Was it because he thought she might need him there for protection, or was it because he himself needed company and reassurance in the long dark hours of the night just passed? Whatever the reason, she decided that it didn't matter. She was glad he was there.

She was wide awake now, and there was little prospect of getting back to sleep. Annoyed, and still tired, she shuffled across to the other side of the bed and swung her feet out over the edge. She lowered them down until they touched the bare varnished floorboards and recoiled at the sudden chill which ran through her as her toes made contact with the ground. The temperature in the room was low and she was cold, despite the fact that she had slept virtually fully dressed. Tiptoeing carefully so she didn't wake Michael, she crept around the room to the window and opened the curtains. Michael stirred and mumbled something unintelligible before rolling over and starting to snore gently.

Leaning up against the glass she looked out over the empty, dead world. An early morning mist clung to the ground, settling heavily in every dip and trough. Birds sang out and flitted between the tops of trees, silhouetted in black against the dull grey sky. For a few moments it was easy for Emma to convince herself that there was nothing much wrong with the rest of the world today. She hadn't often been up and about at four twenty-five (the precise time, according to the alarm clock next to the bed) but she imagined that this was how pretty much every day started.

She spied a lone figure moving slowly across a recently ploughed field just north of the farmhouse, barely able to coordinate its leaden feet over the uneven ground. She had seen thousands of the pitiful creatures over the last few days, but she instantly decided that this one particular stumbling bastard was the one she hated most of all. Her heart sank like a stone when she spotted it tripping languidly through the mist. If she hadn't seen it, then maybe she'd have been able to prolong the illusion of normality for a few minutes longer. But that was all it was now: an illusion of a normality that was long gone and which would never return. And there she was, trapped in the same desperate, incomprehensible nightmare that she'd been stuck in last night and the night before that and the night before that . . .

She began to cry and angrily wiped at her eyes. She felt hollow and empty again, as cold and dead as the body in the distance.

'Everything okay?' a voice suddenly asked from the darkness behind her. Startled, Emma caught her breath and spun around.

Michael stood in front of her, his normally bright eyes still dulled with sleep, his hair matted and unruly.

'I'm all right,' she answered, her heart thumping.

'Did I scare you? I'm sorry, I tried to make as much noise getting up as I could, but you were miles away . . .'

Emma shook her head. It didn't matter. He could have screamed at her and she wouldn't have noticed. She turned back to look out of the window and continued to scan the misty horizon, desperately hoping that she might catch sight of more movement. God, she hoped that they would see something else this morning. Not another one of the loathsome bodies though; she wanted to see someone moving with reason, purpose and direction, like she did. She wanted to find someone else who was truly alive.

'Anything out there?' he asked.

'Nothing. There's nothing left but us.'

19

It was hours later before Michael, Carl and Emma actually stopped and sat down together in the same room. They were in the kitchen, Carl and Emma sitting in silence around a circular pine table while Michael struggled to scrape together some breakfast. The late Mr Jones had obviously been a big eater and he'd left the larder of the farmhouse well-stocked, but the fresh food had spoiled and Michael was no cook.

The atmosphere was heavy and subdued. Michael felt low – perhaps lower than he had done at any time during the last few days – and he was struggling to fully understand why. He'd expected to feel more positive today. The three of them had after all stumbled upon a place where they could shelter safely for a while; a place which offered isolation and protection and yet which was still comfortable and spacious. He looked out through the wide kitchen window as he cooked and decided that it must have been the slight elation they'd felt last night which was making the reality of this morning so hard to accept. The baked beans he'd been heating had started to stick to the bottom of the pan and spoil.

'Something burning?' Carl asked.

Michael grunted and stirred and scraped the beans with a wooden spoon. He hated cooking. The reason he was preparing the meal this morning was the same reason he'd been the first to cook at the community centre back in Northwich. He had no community spirit, no real desire to please the others, but cooking was a distraction. Rescuing the burning beans somehow stopped him from thinking about the world outside and all that he'd lost for a few precious seconds.

Dejected and distant, he served the food. Emma and Carl looked at the breakfasts which clattered down in front of them with disinterest, neither of them feeling particularly hungry. Each plate had on it a large serving of beans, a dollop of scrambled eggs and some Frankfurter sausages which had been boiled in brine. Emma managed half a smile of acknowledgement. Carl sniffed and stared at the food, feeling tired and slightly nauseous.

Each of the survivors seemed to be trying their damnedest not to say or do anything that might result in them having to talk to or even look at the others. Whilst they each craved the security and comfort of conversation, they knew that talking would inevitably lead to them thinking about things that they were doing their best to ignore.

As the minutes dragged on, Emma's patience wore thin. Eventually she cracked. 'Look,' she sighed, 'are we just going to sit here, or should we think about actually trying to do something constructive today?'

Carl finally started to eat. Filling his mouth with burnt beans, undercooked sausage and overcooked eggs gave him an excuse not to have to talk.

'Well?' Emma pressed, annoyed by the lack of response.

'We've got to do something,' Michael agreed. 'I don't know what, but we've got to do something . . .'

'We need some decent food for a start,' she said, pushing her barely touched breakfast away.

'There's plenty of other stuff we need too.'

'Such as?'

'Clothes, tools, petrol . . . all the basics.'

'We've probably already got some of that here.'

Carl watched Emma and Michael intently as they spoke, following the conversation, looking from face to face.

'You're right. First thing we should do is go through this house from top to bottom and see exactly what we've got here.' Michael paused to take a breath. 'Carl, do you know what you'll need for the generator?'

Startled by the sudden mention of his name, Carl dropped his fork. 'What?'

Michael frowned. 'Do you know what you need to get the generator sorted?' he repeated, irrationally annoyed that Carl hadn't been listening.

Carl shook his head and picked up his fork again. 'No, not yet. I'll have a look later and try and work it out.'

'We should get it done straight after breakfast,' Emma suggested. 'I think we should check the house out from top to bottom, then get out, get what we need and get back as quickly as we can.'

'The sooner we get started,' Michael added, 'the sooner we get back.'

Emma was already up and out of her seat. Prompted to move by her sudden actions, Michael also got up and left the kitchen.

Carl was in no rush to go anywhere. He stayed sat at the table toying with the lukewarm food on his plate.

The decision to stay at Penn Farm had already been made, but it was only as they scoured the house for supplies that the full potential of their location finally became apparent to Emma and Michael. Carl was less sure. He wasn't convinced they'd be safe anywhere.

Emma began at the top of the building and worked her way down. She started in the odd-shaped attic bedroom which Carl had claimed as his own yesterday evening. The dull room was lit only by the light which trickled in through a small window at the front of the house. Other than a bed, a wardrobe and a couple of other items of furniture there was little of note to be found there.

Michael worked his way through the rooms on the second floor: three more reasonably sized bedrooms and an old-fashioned but practical bathroom. He uncovered little that he didn't expect to find: clothes (far too old, large and worn for any of them to consider wearing), personal possessions, trinkets and junk. As he sat on the edge of the large double bed that Emma had slept on last night and looked through an obviously antique jewellery box, he found himself suddenly fascinated by the value of the items it held. Less than a month ago the rings, earrings, necklaces, bracelets and brooches (which, he presumed, had belonged to Mrs Jones – what had happened to her?) might have been worth a small fortune. Today they were valueless. Conversely, as far as he was concerned, the comfort of the wooden-framed bed upon which he was now sitting made it worth millions in his eyes.

His daydreams were interrupted by Carl shouting from downstairs, 'Have you two seen this?'

Michael found him in the small ground-floor office. He'd been moving piles of papers off the farmer's desk.

Emma appeared moments later. 'What is it?'

Carl looked at her and scowled. How could she not know what it was? Michael did his best to hide the fact that he wasn't sure either. Was it an amplifier? An alarm?

'It's a radio.'

'And do you know how to use it?'

'Not yet,' he answered, blowing dust off the top of the set, 'but I'll find out. We'll get the power going then I'll have a look at it. The instructions are bound to be around here somewhere.'

Michael watched him as he looked at the radio, trying to make sense of the many buttons and dials on its black face-plate. Maybe he'd do it. It would be good to give him a focus, something to concentrate on. But at the back of his mind, he knew it was a pointless exercise. Even if they got the power on later and Carl managed to work out how to use the radio, what good would it do? Did he really expect to hear anything? With so few people left alive, would any of them really be sat around a radio like this, waiting for someone to make contact?

Michael's plan for the rest of the day was simple. Fill the van with supplies, get back, get safe, then get the generator working. Much as it would painfully remind him of everything he'd lost, his ultimate aim was to get a television or stereo working by the time darkness fell. He wanted to bring beer back to the house so that he could drink and forget. He knew that it would be a pale imitation of normality, but that didn't matter. The three of them were mentally and physically exhausted, and if they didn't soon force themselves to stop, it would be only a matter of time before someone cracked. He'd survived so far and he was damn sure he wasn't about to go under.

20

Less than an hour later, Michael, Carl and Emma were ready to leave the farm. Wrapped in as many layers of clothing as they could find, the three of them stood together at the side of the van and winced as a cold and blustery autumn wind gusted across the yard. Conversation was limited to the occasional grunt or monosyllabic mumble. Michael climbed into the van, turned the key and started the engine. The noise echoed through the desolate countryside.

'Any idea where we're going?' Emma asked from behind him. She shuffled in her seat and slid the key to the farmhouse into the pocket of her tight jeans. They'd locked the door, even though there was no one else left alive to break in.

'No,' Michael replied with admirable honesty. 'Have you?'

'No.'

'Fucking brilliant,' Carl cursed as Michael slammed the van into gear. They slowly moved away down the long rough track which led to the road.

'I'm sure I used to come around here on holiday with my mum and dad when I was younger,' he said, his voice quiet and low.

'So could you find your way around?' Emma asked hopefully.

'No. What I do remember is that there were loads of little towns and villages, all linked up by roads like this. If we keep driving in any one direction we're sure to find something somewhere.'

Carl wasn't impressed, but he kept his opinion to himself as Michael began to accelerate, forcing the van along the twisting track at an increasingly uncomfortable speed.

'Hope we can remember the way back after this,' Emma said, sounding far from sure.

''Course we will,' he replied confidently. 'We'll just keep going in one direction today. We'll get to a village, get what we need, and then just turn around and come back home.'

Home. Carl thought that was a strange word to use because this definitely didn't feel like home to him. Home was a hundred or so miles away. Home was his modest three-bedroom semi-detached house on a council estate in Northwich. Home was where he'd left Sarah and Gemma. Home was definitely not some empty farmhouse out in the middle of nowhere. He closed his eyes, rested his head against the window and tried to concentrate on the sound of the van's engine. Concentrating on the noise stopped him thinking about anything else.

Michael was right. Within fifteen minutes of leaving the farm they'd stumbled upon the small village of Pennmyre. As they approached they saw that it was not so much a village, more just a short row of modest shops with a few car parking spaces. The silent hamlet was so small that the sign which said *Welcome to Pennmyre – Please Drive Carefully* was less than a quarter of a mile from the one which read *Thank You for Visiting Pennmyre – Have a Safe Journey*. But the size of the village was comforting. They could see everything from the main road. There weren't any dark corners or hidden alleyways to worry about.

Michael stopped the van halfway down the main street and got out, leaving the engine running as a precaution. On first impressions the sight that greeted them was disappointingly familiar. It was just what they had expected to find – a few bodies littering the pavements, a couple of crashed cars and the occasional walking corpse, tripping and stumbling around aimlessly.

'Look at their faces,' Carl said as he stepped out into the cold morning air. It was the first time he'd said more than two words since they'd left the farmhouse. He stood on the broken white line in the middle of the road with his hands on his hips, staring in disbelief at the pitiful creatures that staggered past him, oblivious. In the short time since they'd left Northwich, their physical condition seemed to have rapidly deteriorated. 'Christ, they look fucking awful . . .'

Emma walked around the front of the van and stood next to

him. 'Which ones? The ones on the ground or the ones that are moving?'

He thought for a second. 'Both,' he replied at last. 'Doesn't seem to be any difference between them, does there?'

Emma looked down at a body in the gutter by her feet. Its lifeless face bore an expression of frozen, suffocated pain and fear which was still visible despite its grotesque deformation. Its skin appeared strangely saggy and loose, its eyes sunken and hollow, and she noticed that its flesh had a peculiar dappled-green tinge. The first obvious visible signs, she decided, of decay. The other bodies – those still moving around them – had the same unnatural hue to their skin.

There was a sudden dull thump behind Carl and he spun around anxiously to see that one of the awkward stumbling figures had walked into the side of the van. Painfully slowly it pivoted around on stiff legs and then, quite by chance, it began to walk towards him. For a few long seconds Carl didn't react. He just stood there and stared into its emotionless eyes, feeling an icy chill run the entire length of his body.

'Bloody hell. Look at its eyes. Just look at its eyes . . .'

Emma recoiled at the sight of the pitiful creature. It was a man who she guessed must have been about fifty years old when he'd died (although the colour and sheen of his skin made it difficult to estimate with any certainty). The uncoordinated body staggered forward listlessly. The inside of its legs, she noticed with disgust, were wet with decay, its putrefying innards slowly seeping out.

Carl was transfixed, almost hypnotised by a deadly combination of morbid curiosity and uneasy fear. As the cadaver approached he could see that its pupils had dilated to such an extent that the dull iris of each eye seemed almost to have disappeared, leaving just two wide black circles. The eyes moved continually, never settling on any one object; whatever information was being sent to the creature's dead brain was not registering at all. The body moved ever closer to Carl, looking straight through him. It didn't even know he was there.

'For God's sake,' Michael shouted, 'be careful, will you?'

'It's all right. Bloody thing can't even see me.' With that he lifted up his arms and put a hand on each of the dead man's shoulders. The body stopped moving instantly. Rather than resist or react in any way it simply slumped forward. Carl could feel the weight of its entire frame (which was unexpectedly light and emaciated) being supported by his hands.

'They're empty, aren't they?' Emma said under her breath. She took a few tentative steps closer to the corpse and stared into its face. Now that she was closer she could see a fine, milky-white film covering both eyes. There were open sores and fluid filled blisters on its skin (particularly around the mouth and nose) and its greasy hair lay lankly against its skull. Its shirt hung open and she looked down at its willowy torso, staring at the rib cage in vain for any sign of respiration.

Michael had been watching her as intently and with as much fascination as she'd watched the body. 'What do you mean, empty?' he asked.

'Just what I said,' she replied, still staring at the dead man. 'There's nothing to them. They move, but they don't know why. It's like they've died, but no one's told them to stop and lie still.'

Carl dropped his arms and let the corpse go. The second he relaxed his grip it began to stumble away.

'So if they're not thinking, why do they change direction?' he asked.

'Simple,' Emma answered, 'they don't do it consciously. If you watch them, they only change direction when they can't go any further forward.'

He watched as another listless figure clattered comically into a shop window, then turned and walked away.

'I know that, but how did that one know to turn around? Why didn't it just stop?'

'It's just a basic response, isn't it?' Michael suggested.

'Suppose so,' Emma agreed. 'It's just about *the* most basic response. Christ, even amoebas and earthworms can react like that. If they come across an obstruction then they change direction.'

'So are you saying that they're thinking or not thinking?'

'I'm not sure really . . .' she admitted.

'Because you sound like you're saying they might still have some decision-making capabilities . . .'

'Suppose I am.'

'But on the other hand they seem to be on autopilot, just moving because they can.'

Emma was getting a little annoyed by his barrage of unanswerable questions. 'Christ, I don't know. I'm just telling you what I think.'

'So what *do* you think? What do you really think has happened to them?'

'They're almost dead.'

'Almost dead?'

'I think that about ninety-nine per cent of their bodies are dead. They're not breathing, thinking or eating, but there's something still working inside them at the most basic level.'

'Such as?' Michael asked.

'Don't know.'

'Want to take a guess?'

Emma was reluctant. She wasn't at all certain about what she was saying. She was improvising, and having to think on her feet.

'I'm really not sure,' she sighed. 'Christ, it's instinct, I suppose. They have no comprehension of identity or purpose any more, no needs or wants. They just exist. They move because they can. No other reason.'

Conscious that she had become the centre of attention, Emma walked away from the van towards the row of shops to her right. She felt awkward. In the eyes of her two companions her limited medical experience and knowledge made her an expert in a field where no one actually knew anything.

On the ground in front of a bakery the dead body of a frail old man struggled to get up, weak arms flailing uselessly.

'What's the matter with it?' Carl asked, peering cautiously over Emma's shoulder.

Michael, who had followed the other two, nudged Emma and pointed at an upturned wheelchair which was lying a few yards away. She looked from the chair to the body and back again, then crouched down. Fighting to keep control of her stomach (the rotting skin gave out a noxious odour) she pulled back one of the trouser legs and saw that its right leg was artificial. In its weakened state the body couldn't even lift it off the ground.

'See,' she said, standing up again, 'bloody thing doesn't even know it's only got one leg. Poor bugger's probably been in a wheelchair for years.'

Uninterested in the crippled body and feeling queasy, Carl wandered away. He walked alone along the front of the row of silent shops and gazed sadly into the dusty windows of each building he passed. There was a bank – its doors wide open – and next to it an optician's, where two corpses sat motionless, waiting for appointments that would never happen. Next to the optician's was a grocery store. It had been shut for almost a week, and the front of the small shop was a bit of a sun-trap, making the inside dry, stale and unexpectedly warm. The contrast with outside acted like smelling salts and reminded Carl why he was there. Suddenly feeling vulnerable and unsafe, he began to fill cardboard boxes with all the non-perishable food he could find.

Emma and Michael arrived moments later and in a little under fifteen minutes the three of them had transferred much of the grocery store's stock to the back of their van. In less than an hour they were back at Penn Farm.

21

Michael and Emma sat opposite each other at the kitchen table. It was almost four o'clock. Carl had been working outside on the generator for the best part of the afternoon. The back door was open and the house was cold.

'There's got to be something driving them on,' Emma said. 'I can't understand why they keep moving and yet—'

'Bloody hell, give it a rest, will you? What does it matter? Why should we give a damn what they do and why they do it as long as they're not a danger to us? Christ, I don't care if I wake up to find a hundred and one of the fucking things stood around the house doing a bloody song and dance routine as long as they don't—'

'Okay, you've made your point. Sorry if I don't share your short-sightedness.'

'I'm not being short-sighted,' Michael protested.

'Yes you are. You don't give a damn about anyone but yourself—'

'That's not true.'

'Yes it is.'

'No, it isn't. I'm looking out for you and Carl too. I just think we have to face facts, that's all.'

'We don't know any facts, that's the problem. We don't know anything.'

'Yes we do. For a start it's a fact that it doesn't matter what's happened to the rest of the population as long as nothing happens to us. It's a fact that it doesn't matter *why* millions of people died and we're alive. What difference would it make if we knew? What could we do? Even if we found some miracle cure, what would we do? Spend the rest of our lives sorting out fifty-odd million corpses at the expense of ourselves?'

'No, but—'

'But nothing. I'm not being short-sighted, I'm being realistic.'

'I can't help it,' she said quietly, resting her head in her hands. 'It's the medic in me. I wanted to look after people and this goes against the grain—'

Michael stared at her. 'Forget all that. Forget everything. Stop trying to work out what's happened and why. What's gone is gone and we've got to make the most of what's left. We've got to forget everything and everyone else and concentrate on trying to build some kind of future for the three of us.'

'I know. But it's not that simple, is it? I can't just switch off and—'

'But you've *got* to! Christ, how many times do I have to say it? You've got to shut off from the past. That life's over now.'

'I'm trying. Look, I know I can't help anyone else, but I don't think you've thought about this like I have.'

'What do you mean?'

'I want to make sure we're safe, same as you do,' she explained, 'but have you stopped to wonder whether it's really over?'

'What?'

'Who says that's the end of it? Who says that the bodies getting up and moving around was the final act?'

'What are you saying?'

'I'm not sure,' she admitted, slouching forward and massaging her temples. 'Look, Mike, I think you're right, we have to look after ourselves now. But I need to know that whatever it was that happened to the rest of them isn't going to happen to me. Just because we've escaped so far doesn't necessarily mean we're immune, does it?'

'And do you think we should—?'

Michael's words were abruptly cut short by a sudden loud crash from outside which echoed through the otherwise quiet house. He jumped up and ran outside to find Carl sitting on the grass with his head in his hands. Through the half-open shed door he could see an upturned toolbox which had just been kicked over, or maybe thrown in anger.

'Okay?' he asked redundantly.

Carl angrily grunted something under his breath before getting up and disappearing into the shed again.

Emma watched from the back door. 'Is he okay?'

'I think so. Looks like he's having a few problems, that's all.'

She nodded thoughtfully and continued to watch.

Michael slumped against the wall next to her.

'It'll be getting dark soon. He'll have to call it a day.'

Michael didn't answer. He looked up and watched her watching Carl. 'Listen, about what you were just saying . . .'

'What about it?'

'Assuming we are immune and we do survive all of this . . .'

'Yes . . . ?'

'Do you think we'll be able to make something out of what's left?'

Emma thought for a moment before answering, 'Not sure yet. Do you?'

'We can be comfortable here, I'm sure of that much. Christ, we could turn this place into a bloody fortress if we wanted to. Everything we need is out there somewhere. It's just a question of getting off our backsides and finding it . . .'

'Daunting prospect, isn't it?'

'I know. It's not going to be easy but . . .'

'I think the most important thing is deciding whether we want to survive, not whether we can.' She turned around to face Michael. 'Look, I know we could have anything – bloody hell, we could live in Buckingham bloody Palace if we wanted to—'

'—once we'd cleared out the corpses—'

'Okay, but you get my point. We *can* have anything, but we've got to ask ourselves: is there anything that will make any of this easier to deal with? I don't want to bust a gut building something up if we're just going to end up prisoners here, counting the days until we die of old age.'

Her honesty was painful. Michael got up and went back inside. She followed him into the kitchen and watched as he filled a kettle of water and put it on the hob to boil.

'You know what I think we should—' he started, but he stopped speaking suddenly. He could hear something. It couldn't be, could it? He turned the gas burner off. Christ, he could hear machinery: a low, steady mechanical chugging.

Carl breathlessly threw himself through the door. 'Done it! I've fucking done it!'

He proudly flicked the light switch on the wall and the fluorescent strip above them slowly flickered and jumped into life, filling the room with harsh, relentless and completely beautiful electric light.

22

They continued to busy themselves around the house until just after nine o'clock. The availability of electric light had substantially extended the length of their useful day. Once their supplies had been stored and the van and house made secure for the night they stopped, exhausted. Emma made a meal which they ate as they watched a film they'd found.

Michael, who had been sitting on the floor resting with his back against the sofa, looked over his shoulder just after eleven and noticed that both Carl and Emma had fallen asleep. For a while he stared into their faces and watched as the flickering light from the television screen cast unnerving, constantly moving shadows across them.

It had been a strange evening. The apparent normality of sitting and watching television had bothered Michael more than he'd expected. Everything had seemed so ordinary when they'd started watching the film an hour and a half earlier. Within minutes each of them had privately been transported back to a time not so long ago, when the population of the country had numbered millions, not hundreds. Perhaps the night felt so strange and wrong for that very reason. The three of them had again been reminded of everything that they – through no fault of their own – had lost. Carl had admitted that he felt guilty living like this when everyone else was dead.

Michael was bitterly disappointed, although he did his best not to show it. Gone was the time when he'd been able to enjoy the cheap and cheerful comedy film (such as the one they'd just watched) for what it was – a temporary feel-good distraction, anaesthetic for the brain. Now everything that he did and saw forced him to think about issues he didn't want to consider and ask questions he didn't want to answer. Not yet, anyway.

His lack of concentration had been such that he hadn't noticed the film had finished until the end titles had been rolling up the screen for several minutes. Preoccupied by dark thoughts again, he remained sitting on his backside, waiting for the screen to finally fade to black. As the music ended and was replaced by silence he opened another can of beer and stretched out on the floor.

For a while longer he lay still and listened carefully to the world around him. Carl was snoring lightly and Emma fidgeted in her sleep but other than that, the two of them were quiet. Outside there was the constant thumping and banging of the generator in the shed and he could hear a strong wind gusting through the tops of the tall pine trees which surrounded the farm. Beyond all of that Michael could just about hear the ominous low grumble of a distant but fast-approaching storm. Through half-open curtains he watched as the first few drops of rain clattered against the window. He sat up quickly when he glimpsed movement outside the back of the house. Was there something out there?

Suddenly nervous, Michael jumped up and pressed his face against the glass. He peered out into the dark night, wondering whether the mechanical noises being made by the generator had acted like the classical music back in the city, attracting the attention of survivors who would otherwise have remained oblivious to their arrival at Penn Farm. He couldn't see anything. As quickly as he cleared the glass the rain outside and the condensation inside obscured his view again.

The others were still asleep. Michael ran through the house and picked up a torch they had placed on a dresser in the hallway. The torch was bright and he followed the unsteady circle of white light through to the back door of the house. He opened it cautiously and stepped out into the cold evening air, ignoring the heavy rain which quickly drenched his clothes.

There it was again: definite movement around the generator. With his pulse racing he made his way further down the garden, stopping when he was just a few yards short of the shed. Gathered around the walls of the small wooden building were four dishevelled figures. Even with the limited light from the torch and with the distraction of the wind, rain and approaching storm it was obvious that these were victims of the disease, the virus or whatever it was that had devastated the population last week. Michael watched with mingled curiosity and unease as one of the bodies collided with the door. But rather than turning and staggering away again as he'd expected, the bedraggled creature instead began to work its way around the shed, tripping and sliding through the wet grass.

Something wasn't right.

It took Michael the best part of a minute to decide what it was, and then it dawned on him: these corpses weren't going anywhere. Their movements were just as slow and listless as the hundreds of others they'd seen, but they were definitely gravitating around the shed.

When three out of the four bodies were temporarily out of the way of the door, Michael pushed past the one remaining and slipped inside, struggling to think straight over the deafening noise of the generator. He found the controls that regulated the machine and switched it off. After wiping his face and hands dry on a dirty towel and pausing to catch his breath, he went back outside.

By the time he'd shut the door to the shed he was alone. Three of the corpses had already gone and he could see the fourth awkwardly tripping away from the house.

23

Despite having gone to bed exhausted, Michael was awake, up, washed and dressed by six o'clock the following morning. He'd spent another uncomfortable and mostly sleepless night tossing and turning on the hard wooden floor at the side of Emma's bed. He was glad he'd woken up before she had. She hadn't said anything to make him think that she minded him being there, but he was quietly concerned as to what she thought his reasons were. It just made him feel better not to be sleeping alone.

Michael had spent the last dark hours curled up in fear like a frightened child. His mind had been full of irrational nightmares, the like of which hadn't troubled him since he'd been eight or nine years old. In the early morning gloom he'd hidden under his covers from monsters lurking behind the door, then found himself sitting bolt upright in the darkness, certain that something terrible was coming up the stairs to get him. He knew there was nothing there, that the sounds he could hear were just the unfamiliar creaks and groans of the old house, but that didn't make any difference. The fear was impossible to ignore. As a child his parents had always been there to rescue and reassure him, but not today. Today there was nothing and no one to help, and the reality beyond the door of the farmhouse was worse than any dark dream he'd ever had.

As the first light of morning had begun to creep into the house, his confidence had returned. The uncomfortable fear he'd experienced was quickly replaced by a private foolishness, leaving him feeling almost embarrassed that he'd been so frightened in the night. At one point in the long hours just passed, when the howling wind outside had been screaming and whipping fiercely through the trees, he had covered his ears and screwed his eyes tightly shut, praying that he'd fall asleep and wake up somewhere else. Although no one else had seen or heard him, he felt ashamed that he had allowed a chink to appear in his usually unflappable, almost arrogant exterior.

It was a strong, safe and sound house, and Michael knew he need not have worried. In spite of all that he had imagined in the darkness, nothing and no one had managed to reach Penn Farm. Still drugged by sleep he stumbled into the kitchen and lit the gas stove. The constant low roar of the burner was strangely soothing and comforting and he was glad that the heavy silence of the early morning had finally been disturbed. Slightly more relaxed, he boiled a kettle of water and made himself a mug of strong black coffee. He made himself some breakfast but couldn't eat much more than a couple of mouthfuls. Bored, tired and restless, he desperately needed to find something to do. As he had already discovered to his cost, an unoccupied minute these days tended to feel like an hour, and an empty hour seemed to drag on for more than a day.

An open door on the other side of the kitchen led into a large utility room, which Michael wandered into aimlessly. In the furthest corner of the room was a pile of empty boxes and other rubbish that they hadn't yet disposed of. This had been the least important room in the house as far as the three of them had been concerned, and as such, they'd done little more than use it as a temporary store. Michael thought for a second or two about trying to sort it into some kind of order, but he couldn't be bothered. Too much effort, too early in the day.

High on the wall opposite the door he'd just walked through was a wooden shelf, a warped plank of wood held in place by three rusty brackets, and it was piled high with junk. Curious, he dragged a chair across the room and climbed up to have a closer look. On first sight there was little of any interest – some old garden tools and chemicals, faded and yellowed books and newspapers, glass jars full of nails, bolts and screws and the like – but then he came across an unexpected, unmistakable shape. It was the butt of a rifle. Cautiously he pulled the gun free and stood there, balancing precariously on the chair, admiring the cobweb-covered weapon. With the rifle wedged under his arm he reached up again and felt his way along the shelf, first to the left and then to the right, until, with his fingers at full stretch, he grabbed hold of a dusty cardboard box. He teased open the lid and saw that it was full of ammunition. Like a child with a new toy he jumped down and carried his treasure trove back to the kitchen.

Emma rose at half-past eight and Carl got up three-quarters of an hour later. They found Michael sat at the kitchen table, carefully cleaning the rifle. He'd been working on it for almost two hours and the job was almost done. He glanced up at Emma. She looked as tired as he felt. Had she spent the night lying awake too?

'What are you doing?' she eventually asked him, once she'd made herself a drink.

'Found this earlier,' he replied, stifling a yawn. 'Thought I'd have a go at cleaning it up.'

'What's it for?' Carl asked, the first words he'd uttered since coming downstairs.

Without any sarcasm or attempt at humour he replied, deadpan, 'Shooting things.'

'I know that, you idiot, but what are we going to use it for?'

He put the rifle down. 'Don't know. Bloody hell, I hope we never need it.'

The weapon was clearly of interest to Carl. He sat down next to him and picked it up. Having spent all morning working on it, Michael was annoyed that he'd decided to interfere.

'Put it down,' he said, 'I haven't finished with it yet.'

'You ever used one of these?' Carl asked, suddenly awake and much more animated.

'No, but . . .'

'I have,' he continued. 'Used to do some work for a bloke who used to shoot.'

'I don't like it,' Emma said from across the room. She was standing next to the sink, as far away from the table as she could get. 'We don't need it. We should get rid of it.'

'I'm not sure. We don't even know if it's going to work yet . . .'

'Can't see any reason why it shouldn't,' Carl interrupted. 'Mind if I try it out?'

'Yes I do,' Michael said, trying unsuccessfully to get the rifle back off him. 'Bloody hell, I've spent hours getting it—'

Carl wasn't listening. He jumped up from his seat, grabbed a handful of ammunition and headed outside. Michael glanced at Emma and then followed him. By the time they reached the front door he could already hear Carl repeatedly cocking and firing the rifle.

'Is he safe with that thing?' Emma asked quietly as they stepped outside. Michael didn't answer; he was still fuming that the rifle had been taken from him. He watched angrily as Carl loaded it.

'This is okay, you know,' he babbled excitedly. 'This is just what we needed. You never know what's around the corner these days . . .'

'Don't know what frightens me more,' Michael said quietly, 'the fact that there are thousands of dead bodies walking around the countryside or him with that fucking gun.'

Emma managed half a smile which immediately disappeared when Carl lifted up the rifle and held it ready to fire again. He pressed the butt hard into his shoulder, closed one eye and aimed into the distance.

'What the hell are you doing?' Michael shouted. 'Are you stupid? All we need is for that thing to blow back in your face and you're history . . .'

'It's okay,' he answered without moving or lowering the rifle, 'I know about these things. It won't blow back.'

'Just put it down, will you?' said Emma.

'Watch this. I'm going to get him . . .'

Puzzled, Michael moved around to stand behind him and looked along the barrel of the rifle. Carl was aiming through a gap in the trees, out towards a field where a lone figure was tripping clumsily through the mud.

'Just leave it, will you?'

'I'm going to get him,' Carl said again, shuffling his feet and setting the figure square in his sights. 'What's he gonna do about it? Christ, he probably won't even know he's been shot.'

'You've got to hit him first.'

'Oh, I'll hit the bastard,' he said and, with that, he squeezed the trigger and fired. The deafening sound of the shot rang out for what sounded like for ever, echoing endlessly.

'Shit, missed him.'

The figure in the field stopped moving.

'He's stopped,' Michael said, shocked. 'Christ, he heard the shot. He must be alive!'

Stunned, Carl took a few cautious steps forward. 'I didn't hit him, did I?' he asked anxiously. 'Shit, I was only trying to . . .'

'Shut up,' Michael said, 'you didn't hit him.'

As they stared into the distance the figure in the field began to move again. Instead of struggling on across the muddy field, however, he had changed direction. The bedraggled man was walking towards the house. Emma couldn't believe what she was seeing.

'Is he coming this way?'

'Looks like it,' Carl replied. Michael didn't say anything. He continued to watch for a few seconds longer until he was completely certain the man was heading towards them, then sprinted out to meet him. Apart from the survivors back in Northwich, this was the first person he'd seen who had consciously reacted to what was happening around them. And to think, moments earlier Carl had aimed a rifle at him!

Emma chased after Michael, and Carl followed close behind. The view from the farmhouse had been misleading. There was a hidden dip between Michael and the man which added extra distance and an unexpected climb. He continued at speed through the clammy mud, keeping the lone stranger in view every step of the way. He pushed himself to keep running, faster and faster. He wanted to shout, but he couldn't; his mouth was dry and his heart pounded with effort and excitement.

'I'll catch you up,' Carl wheezed, unable to keep up the pace of the sudden, frantic run. Emma glanced back at him over her shoulder then turned back to face Michael, who finally stopped running and walked the last few steps towards the man.

'Christ, mate,' he said between deep, forced breaths, 'the chances of us seeing you out here . . .' He lost his footing in the slimy mud, skidded forward and slipped down onto one knee.

He looked up into the man's face and, in an instant, all the hope and elation he had felt immediately disappeared. It was just another one of those fucking useless corpses, with its emaciated frame, clothed in loose fitting rags, grey-green, pockmarked skin . . . just like every other one of the lamentable bastards they had seen.

Dejected, Michael climbed back to his feet and turned around to tell the others, 'It's no good. It's no fucking good. This bastard's dead, just like the rest of them . . .'

Neither Emma or Carl could hear what he was saying over the blustery, gusting wind. Confused, they watched as the scrawny figure continued to move closer. It lifted its rotting head, seeming almost to be looking at Michael, who was still facing the other way. The corpse's next movements were so unexpected that no one, especially not Michael, had time to prevent it.

The sound of a single sliding footstep squelching through the thick mud alerted him. He spun around and found himself face to face with the foul creature. Before he could react it launched itself at him, its numb left hand thumping into him, its right hand somehow managing to grab hold of his shirt. More from the surprise of the attack than its force, Michael was sent slipping and sprawling to the ground, dragging the body down with him. Suddenly spurred into action, Carl sprinted to his defence and grabbed the shoulders of the corpse as it collapsed on top of him. Although weak, with little strength, the body clung on with savage instinct and unexpected determination. Carl managed to pull its decaying frame up a little way, just far enough for Michael to be able to slide his hands under its bony chest and push it up and away. With brutal force he thrust the body up into the air and rolled away to the side through the mud before it hit the deck again.

'Okay?' Emma yelled, running towards him.

He wiped splashes of foul-smelling mud from his face and nodded, still fighting to catch his breath, trying to understand what had just happened. Tired from running, the unexpected attack had caught him completely off-guard.

'I'm all right.'

The body on the ground lay on its back, squirming and struggling to right itself again. It had just managed to haul itself up onto its elbows when Carl knocked it back down, hitting it square in the face with a well-aimed boot.

'Fucking thing. You stupid fucking thing,' he muttered.

The corpse continued to twist and writhe. Oblivious to Carl's comparative strength it lifted itself up again, and Carl immediately kicked it back down.

'Fucking thing,' he spat for a third time before kicking it in the side of the head.

'Leave it,' Michael said. He had managed to stand up and now he was being pulled back towards the house by Emma. 'Come on, Carl, just leave it.'

Carl wasn't listening. He kicked the mud-covered figure on the ground again and again, sending it rolling over and over away from him.

'Carl!' Emma yelled, 'Carl, come on!'

She could clearly see the hate and frustration in his face, driving him on to keep attacking.

He looked at her for a fraction of a second before returning his full attention to the rotting corpse at his feet. He spat into its vacant face before letting go with another torrent of kicks. The creature was totally unaware of the brutal battering it was taking; every time it was beaten down it tried to get back up again.

Finally, dumbfounded, Carl took a breathless step backwards. 'Just look at this!' he shouted, pointing at the pathetic monstrosity squirming in the mud. One of its arms was broken now and hung useless at its side, though the shoulder was still moving continually. 'Will you just look at this thing? It doesn't know when it's beaten!'

Emma could hear desperate, raw emotion in his voice. He sounded close to tears but she didn't know whether they were tears of pain, anger, fear or grief.

'Come on!' Michael yelled again. 'Don't waste your time. Let's get back to . . .'

He stopped speaking when he noticed there was another figure in the field slowly moving towards them.

Emma grabbed hold of his arm. 'Look!'

'I see it. What the hell's going on?'

The second figure stumbled towards the survivors with the same slothful intent as the first.

'There's another one coming, Carl,' Emma said, trying hard to control her rising panic, 'and another!'

Michael took her hand and half-led, half-dragged her away. 'Get going,' he told her, 'and don't stop until you're inside the house.'

Her eyes filling with frightened tears, she took a couple of hesitant steps away before pausing to look back. One last glance at the approaching bodies and she turned and raced back towards the farmhouse, running for all she was worth.

'Carl!' Michael shouted. 'We're going. Pull yourself together . . .'

Carl looked up and finally saw the two other corpses approaching. In a defiant last outburst of anger and frustration he kicked the still squirming corpse on the ground one more time in the head. He caught it square in the face and felt bones shatter and break under the force of his boot. Thick crimson-black, semi-congealed blood dribbled from a gaping hole where its nose and mouth had been and the creature finally lay still. He turned and ran after the others, almost losing his balance in the mud when a fourth bedraggled body came at him from out of nowhere.

By the time all three of them had made it back to the house, the first battered and blood-soaked body in the field had managed to drag itself up onto its unsteady feet again. It turned around awkwardly and followed eleven others as the dead converged on the isolated building.

24

'What the hell is going on?'

Michael slammed the door and locked it.

Emma slid down the wall at the bottom of the stairs and held her head in her hands, still breathing heavily. 'Christ knows.'

Carl pushed Michael to one side and peered out through the small glass window in the front door. 'Shit, there are loads of them out there, bloody loads of them. I can see at least ten from here.' He seemed pumped full of adrenalin, ready for a fight.

'Take it easy, mate. Calm down . . .'

'We should go out there and get rid of them.'

'We should stay in here and wait until they've gone,' Michael said quickly.

'But . . .'

'But nothing. Stay here.'

He watched Carl anxiously. For a second it looked like he was going to go back outside. He remained stood at the door but he didn't do it. Relieved, Michael sat down on the stairs next to Emma.

'They've changed,' she said, her head still low. 'I don't know what's happened or why but they've changed.'

'I know. I saw it last night when you and Carl were asleep.'

She looked up. 'What happened? What did you see?'

'I went out to shut off the generator and there were four of them hanging around outside the shed.'

'You didn't say anything . . .'

'I didn't think it mattered until now. Anyway, as soon as I'd switched it off they disappeared.'

'Don't think they're coming any closer,' Carl said, his face still pressed hard against the glass, ignorant to their conversation. 'Looks like they're starting to move away again.'

'Which way are they going?' Michael asked.

'Not sure. Towards the back of the house, I think.'

'Back towards the generator?'

'Could be.'

'That's it then, isn't it?' Emma said.

'What is?'

'It's sound, it must be. They're starting to regain their senses.'

'But why? Why now?' Michael asked.

'I don't know. Remember how they suddenly got up and started moving around?'

'Yes . . .'

'So this must be the same thing.'

'What the hell are you talking about?' Carl interrupted, finally turning away from events outside.

'Perhaps they weren't as badly damaged as we first thought.'

'Jesus,' he laughed, unable to believe what he was hearing. 'They couldn't have been much more badly damaged, could they? They're dead, for Christ's sake!'

'I know that, but maybe a small part of them has survived? The only reactions we've seen so far have been basic and instinctive. There's this lump of jelly, right in the middle of the brain, that might be responsible for instinct. Maybe that's the part of them that's still alive?'

'But they didn't attack me last night, did they?' Michael reminded her. 'I walked right past those bastards and—'

'Perhaps they were only just starting to respond last night? This is a gradual thing. From what you've told me it's possible that they've only been like this for a few hours.'

'This sounds like bullshit,' Carl said angrily.

'I know it does,' Emma admitted, 'but you come up with a better explanation and I'll listen. One morning everyone drops down dead. A few days later, half of them get up and start walking around again. A few days after that and they start responding to the outside world and their eyes and ears start working again. You're completely right, Carl, it stinks. It does sound like bullshit—'

'But it's happening,' Michael said. 'Doesn't matter how ridiculous or far-fetched any of it sounds, it's happening out there.'

'I know, but—'

'But nothing. These are the facts and we've got to deal with them. Simple as that.'

The conversation ended abruptly and the house became deathly silent. The lack of noise unnerved Carl.

'So why did that thing attack you?' he asked, looking directly at Michael for answers he knew the other man couldn't give.

'Maybe it didn't really attack – maybe it just reacted to me being there, just threw itself at me . . . ?'

'I'm sure it's sound they respond to first,' Emma said. 'They hear something and turn towards it. Once they see what it is they try and get closer.'

'That makes sense . . .'

'Nothing makes sense,' Carl muttered.

Ignoring him, Michael continued, 'The noise from the generator last night, the gunshot this morning . . .'

'So we've just got to stay quiet and stay out of sight,' Emma said.

'And how the hell are we going to do that?' Carl demanded, suddenly furious. 'Where are you going to get a silent car from? What are we supposed to do? Go out to look for food on fucking push-bikes? Wearing fucking camouflage jackets?'

'Shut up,' Michael said, his voice calm but firm. 'You've got to try and deal with this, Carl.'

'Don't patronise me, you bastard.'

'Look,' Emma said, quickly getting up and positioning herself directly between the two men, 'will both of you just shut up? It's like Michael says, Carl, we've got no option but to try and deal with this as best we can . . .'

'So what are we going to do then?' he asked, a little calmer but with his voice still shaking with an equal mixture of adrenalin-fuelled anger and fear.

'We need to get more supplies in,' Michael answered. 'If they are becoming more aware, then I think we should go out right now and get as much stuff as we can carry. Then we should get ourselves back here and lie low for a while.'

'And how long is that likely to be?' Carl asked, beginning to wind himself up again. 'A week? Two weeks? A month? Ten fucking years . . . ?'

'I *don't know*! Will you stop being such a prick and get a hold of yourself—!'

'Shut up!' Emma yelled, immediately silencing them both. 'For Christ's sake, if neither of you can say anything without arguing, then don't bother saying anything at all.'

'Sorry,' Michael said self-consciously, running his fingers through his matted hair then massaging his temples.

'So what *are* we going to do?' she asked.

Rather than take any further part in the increasingly difficult conversation, Carl turned and walked away.

'Where are you going? Carl, come back here. We need to talk about this . . .'

Halfway up the stairs he stopped and looked back over his shoulder at her. 'What's left to talk about? What's the point?'

'The point is we've got to do something now,' Michael said. 'We don't know what's going to happen next, do we? Things could be a hundred times worse tomorrow.'

'He's right,' agreed Emma. 'We've got enough stuff here to last us for a few days, but we need enough to last us weeks. I think we should get out now and barricade ourselves in when we get back.'

'What do you mean?' asked Carl, sitting down on the step he'd been standing on. 'I don't want to shut myself away in here . . .'

'Maybe we shouldn't,' Michael said. 'Maybe we should try it a different way, try and seal off the farm from the outside.'

'And how are we supposed to do that?' Emma asked.

'Build a fence,' he replied, simply.

'It'd have to be a fucking strong fence,' Carl added.

'Then we'll build a fucking strong fence. We'll get whatever materials we need and make a start. Face it, we're not going to find anywhere better to stay than this place. We need to protect it.'

'We need to protect ourselves,' said Emma, correcting him.

'Let's go,' he said, picking up the keys to the van from a hook on the wall by the front door.

'Now?' asked Carl.

'Now,' Michael replied. He opened the door and went out to the van, stopping only to pick up the rifle from where Carl had left it in the yard in front of the house.

25

Carl drove the van while Michael and Emma sat in the back. It had been a conscious move by Michael to hand the keys over to him. He hadn't liked the way Carl had been acting this morning. Sure, all three of them were right on the edge at the moment, but he seemed more precarious than either of the other two. There was an undeniable edge of uncertainty and fear in his voice whenever he spoke. Michael's logic was that by distracting him and giving him a definite role to focus on, his mind would be occupied and any problems could be temporarily avoided.

They drove towards the village of Byster at a phenomenal speed. Michael tactfully asked Carl to slow down, but he wouldn't. Driving was deceptively difficult now, because although silent, every road was strewn with countless random obstacles – crashed and abandoned cars, burnt-out wrecks, the remains of collapsed buildings and many scattered, motionless corpses. Those which were still moving added another level of difficulty to what had previously been a simple task. When Michael himself had driven he'd found that a steadily increasing, nervous pressure had forced him to keep his foot on the accelerator. He felt sure that Carl was feeling that same clammy, uncomfortable fear too.

Before they reached the village they passed a vast, warehouse-like supermarket on the edge of an industrial estate, brightly painted and completely at odds with the lush green countryside which surrounded it. Carl slammed his foot on the brake, quickly turned the van around and drove back towards the large building. It was a crucial find and would no doubt be stocked with pretty much everything they needed. More importantly, filling the van with supplies there meant that they didn't need to get any closer to the centre of the village. It meant that they could keep their distance from the dead.

'Brilliant. This is fucking brilliant,' Carl said under his breath as he pulled into the car park and stopped the van. Apart from four stationary cars (two empty, one containing three motionless bodies and the other a charred and rusting wreck) and a single body which tripped and stumbled haphazardly towards them, they were alone.

'You want to get as close as you can to the main doors,' Michael advised, looking over Carl's shoulder. 'We need to be out in the open as little as possible.'

After thinking for a second, Carl put the van into first gear and pulled away again, driving away from the building and stopping when the glass entrance doors were directly behind him.

'What's he doing?' Emma asked quietly.

'I think he's going to reverse back,' Michael replied. 'Sensible move. If I was driving I'd try and get us almost touching the doors so that—'

He stopped speaking suddenly when Carl slammed the van into reverse. The force of the sudden and unexpected movement threw Emma and Michael forward in their seats.

'Jesus Christ!' Michael yelled over the scream of the engine and the screeching of tyres, 'what the hell are you doing?'

Carl didn't answer but looked back over his shoulder at the supermarket doors as the engine whined and the van hurtled back towards the building. Emma turned to look behind too, then crouched down with her hands over her head and braced herself for impact. The van smashed into the plate-glass doors, then stopped suddenly. The noise of the engine was immediately replaced by the ear-splitting crash of shattering glass and the ominous groan and grind of metal on metal. When Michael looked up he saw that the back third of the van was inside the building, wedged in the doorway.

'You stupid idiot!' Emma shouted angrily.

Ignoring her, Carl turned off the engine, opened the tailgate using a control lever by his right foot, took the keys from the ignition and clambered out between them over the back seats. He stepped out into the supermarket, his boots crunching on the jagged shards of glass, grinding them into the marble floor.

Michael watched Carl, silently acknowledging that his

unorthodox parking, whilst doing the exterior of their van no good at all, had made their situation much easier. Not only had he got them safely inside the building, he'd also blocked the entrance at the same time, and it would stay blocked until they decided to leave. He was impressed.

They followed him out into the supermarket. The large building smelled stale and dry. It's only going to get worse, Emma thought to herself, as freezers full of defrosted food begin to rot. And as for the bodies . . . Even the thought of it made her retch and heave. She had to fight to control the rising bile in her stomach.

'We need to get a move on. We don't want to be here any longer than we have to,' she said. 'I don't think I can stand much of this . . .'

Her words were viciously truncated as she was knocked off-balance by a lurching, staggering figure which appeared from out of nowhere. Emma screamed and instinctively pushed the corpse away, feeling her hands sink into its putrefying flesh. Michael watched as the remains of an unnaturally gaunt-faced, mousy-haired shop assistant lay still for a second before its emaciated arms and legs began to flail around again as it desperately tried to haul itself back up onto its feet. Before it could get up he kicked it in the face and it dropped back down again.

'We should have a look around,' he said, anxiously looking from side to side. 'There's bound to be more of them in here.'

He was right. The deafening crash of the van as it ploughed through the glass doors had attracted the unwelcome attentions of a further five ragged cadavers which had been trapped inside the building. The clumsy remains of four shop staff and one delivery driver slowly advanced towards Michael, Carl and Emma with slothful speed but undeniable intent. The battered body on the floor reached out a bony hand and grabbed hold of Michael's leg. He shook it free and kicked the creature in the face again.

'We've got to shift them,' he announced. He looked around again and spied a set of double doors behind a bakery display piled high with stale, mouldy bread. He grabbed the body at his feet by the scruff of its neck and dragged it across the floor. He pushed the doors open and threw the remains of the man into a dark room filled with cold, unlit ovens. Making his way back to the others, he caught hold of the next closest corpse (a check-out operator, its uniform stained with dribbles of decay) and disposed of it in exactly the same way.

'Get them shifted,' he shouted as he ran at a third creature. 'Be quick, and they won't have time to react.'

Carl took a deep breath and grabbed hold of the nearest corpse in a tight headlock. With its thrashing limbs carving uncoordinated arcs through the air he hauled it over to the bakery and pushed it through the double doors. It collided with the body of the dead check-out operator which, a fraction of a second earlier, had managed to lift itself back up onto its feet. He looked down at his jacket, covered in dribbles of blood and other unidentifiable discharge, and gagged.

'Move!'

Emma ran towards him and shoved the remains of an elderly cleaner through the doors. Unbeknownst to Carl, it was staggering dangerously near, until Emma dropped her shoulder and charged at the pitiful figure. The unexpected force of the impact sent the shuffling carcase (which had all the weight and resistance of a limp rag-doll) flying into the bakery.

Once the last of the corpses had been safely pushed through the double doors, Michael wheeled a snaking line of twenty or so shopping trolleys in front of the bakery to prevent the dead from pushing their way out.

'Let's move,' he said breathlessly as he wiped his dirty hands on the back of his jeans. 'Just get whatever you can. Load it into boxes and pile it up by the van.'

As Michael packed tins of food into cardboard boxes he looked around nervously, convinced he could hear more bodies approaching. The corpses in the bakery stared back at him through small square windows in the doors, their emotionless, rotting faces clamouring at the safety-glass. Were they watching him?

'Jesus Christ,' Carl said suddenly.

He was standing close to where he'd wedged the van into the entrance doors. His voice echoed eerily around the vast and cavernous store.

'What is it?' Emma asked, immediately concerned.

'You don't want to know what's going on outside,' he replied ominously.

Emma and Michael looked at each other for a fraction of a second before both dropping what they were doing and running over to where Carl was standing.

'Shit,' Michael cursed as he approached. Even from a distance he could see what had happened. Carl had been about to start loading the boxes into the back of the van when he'd noticed a vast crowd outside, the dead faces of countless corpses pressed hard against the windscreen and every other exposed area of glass. More of them tried unsuccessfully to force their way through the slight gap between the sides of the van and the buckled remains of the supermarket doors.

Emma stared through the van at the mass of grotesque faces looking back at her with dark, vacant eyes.

'How did they—?' she started to say. 'Why are there so many—?'

'Heard us breaking in, didn't they,' Michael whispered. 'It's silent out there. They'd have heard the van and the crash for miles around.'

Carl leant further into the van and looked around. 'There are loads of the fucking things here,' he whispered, his voice just loud enough for the others to hear, 'thirty or forty of them at least.'

'And this is just the start of it,' Michael said. 'That was a hell of a noise we made getting in here. The whole building's probably been surrounded by now.'

'We've got to get out of here,' Carl said, stating the obvious.

'Have we got everything we need?' Michael asked.

'Don't care. We've just got to go.'

Between them they began to load boxes and bags of food and supplies into the van.

'You two get inside,' Michael said as he worked. Carl loaded another two boxes then clambered back through to the driver's seat.

'I'll get the engine started.'

'Leave it,' Emma said, grabbing hold of his arm. 'For God's sake, leave it to the last possible second, will you? The more noise we make, the more of those bloody things we'll have to get through.'

He nodded, then climbed through the gap between the front seats and slid down behind the wheel. Emma followed and silently lowered herself into the passenger seat, forcing herself to look anywhere but up into the wall of dead faces gazing back at her. Struggling to concentrate, Carl attempted to put the key into the ignition. His hands were trembling, and the more he tried to ignore the bodies and keep them steady, the more they shook.

'Last couple of boxes,' Michael yelled as he crammed more and more into the back of the van, leaving just enough space for him to be able to climb inside and pull the tailgate shut behind him.

'Forget the rest of it,' Emma said over her shoulder. 'Just get yourself in.'

Carl looked up and made eye-contact with a horrifically decayed cadaver leaning against the window to his right. Its lips were swollen and cracked and dirty brown drool dribbled down the glass. It somehow managed to lift a clumsy hand into the air then drew its fingers together to form a fist. Without warning, it brought it crashing down on the driver's door window, leaving behind a greasy smear.

'Michael, are you in yet?'

'Almost,' he replied.

Carl watched as a second body lifted its hand and smashed it against the side of the van. Then another followed it, and another, and another, as the reaction spread through the ragged crowd like fire through a tinder-dry forest. Within seconds the inside of the van was ringing with a deafening crescendo of dull thumps and crashes. He turned the key and started the engine.

'I'm in,' Michael yelled as he hauled himself up into the van. He reached out, grabbed hold of the tailgate and pulled it down. 'Go!'

Carl pushed down on the accelerator and cautiously lifted his foot off the clutch. For a second nothing happened: the engine strained, but the van refused to move, shackled by the buckled supermarket entrance doors. Then, painfully slowly, they began to gradually inch forward, and he revved the engine again, finally producing enough force to free them from the doors. But progress forward was still difficult, the sheer volume of dead flesh which surrounded the front and sides of the vehicle preventing them from moving away at speed. Terrified, Carl pushed down harder on the accelerator and released the clutch, sending the van careering through the rotting hordes. The bulk of the bodies were pushed away to the sides, but many others couldn't escape and were dragged down under the wheels.

'Bloody hell,' Michael said, his face pressed up against the rear windscreen.

'What's the matter?' Emma asked.

'They won't lie down. *The damn things just won't lie down.*'

He watched in disbelief as the crowd began to surge after them. Although their slow stagger was obviously no match for the speed of the van, their relentlessness and persistence was terrifying. There was no point in them following, but they continued regardless. Those bodies which had fallen were trampled by those which remained standing.

'Almost there,' Carl announced as he steered towards the car park exit. A solitary figure stumbled out in front of the van, and rather than waste precious seconds trying to avoid it, he instead ploughed straight into it. The momentum of the van carried the corpse along for a few yards before it slipped down under the front bumper and was crushed beneath the wheels.

Emma covered her face and began to sob.

'What else was I supposed to do?' Carl demanded. 'It was already dead. They're all dead . . .'

The van bumped down the kerb heavily as they swerved out onto the road. Michael continued to watch the body they'd just knocked down. Its legs were smashed and shattered – that much was clear – and yet still it moved. The furthest-advanced of the following crowd tripped and stumbled over it, and still it continued to move. Oblivious to the horrific injuries it had received and the pain it should have felt, it reached out with twisted, broken fingers and tried to drag itself along the ground, inch by inch by inch.

26

The drive back to the house and the subsequent unloading of supplies happened at a frenetic pace. In just a couple of hours everything had unexpectedly changed; the world had again been turned upside-down. The safety and security that Michael, Carl and Emma had stumbled upon at Penn Farm had been brutally shattered and now they felt more exposed and vulnerable than ever. As the bodies physically deteriorated, so the dead seemed to be becoming more alert and controlled. If they were ready to attack and tear them apart today, what would they be like tomorrow?

Michael looked at the other two as they sat together in silence in the kitchen. Each person's fear was palpable, and impossible to hide. Every unexpected movement caused them to freeze, and every sudden sound made their hearts miss a collective beat. Even the rustle of the wind through the trees and bushes outside and the creaks and groans of the old house around them were no longer just innocuous background noises. Instead they had become whispered warnings, a constant reminder of the unspeakable horror which now surrounded them and dogged their every move.

'So what do we do?' Michael asked as he paced the length of the kitchen floor. The tension in the room had become too much for him to sit still. Carl shrugged his shoulders unhelpfully. Michael looked at Emma, but her response was no better.

'Don't know. We'll be okay if we can just keep them away from the house.'

'And how are we supposed to do that?' Carl asked, struggling to keep his nerves in check.

'Build a wall or a fence? You said we should, didn't you, Michael?'

'I'm not going out there again today,' Carl whined.

'Well, we need to do something,' Michael snapped, 'because if we don't we're going to end up trapped in here. Make enough noise and this place will be crawling with those things.'

'So how do we build a fence without making a sound?' Emma sensibly asked.

'And what are we supposed to use to build it?' Carl added, equally sensibly.

Michael struggled to find an answer. 'We'll just have to use whatever we can find lying round here. This is a bloody farm, for Christ's sake; there's bound to be plenty of stuff if we look for it . . .'

'Enough to go all the way around the house?'

'It doesn't have to, does it? And it doesn't have to be a fence either, just something that's going to stop them. We could dig a trench, or park cars round the perimeter or—'

'You're right,' Emma said, 'it's not as big a job as it sounds. We've got the stream on one side, and the forest, and there's already a fence round the back . . .'

'And there's nothing to them, is there?' Michael continued, gradually regaining his composure. 'Emma, I watched you shoulder-charge the body of a man twice your size today and you virtually threw it across the room. If we act now we can stop them. If we leave it 'til tomorrow . . .'

'Then who knows what they'll be capable of,' she said ominously.

A while later Michael dared to creep outside again. Carrying the rifle he cautiously walked across the yard and began to scout around, looking for anything they might be able to use to barricade the farmhouse and keep the dead at bay. The longer he spent out in the open, the more confident he gradually became. In two large barns on the far side of the yard he found timber, fence-posts and a roll of barbed wire. Then he looked at the barns themselves. They served no practical purpose any more. He decided they could use the wooden walls of the buildings as part of the blockade and strip off the corrugated metal roofs to use to block the gaps. Even if they just assembled a huge pile of debris around the farm, that would probably be enough to hold back the dead. It wasn't impossible. He knew they could do it. With a final burst of effort they'd be able to shut the rest of the world out.

As he walked back towards the house, a single innocent thought wormed its way into his tired, unsuspecting mind from out of nowhere. For the briefest of moments he thought about a friend from work. For a second he allowed himself to picture the face of the girl who sat at the desk opposite his, and that single unexpected recollection suddenly allowed the floodgates to open, quickly becoming an unstoppable torrent of pain and emotion. He hadn't thought about her since everyone had died. She was almost certainly gone now. Had she died at her desk, or on the way to work, or with her boyfriend? Who else from work was dead? All of them? Circumstances had enabled him to suppress these thoughts and feelings for days now, but he'd suddenly been caught off-guard. Like a dam, about to crack under the pressure of the water building behind it, the memory of everything and everyone he'd lost suddenly came sharply into focus. He slumped down on the bottom step in front of the farmhouse door, held his head in his hands and wept for his family, his friends, his customers, his work colleagues, the people at the garage who had fixed his car last month, the woman who'd sold him a paper on his way to school on the first morning, the teacher at the back of the class, the girl who'd been the first to start coughing . . .

Were they wasting their time here? Was survival worth all the effort it was surely going to take? Then, annoyed with himself for thinking such dark thoughts, he picked himself up, wiped his eyes and went back inside.

27

The barrier around the house took the three of them almost all of the following day to complete. They worked constantly, beginning just after the sun first rose and stopping only when the job was finally completed. As the light faded, the work became increasingly difficult. Carl, Michael and Emma individually struggled to keep focused on the task at hand, trying to ignore the mounting fear that the approach of darkness brought. Throughout the day the generator had remained switched off. As far as was possible they worked in the safety of a shroud of silence.

Despite his earlier apparent apathy, Carl worked as hard as the others. They took turns to stand guard with the rifle and, in some ways, that job proved to be the hardest of all. Emma had never held a loaded firearm before and, although Carl had shown her how to prime and fire the weapon, she doubted she would actually be able to use it should the need arise. Frustrating, often contradictory thoughts invaded her mind with an infuriating regularity. She had come to despise the wandering corpses which dragged themselves lethargically through the remains of her world. They were now so sick, so diseased and dysfunctional, that it had become almost impossible for her to comprehend the fact that a short time ago they had each been human beings with names, lives and identities. And yet, should one of them stumble into her sights, she wondered whether she would be able to pull the trigger and shoot it down. She wasn't even sure whether a bullet would have any effect. She had witnessed those creatures being battered and smashed beyond almost all recognition, only to somehow continue to function, apparently ignorant of the pain that their injuries and sickness must surely have caused. No matter what physical damage was inflicted on them, they carried on regardless.

In the long hours spent outside, only a handful of bodies had appeared. Whenever they became aware of movement, Michael, Carl and Emma would drop their tools and disappear into the farmhouse and wait until the withered creatures had passed by or become distracted by another sound and drifted away again.

Michael had impressed himself with his ingenuity and adaptability. As he'd planned, they'd used the stream as a natural barrier along one side of the farmhouse, building up the bank on their side with mud, rocks and boulders from the water. The barns themselves had become an integral part of the blockade on the other side of the yard, with a tall, inwards-facing door from one of them being used to create a strong, padlocked gate across the stone bridge which spanned the width of the stream. Two thick crossbeams provided additional strength and security for the hours they would spend locked away inside the farmhouse. The roofs of the barns helped to reinforce the vital boundary, leaving the exposed rafters sticking up into the air like the ribs of an animal carcase.

In places the barrier was little more than a collection of carefully placed obstructions: piles of farm machinery and unneeded bags of chemicals, all arranged to create what they hoped would be an impenetrable blockade. Michael judged the success of each section of barrier by whether he could get through or over to the other side. If he, a fit, healthy man, struggled, then the decaying bodies would surely have no chance.

As Monday evening drew to a close, Michael stood outside, checking and rechecking that the barrier was secure. Everything he could find that they wouldn't need was placed against the barricade or used to build it higher. As he worked, it occurred to him that it was almost a week since the nightmare had begun. The longest seven days of his life. In that time he had experienced more pain, fear, frustration and outright terror than he would ever have thought possible. He refused to allow himself to think about what might be waiting for him tomorrow.

28

Wednesday night. Nine o'clock. Michael cooked a meal for the three of them. He had allowed himself to relax slightly now that there was a decent physical barrier between them and the rest of the world. Emma noticed that he had started to occupy his time by doing odd jobs around the house. She had casually mentioned that a shelf in an upstairs room was coming loose from the wall. When she'd next walked past the room she noticed that Michael had completed the repair. Each of them had a desperate urge, a need, almost, to keep themselves occupied. Keeping busy helped them to forget (almost to the point of denial) that the world on the other side of their door had crumbled and died.

Carl had busied himself with the radio they'd found in the dead farmer's office. It had taken him several hours to find any instructions, and as long again to get the equipment working. For a while he'd sat alone in the office scanning the dial, desperate to hear another voice. He'd eventually given up when all he'd got was static, but he hadn't lost all hope. Maybe he'd not been doing it right? He decided he'd try again in the morning.

The three of them had been sitting in the kitchen for almost an hour by the time the meal was ready. It was the longest length of time that they'd willingly spent in each other's company since they'd finished barricading the house, and the atmosphere was subdued, the conversation sparse. While Michael was cooking, Emma read a book and Carl, for the most part, did very little.

Emma had discovered a few bottles of wine hidden in a dusty rack wedged between two kitchen units, and she'd wasted no time in uncorking a bottle and pouring out three large glasses, passing one each to Carl and Michael.

Carl normally didn't drink wine, but tonight he was ready to make an exception. He wanted to get drunk. He wanted to be so fucking drunk that he couldn't remember anything. He wanted to pass out on the kitchen floor and forget about everything for as long as he possibly could.

The food was surprisingly good – probably the best meal they'd eaten together – and that, combined with the wine, helped foster an uneasy, fragile sense of normality – but that taste of normality had the unwanted side-effect of helping them to remember everything about the past that they had been trying so hard to ignore.

Michael decided that the best way to deal with what they'd lost was to talk about it. 'So,' he began, chewing thoughtfully as he spoke, 'Wednesday night. What would you two usually have been doing on a Wednesday night?'

There was an awkward silence, the same awkward silence which always appeared whenever anyone dared broach the subject of the way the world had been before last Tuesday.

'I'd either have been studying or drinking,' Emma eventually replied, suddenly realising that it made sense to talk about it if they were to stay sane. 'Probably both,' she added with a wry smile.

'Drinking midweek?'

'I'd drink any night.'

'What about you, Carl?'

Carl toyed with his food and knocked back a large mouthful of wine. 'I was on call,' he said slowly. 'I couldn't drink in the week, but I'd make up for it at the weekend.'

'Were you a pub or a club man?' Emma asked.

'Pub,' he replied, very definitely. 'Used to spend all day in the pub at the weekend.'

'So what about your little girl?'

There was an awkward pause, and Emma wondered whether she'd gone too far, said the wrong thing.

Carl looked down at his food again and swallowed a second mouthful of wine, this one emptying the glass. He grabbed hold of the bottle and helped himself to a refill before continuing, 'Sarah and me, we used to walk down to the local around lunchtime,' he began, his eyes moistening with tears. 'We were part of a crowd. There was always someone in there we knew. We'd stay there 'til Gemma got tired. There were always kids her age there. They had a play area and she had her friends and they used to . . .' The pain became too much to stand.

He stopped speaking and drank more wine.

'Sorry,' Emma said instinctively, 'I shouldn't have said anything. I wasn't thinking.'

Carl didn't respond.

'Why?' Michael asked.

'What?'

'Why are you apologising? And why don't you want to talk about it, Carl?'

Carl looked up and glared at the other man as tears streaked down his face. 'I don't want to talk because it fucking well hurts too much,' he spat, almost having to force the words out. 'You don't know how it feels!'

'I've lost people too—'

'You didn't lose a child, you fucking idiot! You don't know how that feels. You *couldn't* know.'

Michael couldn't argue; he knew Carl was right. Still, he wanted the conversation to continue. How could they move on and rebuild their lives if they couldn't clear the ruins of the past?

'I'd give anything to be back in lectures again,' Emma said, trying to deflect the discussion into safer waters. 'Stupid, isn't it? Before, I used to do everything I could to avoid them, now I just want to—'

'You can't begin to imagine what this feels like,' Carl repeated, interrupting her. 'This is *killing* me. Every morning I wake up and I wish that it was over. Every single day the pain is worse than the last. I still can't accept that they've gone and I just . . .'

'It hurts now, but it will get easier,' Michael said, beginning to regret his earlier words. 'It *must* get easier over time – it has to . . .'

'Will it? You know that for a fact, do you?'

'No, but I . . .'

'Just shut your mouth then and don't fucking patronise me. If you don't know what you're talking about, don't say anything. Don't waste your time trying to make me feel better because you can't. There's nothing either of you can say or do that will make any of this any easier.' And with that he stood up and stormed away from the table.

They heard his heavy footsteps thumping upstairs, followed by the slamming of his attic bedroom door.

'Really fucked up there, didn't I?' Michael said quietly.

She nodded. 'He's struggling. It's my fault. I should never have asked him about his little girl.'

'Maybe not, but I still think he's got to talk. We've all got to deal with everything that's happened. We can't just ignore it and hope it goes away . . .'

'Have you dealt with everything, then?' she asked, cutting across him.

He paused for a moment and then shook his head. 'No. You?'

'I haven't even started. I don't even know where to start.'

'Maybe you should start with what hurts the most. With Carl it's his daughter. What about you?'

She drank more wine and carefully considered his question. 'Don't know really. Everything hurts the same right now.'

'Okay, so when does it get to you the most?'

Again she couldn't answer. After a pause, she murmured, 'I was thinking about my sister's kids yesterday, and that really got to me. I didn't see them that often, but the thought that I'm not going to see them again . . .'

'You might—'

'Don't give me that bullshit. We both know they're gone.'

'Where did they live?'

'Overseas. Jackie's husband got moved to Kuwait with his job for a couple of years. They were due to come back next summer.'

'You don't know. They still might—'

'How do you reckon that, then?'

'Well, we still don't know for certain that any other countries have been affected by this, do we?'

'Not for sure, but . . .'

'But what?'

'But I think we would have heard something by now, don't you?'

'Not necessarily.'

'Oh come on, Michael, I thought you were supposed to be the

realist. If there was anyone left we would have heard something. You said as much back in Northwich last week.'

At the mention of the town they'd just fled from, Michael immediately began to think about the crowd of survivors left behind in the shabby Whitchurch Community Centre. He pictured the faces of Stuart, Ralph, Kate and the others, and wondered what they were doing now. Their irrational fear of the bodies outside had been pitiful and pathetic. They'd probably still be locked inside the dilapidated building, terrified, cold and starving. He felt sorriest for Veronica, the girl who'd come to them looking for help and shelter. She'd have been better off staying away . . .

'So what about your family then?' Emma asked, distracting him.

'What about them?'

'Who do you miss the most? Did you have a partner?'

Michael took a deep breath, then ran his fingers through his hair. 'I'd been seeing a girl for about six months,' he began, 'but you know, I haven't thought about her at all.'

'Why not?'

'We split up last month.'

'Do you miss her?'

'Not any more. I don't miss my best friend either. That's who she was screwing. There are plenty of other people I miss more.'

'Such as?'

'My mum. I was thinking about her last night when I was in bed. You know when you're just about to go to sleep and you think you hear a voice or see a face or something? Well, I thought I heard my mum last night. I can't even tell you what it was I thought she'd said; I just heard her for a split-second. It was like she was lying next to me.'

'That was me,' Emma smiled, trying to lighten a conversation that was becoming increasingly morose.

Michael managed half a smile before returning his attention to his drink.

The conversation in the kitchen continued as long as the wine lasted, but as the hours passed, their discussion became less in-depth and focused and more trivial. By the early hours of Thursday morning, everything they were talking about had become pretty insignificant. Emma and Michael had learnt about each other's strengths, weaknesses, hobbies, interests, phobias and (now pointless) aspirations and ambitions. Then they talked about their favourite books, films, songs, television programmes, singers, actors, food, politicians, authors and comedians. They learnt about other redundant aspects of each other's lives – their religious beliefs, their political views and their moral standings.

They finally made their way up to the bedroom they innocently shared just before three in the morning.

29

During the days which followed Carl spent many hours shut away in isolation in his attic bedroom. He'd taken the radio up there, and when the generator was running, he constantly scanned the dial, endlessly listening to the static, hoping against hope that he would either hear a voice, or that someone would hear him. There wasn't much point in doing anything else – what exactly was he supposed to do? Sure, he could talk to Michael and Emma, but why bother? Every conversation he had with either of them, no matter how it began, seemed to end with him being reminded of all he'd lost. He decided that if he was condemned to spend the rest of his time wallowing in his memories, he'd rather do it alone.

Anyway, he told himself, he had to keep trying because someone *was* out there. He'd heard them when Emma had been in the room with him, either yesterday evening or the night before. It might even have been the night before that. She hadn't heard anything, but she was always too busy talking to listen. She infuriated him: the one time he was sure he'd heard a voice and what did she do? She'd talked right over the top of it. By the time he'd silenced her inane conversation it was gone, lost again in the static and white noise.

Carl's bedroom was wide and spacious, spanning virtually the entire width of the large house. It was well-insulated, and being at the very top of the building meant it was relatively warm and comfortable. Most importantly, as it was the only room in the attic, it was also isolated. There was no need for anyone to come upstairs for any reason other than to see him, and as no one had any need to see him, no one came upstairs at all. That was how he liked it.

Although twee and old-fashioned, the bedroom had been recently occupied. When they'd first arrived Carl had decided that it had last been used as a temporary base for a visiting grandchild, perhaps one sent to the countryside to spend his or her final summer holiday from school on the farm. The furniture was sparse – a single bed, an empty double wardrobe, a chest of drawers, two wooden stools, a bookcase and a battered but comfortable sofa. On top of the wardrobe Carl had found a box containing a collection of toys, some old books and a pair of binoculars which, once he'd cleaned the lenses, he used to watch the world outside his window slowly rot and decay.

It was mid-afternoon, and he could hear Emma and Michael working outside in the yard. He felt absolutely no guilt at not being out there with them because he couldn't see any point in anything they were doing. The time dragged up here, but what else was there to do? Nothing seemed to be worth the risk or effort it would inevitably take.

Carl wasn't even sure what day it was any more. He sat near to the window and tried to work out whether it was Friday, Saturday or Sunday. Back when life had been 'normal' and he'd been at work, each day had felt different, had had its own atmosphere. The week would begin with the dragging purgatory that was Monday morning and then slowly improve as Friday evening and the weekend approached. None of that applied any more. Each new day was the same as the last. Yesterday was as frustrating, dull, grey and pointless as tomorrow would surely also be.

Today – whatever *today* was – had been warm and clear for the time of year. Perched on one of the wooden stools, with the binoculars held up to his eyes, he had been able to see for miles across the rolling fields. He preferred to look into the distance because there were often bodies closer to the house. They were kept safely at bay by the barrier, but they kept on coming regardless. It was the generator that was bringing them here, of course, any fool could see that. He didn't bother telling the others how many there were. What would they have done? As it was, they usually only ran the generator for a few hours in the evenings when it was dark. The silence of the rest of the day and night was long enough to allow most of the corpses to become distracted and disappear again. Most of them had generally gone by daybreak.

The world was so clear and still and free of distractions today that, even from here, he could make out such distant details as the dramatic tower and steeple of a far-off church. As the sun began to slowly drop below the horizon he watched as the colour faded from the steeple and it became an inky-dark shape silhouetted against the light purples and blues of the early evening sky. Strange, he thought, how it all looked so calm and peaceful. Underneath, the world was filled with nothing but death, decay and destruction. Even the greenest fields, seemingly untouched, were breeding grounds filled with fermenting disease and devastation.

A short distance from the church Carl could see a straight length of road, lined on either side with narrow cottages and shops. The stillness of the scene was disturbed by a scrawny dog which suddenly ran into view. The nervous creature slowed down and crept along the road, keeping its nose, tail and belly low as it sniffed bodies and other piles of rubbish. It was obviously hunting for food. As Carl watched, the dog stopped moving. It lifted its muzzle and sniffed the air. It moved its head slowly (obviously following some out-of-view movement) and then cowered away from something in the shadows. The dog jumped up and though Carl couldn't hear it, it was obvious from the dog's movements that it was barking furiously. From its defensive body posture and the repeated angry jerks of its head, it looked like the dog was in danger. Within seconds of the first sound the dog had attracted the attention of a huge crowd of bodies. Carl watched as they surrounded the animal until it disappeared from view, swallowed up by the horde. Even after all that he had seen – the carnage and the loss of thousands of lives – the plight of the dog shocked him. The bodies were becoming more alert and more deadly with each passing day, and he was beginning to think nothing and no one was safe.

He couldn't understand why Michael and Emma were bothering to make such an effort to survive. The odds were stacked against them. What was the point in working so hard to carve out a future existence when it was so obviously a pointless task? Everything was ruined. It was over. So why couldn't they just accept it, see the reality of the situation, like he could? Why continue to make such a fucking noise about nothing?

Carl knew that there would never be salvation, or escape from this vicious, tortured world and all he wanted to do was just stop and switch off. He wanted to let down his guard for a while and not have to be constantly looking over his shoulder. He didn't want to spend the rest of his life running, hiding and fighting.

Outside, in the enclosed area in front of the house, Michael was working on the van. He had checked the tyres, the oil, the water level and just about everything else he could think of checking. The van was their lifeline – without it they would be stranded, trapped at Penn Farm, unable to fetch supplies (which they knew they would have to do at some point in the near future) and unable to get away should anything happen to compromise the safety of their home. And they had almost come to think of it as a home too: in a world full of dark disorientation, within the sturdy walls of the farmhouse they had at last found a little stability.

'Next time we're out we should get another one of these,' Michael said as he ran his hands along the scratched and buckled bodywork. He made it sound as if they could just run down to the shops when they next felt like it, his casual tone completely belying the grim reality of their situation.

'Makes sense,' Emma agreed. She was sitting on the stone steps leading up to the front door. She'd been there for the last hour and a half, watching Michael work.

'Maybe we should get something a little less refined,' he continued. 'This thing has been fine, but if you think about it, we need something that's going to get us out of *any* situation. If we're somewhere and the roads are blocked, chances are we'll need to find another way to get away. We could end up driving through fields or . . .'

'I can't see us leaving here much. Only to get more food or—'

'But you never know, do you? Bloody hell, anything could happen. The only thing we can be sure about is the fact that we can't be sure of anything any more.'

Emma stood up and stretched. 'Silly bugger.'

'I know what you're saying though,' he continued as he

gathered together his tools and began to pack them away. 'We've got everything we need here.'

Emma looked down across the yard and over the barrier, out towards the rapidly darkening countryside. 'Light's fading. Better get inside.'

'I don't think it makes much difference any more,' Michael said quietly, climbing the steps to stand next to her. 'Doesn't matter how dark it is, those things out there don't stop. It might even be safer out here at night. At least they can't see us when it's dark.'

'They can still hear us – might even be able to smell us.'

'Doesn't matter,' he said again, looking into her face, 'they can't get to us.'

Emma nodded and went inside.

Michael followed. 'Carl's in, isn't he?' he asked as he pushed the door shut and locked it.

Emma looked puzzled. 'Of course he's in. He hasn't been out of his room for days. Where else do you think he's going to be?'

'Don't know. He might have gone out back. Just thought I'd check.'

She leant against the wall. The house was dark. 'Take it from me,' she said, her voice tired and low, 'he's inside. I looked up at the window and saw him earlier. He was there again with those bloody binoculars. Christ alone knows what he finds to look at.'

'Do you think he's all right?'

Emma sighed at Michael's pointless question but didn't bother answering.

'He'll come through this,' he said optimistically. 'Give him time and he'll sort himself out.'

'You reckon?'

He thought for a moment. 'Yes. Don't you?'

'I don't know. He's really suffering, that much I'm sure about.'

'We've all suffered.'

'I know that! Bloody hell, we've had this conversation again and again – but he lost more than either of us did. You and I lived on our own. He shared every second of every day with his partner and child.'

'I know, I understand that, but—'

'I'm not sure if you do. I'm not sure if *I* fully understand how much he's hurting. I don't think I ever will.'

Michael was beginning to get annoyed, and he wasn't sure why. Okay, Carl was hurting, but no amount of hoping, praying and crying would bring back anything that any of them had lost. As harsh as it sounded, he knew that the three of them could only survive by looking forward and forgetting everything and everyone that had gone, no matter how painful.

He watched Emma as she took off her coat, hung it over the back of a chair, fetched herself a drink from the kitchen, then went upstairs.

Left alone in the darkness, Michael listened to the sounds of the creaking old house. The wind had picked up and he could hear the first few spots of rain hitting the windows. It was getting colder, and the days were getting shorter. He went out to switch on the generator, thinking more about Carl as he walked through the house. This wasn't just about Carl, he decided. The wellbeing of each of the survivors was of paramount importance to *all* of them. Life was becoming increasingly dangerous and they couldn't afford to take any chances. They all needed to be strong and pull in the same direction if they were to continue to survive.

He was going to have to pull Carl into line. Right now he was their glass jaw, their Achilles heel, and his weakness left them all dangerously exposed.

30

The earlier wind and rain had quickly worsened into another howling storm. By half-past ten the farm was being battered by a furious gale which tore through the trees and rattled and shook sections of the hastily constructed barrier around the building. The driving, torrential rain lashed down, turning the once gently trickling stream beside the house into a wild torrent of white water.

Relatively relaxed, sheltered from the appalling conditions outside, Michael, Emma and Carl sat in the living room together watching a film in the warmth of an open fire. Michael was quickly bored by the feature (a badly dubbed martial arts film which he'd seen several times since they'd taken it from the supermarket in Byster), but he was pleased to be sitting where he was. Whilst what remained of the population suffered outside, he was warm, dry and well fed. Even Carl had been tempted down from the attic for a while. Their evening together had provided a brief but much-needed respite from the alternating pressure and boredom of what remained of their lives.

Emma found it hard to watch the film – not just because it was one of the worst films she'd ever had the misfortune to see, but also because it made her remember again. She couldn't identify with any of it – the characters, their accents, the locations, the plot and the music all seemed completely alien – and yet at the same time everything felt instantly familiar and safe. In a scene depicting a frantic car chase through busy Hong Kong streets, instead of the choreographed violence in the foreground she found herself watching the people in the background going about their everyday business. She watched them with a degree of envy. How novel and unexpected it was to see a clean city, and to see people moving around with reason and purpose, interacting normally with each other. Emma also felt a cold unease in the pit of her stomach. She looked into the faces of each one of the actors and the extras and wondered what had happened to them in the years since the film had been made. She saw hundreds of different people – each one with their own unique identity, family and life – and she knew that virtually all of them would by now be dead.

The end of the film was rapidly approaching, and a huge set-piece battle between the hero and villain was imminent. The filmmakers were less than subtle in their attention-grabbing techniques. The main character had fought his way into a vast warehouse and now found himself alone. The lighting was sparse and moody and the overly dramatic orchestral soundtrack was building to an obvious crescendo. Then the music stopped suddenly and, as the hero waited for his opponent to appear, the film became silent.

Emma jumped out of her seat.

'What's the matter?' Michael asked, immediately concerned. She didn't answer but stood motionless in the middle of the room, her face screwed up with concentration.

'Emma . . . ?'

'Shh . . .' she hissed.

Uninterested, Carl cocked his head to the right so that he could see past Emma, who was standing in the way of the television.

Michael was worried: she looked frightened. 'What is it?' he asked again.

'I heard something . . .' she replied, her voice low.

'It was probably just the film,' he said, trying desperately to play things down. His mouth was dry. He felt nervous. Emma wasn't the type to make a fuss for no reason.

'No. I heard something outside, I'm sure I did.'

The film soundtrack burst into life again, startling her. With her heart in her mouth she reached down and switched off the television.

'I was watching that,' Carl protested.

'For Christ's sake, shut up,' she shouted.

There it was again. A definite, distinct noise coming from outside. It wasn't the wind and it wasn't the rain and she hadn't imagined it. And this time Michael heard it too.

Without saying another word she ran from the living room into the kitchen, weaving around the table and chairs to get to the window. She craned her neck to see outside.

'Anything?' Michael asked, close behind her.

'Nothing,' she replied as she turned and headed back out of the room towards the stairs. She stopped when she was halfway up and turned to face him. 'Listen,' she whispered, lifting a single finger to her lips. 'There, can you hear it?'

He held his breath and listened carefully. For a few moments he couldn't hear anything other than the wind and rain and the constant rhythmic mechanical thumping of the generator outside. Then, just for a fraction of a second, he became aware of a new noise. As his ears locked onto the frequency of the sound it seemed to increase in volume, rising above everything else. As he concentrated on it the noise washed and faded and changed. In turn it was the sound of something being clattered against the wooden gate over the bridge, then another, less obvious noise, then more clattering and thumping. Without saying another word he ran towards Emma and pushed his way past her. She followed as he disappeared into their bedroom. By the time she entered the room he was already standing on the far side, looking out of the window in utter disbelief.

'Bloody hell,' he said as he stared down, 'just look at this . . .'

With trepidation Emma peered over his shoulder. Although it was pitch-black outside and the driving rain blurred her view through the glass, she could clearly see movement on the other side of the barrier. Running the entire length of the barricade were vast crowds of bodies. They had often seen small groups of them there before, but never this many. They had never seen them in such vast and unexpected numbers.

'There are hundreds of them,' Michael whispered, his voice hoarse with fear, 'fucking *hundreds* of them.'

'Why?' Emma asked.

'The generator,' he sighed. 'Even over the weather they must have heard the generator.'

'Christ.'

'And light,' he continued, 'we've had lights on tonight. They must have seen them. And there was the smoke from the fire . . .'

Emma continued to stare down at the rotting crowd gathered

round the house. 'Why tonight, though?' she asked. 'We've had the generator on most nights . . .'

'Maybe they're starting to think again.'

'What?'

'Maybe they know we're in here now. It might not be just the noise that's bringing them here . . .'

'But why so many?'

'Think about it,' he replied. 'The world's dead. It's silent, and at night it's dark. I suppose it just took one or two of them to see or hear us and that was enough. The first few moving towards the house would have attracted the next few and they would have attracted the next and so on and so on . . .'

'So what are you saying?'

Michael didn't answer. As they looked down at the hordes of corpses below, one of the creatures standing on the stone bridge spanning the stream lifted its emaciated arms and began to shake and bang the wooden gate.

'What's going on?' Carl asked, having finally dragged himself upstairs.

'Bodies,' Michael said quietly. 'Fucking *loads* of bodies.'

Carl crept forward and looked out over the yard. 'What do they want?' he whispered.

'Christ knows,' Michael cursed. He stared down at the heaving crowd with morbid fascination until Emma grabbed his arm and pulled him away.

'They won't get through, will they?' she asked quietly. He wanted to reassure her, but he couldn't lie. He said nothing. 'But they haven't got any real strength, have they?' she said, trying hard to convince herself that they were still safe in the house.

'On their own they're nothing,' he replied, 'but there are hundreds of them here. I've got no idea what they're capable of in this kind of number.'

Emma visibly shuddered with fright, and her fright instantly became icy fear as the moon broke through a momentary gap in the heavy cloud layer and illuminated even more of the world around them. Yet more figures were staggering through the fields and forest surrounding the farm, all of them converging on the house.

'What are we going to do?' she asked, watching as part of the crowd along the edge of the stream-come-river surged forward. Several of the creatures, their footing already unsteady in the greasy mud, fell and were carried away by the foaming waters.

Michael looked up into the clouds, trying desperately to clear his mind and shut out all distractions so that he could think straight. Then, without warning, he ran out of the bedroom, down the staircase and sprinted along the hallway to the back door. Taking a deep breath he unlocked the door and ran over to the shed which housed the generator. The conditions were atrocious, and he was soaked through in seconds. Oblivious to the cold and the vicious, swirling wind, he flung open the wooden door and threw the switch which stopped the machine, suddenly silencing its constant thumping and plunging the farmhouse into complete darkness in a single movement.

Emma caught her breath when the lights died. The darkness explained Michael's sudden disappearance and she ran out to the landing to make sure he was safely back indoors. She was relieved when she heard the back door slam shut and lock.

'You okay?' she asked as he dragged himself breathlessly back up to where she waited.

He wiped rainwater from his eyes and cleared his throat. 'I'm okay.'

They stood at the top of the stairs, holding each other tightly. Save for the muffled roar of the wind and rain outside the house was now silent. The lack of any other sound was eerie and unnerving, and Michael took Emma's hand as he led her back to the bedroom.

'What the hell are we going to do?' she whispered. She sat down on the edge of the bed as he stared out of the window and watched the dead.

'We should wait and see if they disappear before we do anything. There's no light or noise to attract them now. If we wait for long enough they should go.'

'But what are we going to *do*?' she asked again. 'We can't live without light. Christ, winter's coming. We'll need fire and light and . . .'

Michael didn't reply. Instead he continued to stare down at the crowd of decomposing corpses. He watched the bodies in the distance, still dragging themselves towards the house, and prayed that they would become disinterested and turn away. Emma was right. What quality of life would they have hiding in a dark house with no light, warmth or other comfort? But what was the alternative? On this cold and desolate night there didn't seem to be any.

Upstairs, Carl stood at his bedroom window with the binoculars, silently watching the milling crowds beyond the barricade with fear and mounting hate.

31

Emma woke suddenly from a nightmare, soaked through with an ice-cold sweat and almost too afraid to move. Once she'd convinced herself that it had only been a dream and she was safe (or as safe as she could expect to be), she leant over to check that Michael was still lying on the floor beside her. She was so relieved when she reached out her hand and rested it on his shoulder that she held it there for a few seconds until she was completely sure that all was well. The gentle, rhythmic movements of his sleeping body as he breathed were remarkably calming and reassuring.

In the days, months and years before her world had been turned upside down, Emma had often tried to analyse the hidden meaning of dreams. She had read numerous books that offered supposed explanations for the metaphors and images which filled her mind while she slept. Her dreams had changed since they'd arrived at Penn Farm. There was nothing subtle or hidden in the visions she'd seen in her sleep this morning. They showed her, in no uncertain terms, a terrifying vision of an all-too-plausible future. There simply wasn't anything more frightening than the world outside the farmhouse.

Taking care not to disturb Michael, she climbed out of bed, walked over to the window and pulled back the curtains. She kept her eyes shut for a few seconds, partly because of the bright light suddenly flooding into the room, but mostly because she was terrified of what she might see outside. She breathed a sigh of relief when she finally dared to look and saw that only thirty or forty ragged figures remained on the other side of the barrier. The majority of the huge crowd which had gathered last night had wandered away into the wilderness again, distracted by some other sound or movement. Since they had switched off the generator the farmhouse now looked as dead and as empty as any other building.

Emma heard noises downstairs. It was almost eight o'clock, so she pulled on some clothes and stumbled into the kitchen, where she found Carl.

'Morning,' she said as she yawned and stretched.

Carl mumbled something indistinct, but he didn't look up, or stop what he was doing. Emma stood and watched him. He was fully dressed, and he had washed and shaved. He was searching through the kitchen cupboards and had collected a pile of food and supplies on the table.

'What are you doing?' she asked cautiously.

'Nothing,' he answered, still not looking up at her.

'Doesn't look like nothing to me.'

Carl didn't reply. Emma moved over to the cooker, lifted the kettle and shook it. There was enough water, so she put it down again and lit the gas burner. Both kettle and stove were cold, so whatever it was Carl was doing, it was obviously important because he hadn't bothered to make himself a drink since getting up – the one thing that the three of them had quickly discovered was their shared need for a hot drink inside them before they could function in the morning.

'Want a coffee?' she asked amiably, determined not to let his hostility deter her.

'No,' he replied abruptly, shoving food into a small bag. 'No thanks.'

Emma spooned coffee granules into two mugs, one for her and one for Michael.

'Carl,' she said, her patience wearing thin, 'what exactly are you doing? And please don't insult my intelligence by telling me it's nothing when it's bloody obvious that it's not.'

He continued to ignore her, and now she noticed that there was a well-packed rucksack resting against a wall in the storeroom adjacent to the kitchen.

'Where are you going?'

Still no response.

The kettle started to boil. Emma made her coffee and sipped at her scalding-hot drink. She watched Carl over the brim of her mug. 'Where are you going to go?' she asked again, her voice deliberately low and calm.

Carl turned his back on her and leant against the nearest kitchen unit. 'I don't know,' he eventually replied. It was obvious that he knew exactly where he was going and what he was planning to do.

'Come on, do you really expect me to believe that?'

'Believe what you want,' he snapped. 'Doesn't matter to me.'

'You can't leave the house, it's too dangerous. Bloody hell, you saw how many of those things managed to get here last night. If you really think you—'

'That's the whole fucking problem, isn't it?' he said angrily, finally turning around to face her. 'I saw how many bodies were here last night and there were too bloody many. It's not safe to stay here any more.'

'It's not safe anywhere these days. Face it, Carl, this place is as good as you're going to get.'

'No, it isn't. We're out on a limb here. There's nowhere to run. If that barrier comes down we're completely fucked—'

'But can't you see that we can get over that? When they're here in large numbers we just shut up and sit tight. If we stay silent and out of sight for long enough they'll disappear.'

'That doesn't work any more. They're still outside, you know.'

'Not as many as there were last night—'

'Anyway, is that what you want? Are you happy to sit and hide for hours every time those bloody things get close? They're getting stronger every day and it won't be long before—'

'Of course it's not ideal, but what's the alternative?'

'The alternative is to go back home. I know Northwich like the back of my hand and I know that there are other survivors there. I think I'll have more of a chance back in the city. It was a mistake coming out here.'

Emma struggled to comprehend what she was hearing. 'Are you *crazy*? Do you know the risks you'll be taking—?'

'I know, but it'll be okay—'

'How do you know that?'

'There are still people out there.'

'But how do you *know*?'

'Because I heard them, remember? The other day when you came into my room, I heard them on the radio!'

'Carl, all you heard was—'

'Emma, I'm going. If you haven't got anything constructive to say, then do me a favour and don't say anything at all. Stuart, Ralph and the others were right. There's safety in numbers. Those bloody things out there proved it last night, didn't they? More survivors has got to equal more of a chance in my book—'

'You're wrong,' Michael interrupted. He was standing in the kitchen doorway. Neither Emma nor Carl knew how long he'd been there or how much he'd heard. He leant against the doorframe with his arms crossed in front of him.

Carl shook his head vehemently. 'I'm not.'

'Leaving here would be a fucking stupid thing to do.'

'Staying here seems like a fucking stupid thing to do too.'

Michael took a deep breath and walked into the kitchen. He sat on the edge of the kitchen table and watched Carl as he tried desperately to ignore him. 'Convince me,' he said as he took his coffee from Emma. 'Just how much have you thought about this?'

'I don't have to convince you of anything,' he replied, annoyed, 'but I've thought long and hard about it, ever since I heard the voice on the radio. It isn't something that I've just decided on a whim.'

'But you don't know who that was. You don't know where they are—'

'I do know.'

'So what's the plan?'

'Get back to Northwich and try and get to the community centre. See who's still there—'

'And then?'

'And then find somewhere secure to base myself.'

'But you said you didn't want to lock yourself away and hide. Aren't you going to be doing exactly that, just somewhere else instead of here?' Emma asked.

'There's a council works depot between the community centre and where I used to live. There's a ten-foot-high wall all the way around it. Once we're in there we're safe. There's trucks and all kinds of things there.'

'How're you going to get in?'

'I'll get in.'

'And what if there's no one at the community centre?'

'I'll keep going to the depot on my own.'

'So when were you thinking of going?' Michael wondered.

'We've got to go out for supplies at some point in the next few days,' Carl answered quickly. 'I figured I'd try and get some transport while we were away from the house and then I'll take it from there.'

'We could go and get supplies today,' Michael said, surprising Emma, who looked at him with an expression of utter disbelief on her face.

'What the hell are you doing? Christ, are you planning to go too?'

'Seems to me that Carl's going to go, no matter what we say or do to try and stop him.'

Carl nodded. 'Damn right. I'd go now if I could.'

'Then there doesn't seem to be any point in Emma or me wasting our time trying to convince you that you're making a fucking huge mistake.'

'I don't think I am. And you're right: you'd be wasting your time.'

'And if we try and stop you leaving we'll probably end up beating the crap out of each other and the result will be that you still leave. Am I right?'

'You're right.'

He turned to face Emma. 'So we don't have a lot of choice, do we?'

'But he'll end up *dead*,' she said, nearly in tears. 'He won't last five minutes out there.'

Michael sighed and watched Carl disappear into the storeroom. 'That's not our problem,' he said softly. 'Our priority is to keep ourselves safe, and if that means letting him go, then that's what we do. Think of him as a messenger. We'll send him on his way today and if things don't work out he'll bring the rest of the survivors from Northwich back here with him.'

Emma understood everything Michael was saying, but she was finding it very hard to accept. 'He's a stupid fucking idiot,' she muttered.

'I know.'

'There was no voice on the radio—'

'I know. He didn't hear anything – he couldn't've. He told me about it, but it's impossible.'

'Why? What do you mean?'

'He took the radio upstairs, but he left the antenna behind. He couldn't have heard anything.'

32

Once they had accepted the fact that Carl was leaving for the city as inevitable, they quickly forced themselves into action. Carl was keen to get away, and Michael and Emma were keen to make the most of having him around. A trip away from the house was essential to all of them, whether they were staying or going. Having three pairs of hands meant they could collect more supplies, and that deferred the next trip out for a few precious days longer.

But Emma was still uncomfortable with Carl going. Three was a safe number – if one of them was injured, then the other two could help. Left alone with Michael, she knew that they would be in serious trouble if anything happened to either of them. And the chances of Carl surviving on his own in an accident were next to nil. By leaving he was putting them all at risk.

It was a cold, wet, miserable Sunday morning. They drove through Pennmyre, the first village they'd visited after finding Penn Farm last week, then continued along the same road until they reached the outskirts of a neighbouring small town. The tension in the van mounted as they approached the town. It was considerably larger than anywhere else they'd recently foraged for supplies, and that inevitably meant the risks were increased. But this journey was important, and each of them felt the risks were justified.

It came as no surprise to find that as the sound of their arrival at the edge of the town shattered the fragile silence, the unwanted interest of scores of deplorable creatures nearby was aroused. Michael stopped the van adjacent to a row of shops, then leant over his seat and scrabbled around in the back, grabbing a wrench from the toolbox they carried. Once he'd got his nerve up, he opened the sunroof and stretched his arm out. With a grunt of effort he threw the wrench across the street, dropping back into his seat as it shattered a shop window with a satisfyingly loud clatter and crash. His vandalism had the desired effect as the dumb but inquisitive bodies gradually dragged themselves over to the other side of the street to investigate the noise.

Emma, Carl and Michael, all crouched down beneath the windows, waited until they had all disappeared, following each other like sheep over to the smashed window. Even from a distance it was clear that the condition of the bodies had continued to deteriorate. They hadn't been this close to any of them in days. Michael watched one of the nearest of them with mounting disgust. Its skin, now marbled dark green in places, flecked red with jagged lines from broken veins and capillaries, no longer seemed to fit its frame. Clumps of hair had fallen from its scalp. Even from inside the van they could smell the increasing decay, and they could hear the sound of buzzing insects: a constant, high-pitched thrum.

Michael had parked next to a small supermarket at the far end of this street. Once the crowds around the van had dispersed, Emma carefully and quietly opened the door, slid out, still crouched, and quietly disappeared inside the shop. Michael and Carl exited just as silently, then crept off to search for alternative transport. Emma collected as many tins of food and other non-perishable supplies as she could find and loaded them into the back of the van. Each movement she made was slow and considered, every step was carefully calculated so that she remained silent and invisible to the rest of the world, frequently stopping and slipping back into the shadows whenever a corpse staggered too close for comfort.

There was a large garage at the other end of a side-street near to the supermarket where Michael found a Land Rover that perfectly suited his needs. He found the keys from the office, then set about ensuring that the tank was filled with petrol. He siphoned extra fuel from the other vehicles parked on the forecourt into metal cans and loaded them into the back of his new transport, cringing whenever he made the slightest sound.

Lethargic bodies occasionally staggered by as he worked, and like Emma, every time he stood still and watched them until they'd gone. He was sure several of them saw him, but they didn't react. On his own he didn't appear to be a threat. Perhaps their rotting brains were unable to distinguish between him and the millions of other diseased bodies dragging themselves along the silent streets. Don't make any noise, he silently told himself, no fast movements . . .

Quite by chance, Carl stumbled across the perfect vehicle to get him back to the city: a motorbike. He found it sitting in a small concrete yard behind a narrow terraced house. It looked well-maintained and powerful. It had been a while since he'd ridden a motorbike regularly and he knew it would take some getting used to, but he also knew it would give him far more speed and manoeuvrability than any four-wheeled vehicle ever could. He found the keys to the bike in the pocket of a leather-clad corpse wedged in a half-open doorway. Understanding the need for protection, and not having the time or inclination to look elsewhere, he gritted his teeth and stripped the leathers from the decaying body before gingerly removing the helmet, using a long-dry towel from a washing line to wipe it clear of seepage. He didn't dare to start the engine, but he released the brake and pushed the bike back out to the supermarket where Emma was waiting anxiously.

As he approached, she climbed into the driver's seat of the van, keen to get away.

'Got this,' he said quietly. 'Should do me nicely.'

She nodded but didn't answer.

'What do you think of this thing?' Carl said to Michael as he returned to the van, but he didn't pretend to be interested in either the bike or Carl, acknowledging him only with a grunt.

'Ready to get going?' Michael asked, clearly directing his question at Emma.

'I'm ready. Let's get out of here.'

'I've found a Land Rover,' he continued. 'You start the van up and I'll try and get it going. Give me a couple of minutes. If I can't get it started I'll be back here for a lift, okay?'

'Okay.' She managed a momentary smile, though her throat was dry and her heart had started to thump in her chest. She knew that as soon as she started the engine she'd immediately become the centre of attention, and bodies from all around would start swarming towards her.

'I'll follow on behind,' Carl said.

'Whatever,' Michael muttered. He checked the road was clear, gave Emma a thumbs-up, then turned and jogged back to the Land Rover. As soon as he was out of sight she started the engine, watching anxiously as every corpse she could see slowly turned and advanced in her direction. The nearest few were upon her in seconds and started slamming their fists against the windows relentlessly. She nudged forward as they began to crowd around the front of the van, accelerating just enough to shunt them out of the way, keeping her escape route clear. The van had been surrounded horribly quickly. She instinctively revved the engine to force some of the dead away, knowing all she was really doing was attracting more towards her. Then, through a momentary gap in the encroaching horde, she saw some of them were beginning to move away. Before she'd had time to work out why, Michael had careered past the front of the van in his Land Rover and swerved down the high street, deliberately weaving from side to side, mowing down as many cadavers as he was able.

Now Emma accelerated, pushing the van through the depleted crowd and following in his bloody wake.

Behind them, Carl was struggling to start the bike. Though most of the walking cadavers had followed the van, some had been slower to move and now six of the dead bodies were focusing on him. He was trying not to panic as sound rang out with every attempt to start the machine, drawing more and more attention, until the bike's spluttering engine finally burst into life, its deafening roar uncomfortably loud.

Overwhelmingly relieved, Carl attempted to move forward. The bike was far more powerful than he'd expected, and the unexpected force caught him off guard. For a second he almost lost control. Shaking hard, he paused and steadied himself, trying to calm his nerves, just as the nearest corpse lurched towards him and caught hold of the back of his jacket. Terrified, he lifted his feet off the ground, pointed the bike in the direction the van and Land Rover had taken and accelerated off down the road, leaving the corpse stumbling pointlessly after him.

*

Carl had driven slowly for the first few miles, getting his confidence, before he felt ready to try the bike's full potential. He followed the route the others had taken until he'd caught up with them, then practised racing the van and the Land Rover, overtaking and then dropping back, cutting between them and weaving around the endless wrecks, bodies and ruins which lay in his path. By the time they'd reached the track from the main road back up to Penn Farm he felt confident enough to surge ahead. He rode across the stone bridge, unlocked the gate and waited for Emma and Michael. The moment they were both through and safely within the confines of the barricade he slammed the heavy gate shut and snap-locked the chunky padlock which they used to keep it secure.

Already there were bodies close by, the remnants of last night's immense crowds, and as he closed the gate, he saw many more grotesque, shadowy shapes appear from the forest and start to move towards the barricade. A week ago, all they could do was wander aimlessly and without direction. Although still clumsy and lethargic, now they moved with an unnerving determination and purpose.

Carl pushed the bike closer to the house, heaved it onto its stand, then knelt down and began to check it over. He didn't want to go inside. Now that he'd made his decision to leave, he felt strangely disconnected from the other two. Out of the corner of his eye he noticed that Emma was walking over to speak to him.

'You okay?' she asked. Her voice sounded tired and emotionless, almost abrupt.

He stood up and brushed himself down. 'I'm all right,' he replied. 'You?' He thought she was talking to him more out of duty than any real desire.

'Look,' she began, 'I know you've said that you're sure about this, but have you stopped to think—?'

'I don't want to hear this, Emma,' he interrupted, silencing her.

'You don't know what I'm going to say—'

'I can guess.'

She sighed and turned away. After thinking for a second she

turned back, determined to make her point. 'Are you sure about what you're doing?'

'As sure as anyone can be about anything at the moment . . .'

'But you're taking such a chance. You don't have to leave. We could stay here for a while longer and maybe go back to the city together later. We could bring the others back here. There might even be more of them by then . . .'

'Emma, I've *got* to go. It's not just about surviving any more. I've already done that.'

'So why leave now?'

'Take a look around you,' he said, gesturing towards the house and the ramshackle barrier which surrounded it. 'Is this enough for you? Does this give you all the protection and security you need?'

'I think we're as safe as we can be—'

'I don't. Christ, last night we were *surrounded*.'

'Yes, but—'

'Just answer me this, Emma. What would you do if those things got through the barricade and got into the house? As far as I can see you wouldn't have many choices. You could lock yourselves into a room and sit tight, or you could try and get to the van and get away. Or you could just run for it.'

'You'd have no chance on foot—'

'That's exactly my point. This house is surrounded by miles and miles of absolutely nothing. There's nowhere to run to.'

'But we don't need to run . . .'

'Not yet you don't, but you might. Back in the city there are a hundred places to hide on every street. I don't want to spend the rest of my life locked away in this bloody house.'

Emma sat down on the steps in front of the house, dejected and frustrated. She shuffled over to one side as Michael began to unload the supplies from the back of the van. He was doing his best to stay clear of Carl.

'I'm worried about you, that's all,' she said quietly. 'I just hope you realise that if anything happens to you on your own, that's it, you've had it.'

'I know that.'

'And you're still willing to take the chance?'

'Yes.' He leant against the bike and looked into Emma's face.

She stared back at him. She felt desperately sorry for Carl. He was nothing more than a shell: he'd lost everything – including, so it seemed, all commonsense and reason. She knew he wasn't really bothered about surviving any more; all his talk of finding shelter and of reaching the survivors was bullshit. All he wanted to do was go home.

33

'Sure you're going to do this?' Michael asked, forcing himself to speak. They'd been back from Pennmyre an hour or more and Carl was still outside, refuelling and checking over the bike.

He looked up. 'I'm sure.'

'You're taking a hell of a risk.'

'We're all taking risks whatever we do,' he answered. 'I don't think it matters any more.'

'Well, I think you're asking for trouble.'

'I'll be all right.'

'Fine then.'

'Good.'

Michael sat down on the steps and looked around the yard, automatically checking that the barrier round the house was secure, then looking up high, staring into the surrounding trees, listening to drops of water from the earlier rain dripping through the leaves.

'Look,' he said, feeling he had a duty to try to persuade the other man not to leave, 'why don't you just give it another couple of days and—'

Carl sighed. 'Christ, not you as well. I had enough of this bullshit from Emma earlier— I'm leaving first thing in the morning.'

'It's *not* bullshit. We're just worried that—'

'Worried that *what*?'

'Worried that you're doing the wrong thing. I've heard everything you've said about wanting to go back to the community centre and I understand why you think you need to go but—'

Carl stopped what he was doing and looked at Michael. 'But . . . ?'

'I think you're confused. I think you've been through too much to cope with and you're having trouble dealing with it all. I don't think you're capable of making the right decisions at the moment and—'

'I'm not a fucking lunatic if that's what you think,' Carl snapped, 'and I know exactly what I'm doing. The fact is I just don't feel safe here. And before you say it, I know we're not safe anywhere any more, but I obviously feel differently about this place than you two. That excuse for a fence we built doesn't make me feel any better—'

'That excuse for a fence,' Michael said, annoyed, 'kept a thousand of those bastards out last night.'

'Yes, I know – but there are *millions* of them out there, and they are going to get through eventually.'

'I don't agree.'

'We'll put a bet on it now and I'll come back next year and see how you're doing.'

Michael didn't find Carl's attempt at humour amusing. 'Okay, so we're not as isolated as we thought we were here, but we've done all right so far, haven't we?'

'Better than I ever thought we would,' he accepted.

'So why leave now? You're going to get ripped to pieces out there.'

Carl thought for a moment. He'd done a good job of keeping his true feelings hidden from the other two for most of the last week. The pair of them had been so wrapped up in securing and protecting their precious ivory tower that they'd forgotten everything else that was important. 'Surviving is one thing,' he said quietly, his voice suddenly calmer, 'but you've got to have a reason to do it. There's no point living if you don't have anything worth living for.'

34

The sun rose just after seven on a blustery and overcast morning. After a fitful, interrupted sleep, Carl was finally ready to leave. His bike, loaded with carefully packed bags, stood next to the gate. Dressed in the leathers and boots he'd taken yesterday afternoon and carrying the freshly disinfected crash helmet in his hand, he stood at the front door of the farmhouse with Emma and Michael. This was it. There was no turning back now, and no point delaying the inevitable.

'Are you ready?' Emma asked.

He swallowed. His mouth was dry. It was a dull morning, and a swirling, biting wind whipped around the farm. Emma zipped up her fleecy jacket and thrust her hands deep into her pockets.

'Last time I ask,' Michael said, fighting to make himself heard over the wind. 'Are you sure about this?'

'Better get on with it,' Carl said in answer, and with that he pulled on his crash helmet, hiding his face.

'I'll open the gate,' Michael said as they walked towards the bike. 'You wheel the bike through and start it. Once I hear the engine and see you move off I'm locking up, okay?'

Carl raised a leather-clad hand and lifted his thumb to show that he understood. He took one last look over his shoulder at Emma and the farmhouse and climbed onto the bike. He flicked up the kick-stand with his foot and tentatively rolled forward a couple of yards. Michael carefully unlocked the padlock and lifted the wooden bar securing the gate.

'Okay?' he asked.

Carl stood astride the bike, his hands tightly gripping the handlebars. He nodded, and Michael pushed open the gate. Carl rolled the bike forward again and stopped on the other side of the bridge. He'd only been out in the open for a few seconds, but already there was activity in the bushes all around him. Dead bodies reacted to the movement and noise, in turn attracting the attention of even more dark, decaying figures.

Struggling to keep his nerve, Carl started the bike. The engine spluttered and roared into life, sending a cloud of hot fumes billowing back towards Michael. As the first few corpses broke cover and emerged from the shadows, Carl accelerated away. Michael quickly pulled the gate shut, just glimpsing the bike swerve as Carl avoided a body which had staggered into his path. With shaking hands he lowered the wooden bar back into place and snap-locked the heavy padlock.

Emma had walked over and was standing just behind him. He turned around and her unexpected closeness startled him. He caught his breath and then, instinctively, reached out for her and held her tight. The warmth of her body was reassuring. Despite all their efforts, he felt racked with guilt that he'd let Carl leave.

The sound of the motorbike took for ever to finally fade into the distance. Emma shivered as she imagined the effect the noise would have on the lamentable remains of the population of the shattered world through which Carl was about to travel. The roar of the engine would attract the attention of hundreds, probably thousands of bodies, every last one of which would stagger after Carl until he was out of view or earshot. But he would have to stop the bike eventually, and what would happen then? It didn't bear thinking about.

Once they were completely sure that they could no longer hear the distant rumble of Carl's vehicle, Emma and Michael went inside and locked the door of the farmhouse behind them.

35

Carl raced along countless twisting, turning narrow roads, praying that he was travelling in the right direction and hoping that he would soon see a road sign or some other waypost to confirm that he was heading the right way. He needed to get onto the motorway which would take him south-east across the country and almost directly into the heart of Northwich, the city from which he, Emma and Michael had earlier been so keen to escape. He reassured himself that he'd be able to cover the distance in half the time it had taken the three of them to drive out here. Their route away from the city had been meandering and haphazard. He had a definite place to aim for.

Driving at such a speed was harder and required more concentration than he'd expected, and his tiredness made it harder yet to control the powerful bike. The state of the roads made the journey even more dangerous. Although clear of any other moving traffic, they were still hazardous, littered with the twisted, rusting remains of wrecked vehicles and rotting human bodies. As well as the numerous motionless obstructions, Carl was constantly aware of shuffling, shadowy figures all around him. Although they could do nothing to harm him while he travelled at speed, their ominous presence alone was enough to unnerve him. He knew that one slip was all that it would take; one lapse of concentration and he would lose control of the bike – and if that happened, he'd have just seconds to get himself back in command of the powerful machine before he was surrounded.

In spite of all that he had seen over the last few hours, days and weeks, still some of the sights he glimpsed as the world filled with grey morning light chilled him to the bone. As he approached one car, its dead driver lifted its rapidly decomposing head and stared at him. In the fraction of a second it was visible, he knew that the body had not looked past him; it had looked directly at him. In those lifeless eyes he saw both a complete lack of emotion and, at the same time, paradoxically, savage hate. Such abhorrent visions, and the fact that he knew he was utterly alone for the first time since this nightmare had begun, made the cold, dark night even colder and darker still.

Thousands upon thousands of grotesque bodies turned and started stumbling awkwardly towards the source of the sound that shattered the fragile silence. Most of the time they were too slow, and when they finally reached the road, Carl was long gone. Occasionally, however, fate and circumstance contrived to allow some of the obnoxious creatures to get dangerously close to him. He quickly learnt that the best way to deal with them was to simply plough straight through them at maximum speed and with maximum ferocity. The empty husks offered no resistance. The body of a teenage girl stumbled out into the middle of the road and began to walk towards the bike. Rather than waste time and effort swerving to avoid her, Carl instead forced the bike to move faster and faster until he collided with the body full-on, sending it flying across the tarmac.

He couldn't stop, not even for a second; his only option was to keep driving until he reached the survivors' base in Northwich. They should never have left the city.

36

The farmhouse felt empty. For hours Michael and Emma sat together in almost complete silence, both of them thinking constantly about Carl. They understood why he'd decided to leave, but neither agreed with what he'd done. Michael's home felt a million miles away, and there was nothing there worth going back for. All that he had left behind him was familiarity, property and possessions, none of which counted for anything today. There were things which had sentimental value, and he would have been happy to have them with him now, but those few precious belongings weren't worth risking his life for. Carl was different. Carl had left behind far more than either he or Emma had.

Despite the fact that Carl had spent most of the last few days shut away in his room, it was painfully obvious that he was missing. Everything felt incomplete. More than that, all Emma and Michael could think about was what might be happening to him out on the road. Had he made it to Northwich yet? Was he with the others at the community centre – or had something happened to him along the way? Had the vast numbers of ambulant bodies in the city been too much for him to deal with? Was he even still alive?

Neither of them could clear these constant dark thoughts from their minds, and at last the oppressive atmosphere proved too much for Emma, who went to her room, wanting to be alone for a while.

Michael wanted to rest, to catch up on the sleep he'd missed last night, but he couldn't be bothered to move. He stayed downstairs, made himself a drink, lit a fire in the hearth and sat down to read a book in an attempt to clear his head. It worked for a while, but he was disturbed a short time later when Emma tiptoed back into the living room. Finding him curled up in a ball in front of the fire and thinking he was asleep, she reached out and gently shook his shoulder.

'Bloody hell!' he said, spinning around and sitting up in a single frightened movement. 'Jesus, Emma! You scared the shit out of me! I didn't know you'd come back down—'

Emma was taken aback by the unexpected strength of his reaction. She slumped into the nearest chair, pulled her knees up to her chest and consciously tried to shrink her body down to the smallest possible size.

'Sorry,' she mumbled, shivering in spite of the fire, for the house was still bitterly cold. The room was dark, the curtains left shut to stop the light from the fire being seen and drawing more of the wandering bodies closer to the house. The pressure to stay silent and out of sight was more intense than ever. They spoke in hushed whispers, and when they needed to go into another part of the house they crept quietly, taking care not to make a single unnecessary sound.

Michael was beginning to feel uncomfortably claustrophobic, like a prisoner serving a sentence of undetermined length. He wanted to scream or shout, or play some music, or laugh out loud, or do pretty much anything other than just sit there and watch the hands on the clock on the wall slowly tick off another hour. But they both knew they couldn't afford to take any chances.

He looked at Emma, sitting hunched up on the chair. She looked tired and sad. Her eyes were heavy, and she was deep in thought.

'Come here,' he said warmly, holding out his arms to her. Not needing any further encouragement, she slid down from her seat and sat next to him. He put his arms around her shoulders and pulled her close, lightly kissing the top of her head.

'It's really cold today,' she whispered. 'I can't switch off. Too much going round in my head.'

'Don't need to ask what you're thinking about, do I?'

'Not really. Impossible to think about anything else, isn't it?'

Michael held her a little tighter still. 'Just wish he'd stopped,' he said, his strained voice suddenly cracked with emotion. 'I still think I should have stopped him. I should have locked the stupid bastard in his room and not let him leave. I should have—'

‘Shh,’ Emma whispered. She pulled back slightly from Michael to allow herself to look deep into his eyes. The low orange flames of the fire revealed the glistening tears which ran freely down his face. ‘There was nothing that either of us could have done, and talking like this is just pointless. We’ve already had this conversation. We both know we would have done more harm than good if we’d tried to stop him—’

‘I just wish he was here now,’ Michael continued, having to force his words out, trying not to dissolve into sobbing.

‘I know,’ she said quietly, her low voice soothing.

After a brief moment of awkwardness and reluctance they both began to cry freely. There had been private tears before, but now, for the first time since they’d lost everything on that desperate autumn morning two weeks ago, they both finally dropped their guard in front of one another. They cried together for all they’d lost and left behind, they cried for their absent friend and they cried for each other.

37

After two hours on the road, Carl was fast approaching the outskirts of Northwich. He had driven at an increasingly cautious speed; as his journey had progressed, so his fatigue had worsened. As his tiredness reached dangerous levels he'd been forced to concentrate even harder on the road, and that extra concentration further drained his already depleted energy reserves.

As the dark shadows of the once-familiar city engulfed him, his heart began to pound in his chest with renewed vigour. Conflicting emotions raged constantly through his tired mind; he felt comforted that the journey was almost at an end, but at the same time he was filled with dread and trepidation at the thought of what might be waiting for him in the desolate streets of Northwich.

Everything looked depressingly featureless this morning, until the greenery of the countryside finally gave way to the harsh plastic and concrete of the decaying city.

He slowed the bike to the lowest speed he dared and started desperately looking from side to side, searching for something recognisable to point him in the right direction. He'd told Michael and Emma he knew the city like the back of his hand, but this morning he couldn't see anything familiar. It all looked so very different to how he remembered, and even with his reduced speed he was still passing the road signs too quickly to be able to read any of them.

The motorway he'd been following bisected the city from east to west, and he knew he'd need to get off the road before he reached the centre of town. He cursed as he raced past a junction and, too late, recognised the curve of the road ahead. He'd come further than he'd thought and just missed the exit which would have taken him close to the Whitchurch Community Centre – and from there, to the suburb of Hadley, where he and his family had lived. Taking care to avoid the wreckage and a handful of corpses which were just staggering out after him, he turned the bike around and doubled back on himself. He found himself smiling wryly at the chaos such a manoeuvre would have caused had he tried to do that a month ago. Even today it didn't feel right to be driving the wrong way down such a major road.

Once off the motorway the number of obstacles in Carl's path increased. The tall office blocks, mansion flats and shops that lined the sides of the dual carriageway he was following were making him feel claustrophobic. He turned right towards Hadley and the community centre – and was forced to slam on the brakes when he suddenly found the road ahead blocked across its entire width by a petrol tanker. He didn't see the wreck until he was almost on top of it, and he braked and pulled back and steered the bike as best he could, leaning over to one side with all his weight, trying desperately to force the machine into the tightest possible turn—

Just as he thought he'd succeeded in avoiding a collision, the bike kicked out from underneath him, sending him tumbling across the uneven tarmac and he crashed into an overturned car. He lay helpless for the briefest of moments, stunned, unable to move. Through blurred eyes he watched the bike sending a shower of sparks shooting up into the cold air as it skidded across the ground towards the tanker, which had jack-knifed and was now on its side, looking like the corpse of a beached whale.

Still dazed, he hauled himself to his feet and ran unsteadily over to the bike. Groaning with pain he lifted it up and restarted the stalled engine, trying to ignore the dark mass of bodies already shuffling towards him. With precious seconds to spare he accelerated through and around the dead, evading their clumsy, barely coordinated attempts to stop him. He had been off the bike and on the ground for less than thirty seconds, but already dozens of the creatures had converged on him, and even more were swarming nearby.

Now he had an idea of where he actually was, and the roads were looking more familiar. He was sure he was infuriatingly close to the community centre. There was continual movement all around him, and that meant there were hundreds, maybe thousands of bodies nearby. He was about to turn around again, convinced he must have been heading in the wrong direction, when he finally saw the road he had been looking for. One last turning, followed immediately by a sharp right, and he would be there.

Momentarily ecstatic, he entered the car park and steered around familiar cars (Stuart Jeffries' car, which had been used as a beacon that first night, and the expensive vehicle he himself had arrived in) and screeched to a halt outside the community centre. He banged his fist on the door.

'Open up!' he yelled desperately, fighting to make himself heard over the roar of the bike. 'Open the bloody door!'

He glanced back anxiously over his shoulder and saw that an incalculable number of stumbling figures were pouring into the car park after him. Despite their laborious movements, they were bearing down on him with frightening speed and definite determination, the stronger, less damaged corpses dragging down the weakest of them as they lunged towards him.

'Open the fucking door!' he screamed. He grabbed hold of the handle and yanked it downwards, and to his surprise it opened immediately. He rocked the bike back, accelerated, and drove into the hall, then jumped off the machine and slammed the door shut behind him, feeling thud after thud after sickening thud as the loathsome creatures outside crashed into the building. Shaking with fear he secured the entrance and leant back against the wall, exhausted. He threw off his helmet, slid down to the ground and held his head in his hands.

The bike had fallen across the width of the entrance hall. Its engine had died, but the wheels were still spinning furiously. He could hear no movement in the hall. Despite the panic and noise of his sudden, unannounced arrival, no one had moved.

Fear and fatigue had turned his legs leaden, but he clambered to his feet, using the wall behind him for support. His mouth was dry, and he could no longer speak. He stepped over the bike, stumbled past the silent kitchen and toilets and into the main hall.

Then he stopped and stared. At first Carl was unable to comprehend the horror of what he was seeing, then his unprepared stomach started churning and bile rose in his throat as the dry heaves started.

For as far as he could see, the floor of the community centre was carpeted with human remains.

Without conscious thought Carl stood up again and took a few uncertain steps forward. Bone crunched beneath his feet as he picked his way through a macabre maze of cold, grey flesh and crimson gore, barely dried. His mind began to race, searching desperately for explanations other than the obvious. Perhaps the corpses were the remains of creatures from outside? Maybe they'd somehow found a way into the community centre and the survivors had slaughtered them?

There was a half-dressed body on the ground in front of him, a young man. Fighting to regain control of his stomach, Carl reached down and grabbed hold of the shoulder and pulled the man onto his back. He didn't recognise the corpse, but he could see immediately that this had not been one of the horrifically diseased bastards from outside. Much of the exposed skin had been torn to shreds, but there was a little untouched flesh on his face which had none of the disintegration of the walking cadavers. Apart from the obvious injuries, this young man had been otherwise healthy and normal. There was no doubt that this was the body of one of the survivors.

Carl began to sob. As he stood in the centre of the room, shaking with anger, cold and fear, he gradually became aware of sounds coming from the darkness somewhere up ahead of him, close to the little storeroom to which he had often escaped. Maybe someone had survived this bloodbath after all?

'Is anyone there?' he whispered.

Silence.

'Hello . . . Is anyone there?'

A figure appeared from the shadows, and, suddenly elated, Carl moved forward. 'Thank Christ,' he called, 'what the hell happened here? How did they manage to get inside?'

The figure inched closer, every step bringing it further into the light . . . until it was close enough for Carl to see that its head was lolling heavily on its shoulders. It slowly looked up and gazed at him with dead, emotionless eyes. Then it lunged towards him without warning—

'*Shit!*' he yelled as he side-stepped the creature's clumsy attack. It lost its already unsteady footing in a puddle of dark, coagulated blood and dropped to its knees in front of him. Carl, his heart pounding, stared down at the wretched corpse as it floundered about, struggling to pick itself back up. He took a step closer and kicked it in the face, the full force of his boot hitting it square on the jaw. The strike sent it flying backwards, skidding through the blood and body parts, but it immediately began to right itself again, feet and hands slipping in the gruesome mire.

Before it could get up Carl strode towards it and unleashed his full fury and frustration on the foul carcase, pounding it until he had broken enough bones to ensure it couldn't get up again. It was rapidly decomposing, and by the time he'd finished with it very little remained recognisable.

Filled with pain, exhausted and disconsolate, Carl walked back towards the bike. His options were now severely limited; he could either stay here in the community centre or take his chances outside, where there would no doubt be crowds already waiting for him. He'd been travelling for hours, and he didn't think he could face going back out there again yet.

He made his way to the small rooms at the far end of the building. Summoning the very last dregs of energy he could manage, he climbed through the skylight and out onto the flat roof, where he sat with the cold wind gusting into his face, watching the city and its dead population decaying all around him.

38

Carl waited for an hour, no longer, curled up in a ball on the roof. The vicious wind substantially reduced the temperature, but it felt infinitely better to suffer the cold outside than to face the carnage inside the hall. He knew he'd have to go through that hellish room eventually, to get to the bike and get out, but not yet.

Everything about the world looked grey this morning; a misty rain covered the city, and the sky, the buildings and the streets, even the bodies were drained of colour, all energy and life leached away. Carl was soaked through as he lay on his side and stared into the distance, trying to decide what to do next. He had cramp in both legs, and he ached all over. He was shivering from cold and exhaustion . . . was it worth trying to do *anything*? He began to question whether he should even bother. He considered suicide, but he lacked any obvious means to end his torment. He didn't have any pills or drink, and the roof of the community centre wasn't high enough for him to jump to his death. He had a knife, but he couldn't bring himself to use it. Carbon monoxide poisoning was a possibility, but that meant going back down there first . . .

Carl forced himself to get up again. He shielded his eyes from the rain and looked out towards Hadley, where he'd lived with Sarah and Gemma. When he pictured their faces he felt unexpectedly ashamed. What would Sarah have thought of him if she'd known what he'd been considering just a few seconds earlier? And what kind of a father would throw his life away so casually and pointlessly? As he thought about the family he'd lost he came to a decision. It was time to go home.

Without stopping to think about the massacre in the hall, or what might be waiting for him on the other side of the main door, he climbed back down through the skylight. He marched through the building, picked up the bike and put on his helmet. He gently pushed open the door, then started the engine. A crowd of corpses, twenty or more, immediately reacted to the noise, but by the time they'd turned themselves around so they were facing the community centre, Carl had already gone.

He reached Hadley in a matter of minutes. He drove up and over a steep incline, and there it was, the estate where he'd lived, nestled at the foot of the hill. He cut the engine and freewheeled down, his anxiety increasing as he moved through the area which was both reassuringly familiar and disturbingly different at the same time. He passed the pub where he'd spent his last 'normal' Saturday night with his family and friends, and was surprised at the number of rats scavenging for food around the bins outside. The building itself was dark and uninviting. Last time he'd been there it had been full of life, filled with people and noise.

Fortunately there were hardly any bodies around. He jumped off the bike and pushed it towards his house at the end of a short cul-de-sac. It broke his heart to see his home again, and he felt strangely guilty – ashamed, even – that he'd run away with Michael and Emma. Part of him wanted to turn and run again, but he had to see Sarah and Gemma again, to know that they were safe. The thought of what remained of his little girl dragging herself endlessly around the desolate streets was almost too much to stand.

Carl left the bike at the end of the drive and walked up to the front door. There was post on the mat in the porch, and he instinctively picked it up and opened it: a gas bill, and his monthly credit card statement. He started to check how much he owed before realising how pointless his actions were. He took the keys from his pocket (he'd carried them with him constantly) and, with his hands shaking, opened the door and went inside.

The house was just as he'd left it. Everything was where it should have been. Gemma's shoes were by the door; Sarah's coat was hanging over the post at the bottom of the banister. Apart from a faint smell of decay and a fine layer of dust which coated everything, it looked like nothing had ever happened here. It still looked like home.

Carl stood at the bottom of the staircase. This was the real reason he'd come back. He knew he couldn't do anything for either of them, but he had to see them. He climbed the stairs slowly, listening for any movement in the house, having to fight to hold his nerve and not turn and run. Eventually he reached the bedroom door. He stopped again, leant against it and listened carefully. No noise. With his mind filled with memories of his family he pushed the door open and waited. Still nothing.

The bodies of his wife and child were lying where he'd left them. As much as he wanted to see them again, he didn't dare lift the sheet which still covered them. He wanted to remember them as he'd last seen them, not as they surely were now, their perfect faces distorted beyond recognition by decay.

Carl kissed his wife and child through the bedclothes, told them both that he loved them, and promised them that he'd always be thinking of them.

He couldn't stay in the house. It hurt too much. He knew that his family were safe, and that was all that mattered, but he couldn't stay here with them like that. But where to go? The community centre was gone, and now that he was alone and the city was swarming with animated corpses, the council depot was less of an attractive option.

His head was spinning and he couldn't think straight. With mixed frustration and resignation, Carl admitted to himself that Michael and Emma had been right. The farmhouse he'd just come from was the safest place left.

39

Michael and Emma forced themselves to keep busy. When they stopped working they started thinking, and whether they thought about the past, the present or the future, it hurt. Concentrating on trivial, practical things helped them to get through the day. They cleaned the farmhouse together, even moving the furniture around in some of the rooms.

Emma decided to organise their supplies in the storeroom, while Michael went to work on their vehicles, but he'd been outside for less than ten minutes when he came barging back inside.

'What's the matter?' Emma asked, hearing the front door fly open.

'We've got a problem,' he told her, looking grim. 'It's the van. It's completely fucked. There's oil and stuff leaking out. Looks like something's cracked underneath.'

'Can you fix it?' she asked.

'Haven't got a clue where to start,' Michael admitted. 'I can change a tyre and check the oil and water, but that's about it. Something like this is way beyond me.'

'So what do we do? Can we get by without it?'

'We can, but we'd be taking a hell of a chance. What if the same thing happens to the Land Rover?'

'So what do we do?' she asked.

'We go out and get ourselves another van,' he replied.

Less than an hour later, Michael and Emma found themselves once again leaving the relative safety of Penn Farm and heading out in search of a new vehicle in one of the dead villages dotted around the decaying countryside.

For once Michael's usually keen sense of direction let him down. Distracted by a body lurching at them from out of nowhere at a crossroads, he took a wrong turn. The road they followed was long and straight. It climbed for more than a mile before levelling off. At the top of the climb the trees and bushes which had obscured their view on the way up suddenly gave way to open ground and it felt unexpectedly spacious and open. Intrigued, Michael drove through an open gate and into a wide field dotted with a handful of cars: a cliff-top car park where, from the far side of the field, they could see out over the ocean.

Emma and Michael were both taken aback. They had no idea they were so close to the coast; in the confusion and disorientation of the last few weeks their whole world had begun to feel like it had been pulled and twisted out of shape beyond all recognition. Maps and atlases had been forgotten, put to one side as they had struggled to survive from day to day. The ocean was the last thing Michael had expected to see.

Feeling more relaxed than they had for ages – the car park was remote, and they could see for miles; for once they couldn't spot a single body – they drove to the edge and stopped. There was an amazing view of the endless expanse of water below. Michael switched off the engine and slumped back in his seat.

'Well, screwed that up, didn't I?'

'Doesn't matter,' Emma said as she wound down her window. It was cold, but the smell of the clean, salty air was welcome, as was the noise of the waves crashing on the beach below – as well as disturbing the otherwise all-consuming silence of the dead world, it was loud enough to allow them to talk without attracting the unwanted attention of any nearby corpses.

The sight of the ocean filled Michael with an unexpected combination of emotions. He had always loved the sea, and seeing it now brought memories of childhood holidays flooding back: endless days when the sky had always been deep blue and the sun huge and hot. The memory of those long-gone days of innocence filled him with a familiar sadness, but now also it was tinged with a slight elation because for a while at least, the two of them were free from the confines of the farmhouse and the thousands of corpses which plagued their daily lives.

'Safest thing to do would be to take one of these cars,' he said, gesturing out across the car park. 'We'll find the one that's in the best condition, empty it, and then drive it back.'

Emma continued to look out over the sea. 'D'you think it's safe to get out?' she asked.

'Well, there's nothing about,' he replied. 'As long as we stay close we should be okay.'

Needing no further encouragement, Emma opened the door and stepped outside. She stared towards the horizon, and for a few seconds she dared to imagine that nothing had happened. She'd tried to do that before, but there had always been something in her line of vision to remind her of the shattered shell of a world in which she now lived. Now, though, looking out over the uninterrupted expanse of water, it was easy to pretend that everything was okay.

She walked forward, just a few steps, and looked down onto a stretch of sandy beach, but her heart sank as she spotted a single clumsy body stumbling through the frothing surf. Each wave knocked the pathetic creature off-balance, and it struggled to stand up again, only to be knocked down again when the next wave came. There was a second body in the water, this one bloated and discoloured, and wearing swimming trunks, obviously the unfortunate remains of an early-morning bather. And in the distance, she noticed with increasing disappointment, was the grey hull of a capsized boat. The illusion of normality had been shattered.

Michael hadn't seen the bodies or the boat. He was still daydreaming as he sat down on the grass next to their vehicle. He stretched out, lying back and resting on his elbows, then looked up at her and smiled. 'Know what I want?'

'What?'

'A sandwich.'

'A sandwich?'

'Yep, I want a big, thick, doorstop of a sandwich on freshly baked, crusty bread. I want salad, sliced ham, grated cheese and mayonnaise. Oh, and I'll have a glass of freshly squeezed orange juice to wash it down with.'

'We've got tinned ham and about thirty jars of mayo back at

the farm,' Emma said, sitting down next to him. 'And we've got orange cordial.'

'Not the same, really, is it?'

'Not really. Think we'll ever eat like that again?'

'We might. I bet we could make bread and cheese eventually, and we could have ham; we just need to catch and kill a pig. And I suppose we could grow fruit and vegetables if we set up a greenhouse . . .'

'You should get yourself an allotment,' she joked.

'We've got a bloody farm!' Michael laughed. He sighed and looked up into the sky. 'It's stupid, isn't it?'

'What is?'

'Everything we've just said. In a few seconds we've managed to come up with about six months' work. Six months, to get a salad sandwich and a glass of orange juice . . .'

'I know.'

Michael yawned and stretched. He looked across at Emma, who was suddenly deep in thought.

'You okay?' he asked.

She smiled. 'I'm fine,' she replied.

'But . . . ?' he pressed. He had the feeling that she needed to talk. He stared at her, trying to make eye contact.

Emma realised that she couldn't avoid answering. 'I was just thinking,' she started hesitantly, 'are we really doing the right thing here?'

'What, sitting in a car park looking at the sea?' he answered flippantly.

She smiled. 'No, I'm talking about the house, being out in the countryside.'

The sudden seriousness in her voice made Michael sit up. 'Of *course* we are – why? Are you starting to have doubts?'

'What is there to have doubts about?'

'Whether we should ever have left the city? Whether Carl was right to go back there?'

'No, I'm not having doubts, exactly . . .'

'So what is it then? Don't you think we can make this work?'

'I'm not sure. Do you?'

'We might be able to. The bodies are rotting, aren't they? Over time they should disappear, and if we can stay safe until then—'

'What about disease?'

'There are a thousand hospitals up and down the country, and all of them are full of drugs.'

'But we don't know which drugs to use, do we?'

'We can find out – and weren't you training to be a doctor?'

'I'd only just started. And anyway, if we're sick and we need to get drugs, we'll need to know what disease we've got, won't we? How do we diagnose that? Do you know the difference between malaria, typhoid and gout, for God's sake?'

'No, but there are books—'

'What, so we just nip out to the library?'

'Now you're just being stupid—'

'No, I'm not.'

'You are.'

'I'm not! I'm just trying to be realistic about our chances, that's all.'

Michael moved closer to her. Although she was still trying to avoid eye contact, he positioned himself directly in front of her so that she had no choice but to look into his face.

'Emma, we do have a chance,' he said, his voice quiet and sounding strangely hurt, 'and that's more than pretty much everyone else has.'

'I know,' she sighed. 'I'm sorry . . .'

They were silent for a few seconds, both staring into the eyes of the other, their minds full of confused, conflicting thoughts.

'Look, let's get back to the house,' Michael said eventually. 'We really shouldn't be out here like this.'

With that he got up and looked around the car park. About a hundred yards away from them was a car – nothing special, just an ordinary family-sized saloon – but it was the newest car in the field. He walked over to it and opened the door. The remains of the driver and his female passenger sat motionless in their seats. They were both dressed in business clothes, which made Michael wonder what they had been doing, sitting in this exposed and isolated place so early on a Tuesday morning. An illicit office affair perhaps? Or maybe a married couple spending a few precious minutes together before heading off to work? He leant inside and undid both seat belts, then dragged the corpses out. He positioned them so they were lying next to each other on the grass. The keys were still in the ignition. He started the engine, checked the display, and gestured for Emma to come over.

'Fuel tank's three-quarters full,' he said, suddenly feeling uncomfortably vulnerable, now that they were making a loud enough noise to be heard by any nearby bodies. 'Follow me back, okay?'

She nodded and got in behind the wheel. Michael ran back over to the Land Rover, started it up and pulled away. They drove out of the car park in convoy and retraced their route back towards the farm.

40

Michael's earlier disorientation worsened as they drove home. The roads they were following looked even more unfamiliar as he tried to navigate his way back to the farmhouse, and the journey was made more difficult by the fact that he was constantly checking the rear-view mirror, making sure that Emma was still behind. He felt surprisingly uncomfortable without her in the seat next to him, vulnerable even. He hadn't realised how much he'd come to rely on having her around. In many ways he hardly knew her, but now he realised he'd shared more pain, despair and raw emotion with her than any other person in his whole life.

He threw the Land Rover around a sharp bend, then steered hard in the opposite direction to avoid hitting the back of a crashed milk float. Ahead of him the winding road gradually opened out and straightened, and in the distance he could see a row of three grey cottages. From one of the buildings (the middle one, he thought) a single figure emerged and staggered out into the middle of the road. It stopped and turned to face him.

'Stupid fucking thing,' he said under his breath as he stared at the wretched body up ahead. He pushed his foot down on the accelerator, and the Land Rover quickly gained momentum. He focused all his pent-up anger and frustration on that one creature up ahead, deciding that destroying it would somehow make amends for the loss of everything that had ever mattered to him. As he raced ahead, the distance between the Land Rover and Emma's car behind increased. Confused and concerned, certain that something was wrong, Emma struggled to keep up.

The body in the middle of the road lifted its arms above its head and began to wave Michael down.

'Jesus Christ. What the hell . . . ?'

It took a few seconds for the full importance of what he was seeing to sink in, and by that time he'd almost reached the body. It was moving with more direction, purpose and intent than he'd seen from any of the corpses before and he slammed on the brakes, bringing the Land Rover to a sudden skidding halt just yards away from the ragged figure. He knew even before he'd stopped that it was another survivor. He could tell from the way the body moved, and when he got close enough, by the expression on the man's face, that he was still alive.

'Thank God!' the diminutive figure cried as he approached Michael, and as Emma stopped her car a short distance behind the Land Rover, 'Thank God,' he cried again, 'you're the first people I've seen in weeks . . . !'

'Are you all right?' Emma asked. She was already out of the car and running towards him.

'I'm fine,' he replied quickly, chattering like a nervous child, 'so much better now I've seen you two. I thought I was the only one left. I was going to—'

'What's your name?' Michael asked, cutting across him.

'Philip, Philip Evans.'

'And where do you live?'

The little man gestured towards his house. 'Here,' he said simply.

'Then let's get inside. It's not a good idea to be standing out here like this.'

Philip Evans obediently turned and led the others back towards his cottage. Emma looked him over as she followed him indoors. He was thin, and shabbily dressed; his grubby clothes were well worn and had obviously not been washed or even changed for several days, maybe longer. A noticeable stoop made him appear much shorter than he actually was. His tired face was ruddy, pockmarked and unshaven, and his uncombed hair looked greasy and unkempt. She noticed he kept scratching himself.

As they walked through the low front door, Michael baulked at the stench. Inside, the house was as squalid as its owner, and he wanted to turn and leave immediately – but he knew that he couldn't. No matter how he looked, Philip Evans was a survivor, and Michael felt duty-bound to try and help him. They were all in the same boat now.

'Sit down,' Philip said as he closed the door behind them and ushered them both into the living room. 'Please sit down and make yourselves comfortable.'

Emma glanced down at the sofa next to her and decided to stay standing. It was covered with bits of food, crumpled wrappers and other, less easily identifiable rubbish.

'Can I get you a drink?' he asked politely. 'I'm sorry, I'm just so surprised to see you both. When I heard the noise of your engines I thought that someone in the village must have . . .'

He continued to talk, his words fading as he disappeared into the kitchen to fetch drinks (though neither of them had taken him up on his offer).

Michael, glad to be alone for a moment, seized the opportunity. 'So what do you think?' he whispered.

'About what?'

'About him – what do you think we should do?'

She thought for a moment. She knew what she had to say, though she really didn't want to say it. 'He's a survivor, and we should offer to take him with us,' she said finally, with obvious reluctance.

'But . . . ?'

'But look at the state of this place,' she said, shuddering as she gestured at their filthy surroundings. 'Christ, this house is disgusting. I feel like throwing up just standing here. By the look of him he's probably contagious, isn't he?'

'We don't know that for certain, though, do we? We've got to try and do something for him . . .'

She nodded dejectedly and then changed the sour expression on her face to a forced smile as Philip returned to the room, still talking.

'—and after that when we couldn't find him we decided that something was definitely wrong,' he babbled. His voice sounded tired, and he paused for a moment to cough, a violent, hacking noise, like the rasp of a heavy smoker first thing in the morning. He was obviously struggling to catch his breath.

'You all right?' Michael asked.

Philip looked up and nodded, his face flushed and red. He spat a lump of yellow phlegm onto the carpet behind the TV.

'Fine,' he wheezed, wiping his mouth, 'just picked up a bit of an infection, I think.'

He carried a circular metal tray which he put down on the table after sweeping away a pile of rubbish with his arm. He handed Emma a chipped mug and passed another to Michael. Emma peered into her cup and sniffed it. She wasn't sure what it was . . . fruit juice concentrate? Something alcoholic? She glanced over at Michael who discreetly shook his head and gestured for her to put it down.

'Do you know what's happened?' Philip asked.

'Haven't got a clue,' Michael replied.

'I searched the village, but I couldn't find anyone else. I can't drive, so I haven't been able to get into town. I've just been stuck here waiting for someone to come . . .' He stopped talking for a second and looked at Michael again. 'Are you two from town? Are there many of you there?'

Emma and Michael looked at each other, then she said gently, 'We came here from Northwich just over a week ago, and there are just the two of us now. We left a few people there, but other than them we hadn't seen anyone until we found you.'

Philip sank down into an armchair with an expression of bitter disappointment on his face. 'That's not good news,' he muttered. 'I've been stuck here waiting and I haven't been able to do anything. The electricity and gas have been cut off, and my telephone's not working . . .'

'Philip,' Michael interrupted, 'just listen to me for a minute, will you? It's important that you pay attention. Whatever's happened here has happened right across the country, as far as we know. Just about everyone is dead—'

'No, no, I've seen some people,' he interrupted excitedly, not taking in Michael's words, 'but they're not right. They come when they hear me, but they're sick, see. They bang on the door for hours trying to get inside, but I just lock it and sit in the back room until they go.'

'Philip, we think you should come with us. We're living in a farmhouse a few miles from here, and we both think it would be better for you if you were to—'

But Philip still wasn't listening.

'Do you know what makes them act like that? I really don't like it. Mother's not well, and it upsets her—'

'Your mother's here as well?' Emma broke in, shocked.

'Of course she is!'

'She can come with us,' Michael suggested. 'We should get your things together and get out of here as quickly as we can.'

'She won't like leaving,' Philip sighed, his voice much quieter. 'She's lived here since she and Dad got married. He bought this house when they were courting.'

'Maybe you'll be able to come back,' Emma said. She guessed that Michael was keen to get moving, and she was doing her best to persuade Philip to leave.

He thought for a moment then said, 'You're right, it's probably for the best if we all stick together. I'll go and talk to Mum.' With that he got up and walked through a door in the corner of the room which opened onto a steep, narrow staircase.

Emma instinctively started to follow, but Michael stopped her.

'What's the matter?'

'Let me go first,' he whispered, putting her behind him.

Philip was already at the top of the stairs, and as Michael approached he lifted a finger to his chapped lips. 'Wait here please,' he whispered. 'Mum's found all of this a little hard to deal with and I don't want to frighten her. She's very old, and she's not been well these last few months.'

There was a rancid smell at the top of the stairs and Michael could clearly hear the ominous humming of a mass of flies close nearby.

Philip pushed the door open slightly and stuck his head into his mother's room, then he turned back to face the other two. 'Give me a minute with her, will you?' he asked. He disappeared into the room and started to push the door shut behind him, but Michael followed immediately.

Philip didn't notice. 'Mum,' he said softly as he crouched down at the side of the bed, 'Mum, there are some people here who can help us. We're going to go with them for a few days, just until things settle down again.'

Michael was standing just behind Philip as Emma entered the room. As she started to move towards him, he turned around and quickly pushed her back. 'Go downstairs,' he said quietly.

'Why?' she asked, and pushed her way past him to get a better view of Philip's mother—

—and recoiled immediately, covering her mouth in horror. Flies buzzed around Mrs Evans' decomposing flesh and fed on her constantly writhing body.

Michael went to the bed and, ignoring Philip's protestations, pulled back the soiled sheets. He stared down at the old woman's emaciated body. She was tied down with ropes, which were stretched tight across her stained nightdress and cut deep into her rotting flesh. She'd obviously been dead since the first morning.

'I had to do it,' Philip stammered anxiously, desperate to explain. 'She wouldn't stay in bed, and when the doctor saw her last, he said she had to stay in bed until she was better—'

'Philip, your mum's dead,' Michael said firmly.

'Don't be stupid,' he scoffed, 'how can she be dead? She's not well, that's all. Bloody hell, how can she be *dead*, you daft bugger?'

'Philip, this has happened to *millions* of people,' Emma said, fighting to keep control of her nerves and her stomach. 'I know it sounds crazy—'

'Dead people can't move,' he shouted, resting his hand on his mother's squirming shoulder.

'And living people don't rot,' Michael shouted back. 'She's *dead*, man! Your choice is simple. You either leave her here and come with us now, or you stay here.'

'I can't go without Mum,' he whined, 'I can't leave her here on her own, can I?'

Michael took hold of Emma's arm and pushed her back towards the stairs.

'Wait for me by the front door,' he said, then turned back to try and reason with the strange little man.

'Philip, you have to accept this. Your mother is dead. She might still be moving, but she's dead. She's the same as those other people you've seen outside, the ones who come and bang on your door.'

Emma listened anxiously as she waited on the bottom step for Michael.

'What are you going to do if you stay here?' he continued. 'You probably haven't got much food or drink, have you? And I can see you're ill yourself. We're your best chance, Philip – we're your *only* chance. Get your stuff together and come with us.'

'Not without Mum. I can't leave without her,' he said stubbornly.

Michael shook his head dejectedly. 'No,' he said simply.

Something inside Philip snapped, and in a fraction of a second the meek little man became an uncontrolled animal as the weeks of pent-up fear and frustration were suddenly too much for him to bear and he lunged, sending Michael flying across the bedroom. He lost his balance, surprised by the unexpected force and the venom of the attack, and tripped backwards through the doorway, Philip still holding onto him desperately.

The two men tumbled down the stairs and fell in a heap at Emma's feet.

'Get back to the car!' Michael yelled as he struggled to hold the other man down. 'Get the fucking engine started!'

Despite having the speed and intentions of a man possessed, Philip was weak and malnourished, and it took little effort for Michael to overpower him. He wrenched him around and grasped his scrawny neck in a dangerously tight headlock, then dragged him towards the front door of the cottage.

There were three bodies in the road between the car and the van. Emma ran past them and climbed into the car and started the engine. In those few moments the first corpses had already been joined by five more, which had emerged from the shadows nearby, and they began to crowd around her as she waited anxiously for Michael to appear.

Now new bodies were appearing, reacting to the sounds of the violent struggle inside the building. They started heading towards the cottage, and Emma revved the engine, hoping the noise would distract enough of them to give Michael a chance to get himself and Philip out. A handful of figures turned around awkwardly and staggered back towards the car, but an equal number continued to move towards the house.

Michael dragged Philip across the living room, but he jerked to a halt when Philip grabbed hold of the arm of the sofa and clung on desperately. Michael looked up to see corpses in the doorway, and Philip took advantage of Michael's momentary distraction to squirm free. He took a few steps and wiped tears from his eyes. He was completely oblivious to the danger of the approaching cadavers.

'Why can't I bring her with me?' he demanded, still refusing to accept the truth.

Michael didn't answer, just reached for his arm, but Philip recoiled and twisted himself free – just as one of the cadavers in the doorway reached out and grabbed hold of his shoulders. Another caught hold of one of his legs, and Philip, now truly terrified, began to kick and scream.

'Get them off me!' he yelled, '*please*, get them off!'

Michael tore the creatures away and shoved them back out into the street, using their skeletal frames to push the others back out through the door. He looked around briefly and saw there were already two dozen or more figures around Emma's car. He had to make an immediate choice: continue trying to persuade Philip to leave without his dead mother – or leave him and just go.

He glanced back at the pathetic shell of a man, who was now lying curled into the foetal position in the middle of his filthy living room carpet, whimpering and snivelling. The decision was simple. He ran out of the cottage, pausing only to pull the door shut behind him, then barged more of the stumbling bodies out of the way as he fought his way through the rancid crowd. Their comparative weakness and dulled reactions were no match for his strength and fury.

He climbed into the Land Rover and started the engine, and as he did so the dead hammered on the car and crowded around him until all he could see was a mass of grotesque, decaying faces staring back from every angle. He gave a couple of short blasts on the horn, and when he heard Emma do the same, he pushed down on the accelerator and moved forward, driving blind until all the decomposing bodies had been pushed to the side or driven over. One managed somehow to cling onto the bonnet, but within a few yards it too was gone, dragged down under the wheels of the car.

He watched in the rear-view mirror until he was certain Emma was safely away, then he put his own foot down.

41

Michael found the maze of twisting country lanes which connected Penn Farm to the numerous villages and small towns around horribly confusing. He was disorientated, and was finding it harder than ever to concentrate. Had he done the right thing in leaving Philip behind, or should he have forcibly dragged the man from his home? There was no way that poor mad bastard was going to abandon his rotting mother, not without a damn sight more persuasion, and there hadn't been time to argue. In the end it had boiled down to a clear-cut choice between Philip's safety and his own and Emma's, and he couldn't stand the thought of putting her at risk, not for even a second . . . but at the same time, he felt racked with guilt when he remembered the frightened little man he'd left quivering alone in the squalid confines of his dead mother's house.

A while earlier in the car park, in those few precious minutes when he had dared to stand out in the open air with Emma, he'd allowed himself to feel a faint flicker of optimism. For that moment they had been miles away from the farmhouse and the bodies and the disease and everything else, and he'd felt strong and alive, breathing in that clean sea air.

Now he'd been brought back to reality with a vengeance, and those all-too-familiar feelings of claustrophobia and despair had returned.

A T-junction in the road loomed up ahead, and Michael thought it looked familiar; they were finally heading in the right direction. Then came a signpost he'd definitely seen before, then the rusting wreck of a blue estate car which had crashed into the base of an old oak tree . . . Yes, they were back on the road that would take them home.

Carl was driving back along the same road, but approaching the farm from the opposite direction. He felt numb, and weak with tiredness, and every muscle in his body ached, but he refused to slow down. He hadn't planned on making two long trips, not on the same tank of petrol, and the needle on the fuel gauge had dropped to the lowest possible level. He was riding on fumes. But he forced himself to keep going. He swerved around another putrefying cadaver as the body swung round awkwardly and grabbed at the carbon monoxide-filled air where the bike had just been.

Almost there. Just a couple of hundred yards left until he reached the turning onto the track to the farm. He was scanning the side of the road constantly, searching for the elusive gap in the hedgerow. There were bodies all around him now, spilling out into the road from every direction, for the all-consuming silence of the dead world had again amplified the noise the motorbike made out of all proportion.

The bike briefly juddered and shook as the engine began to splutter and die. He glanced down at the controls, but it was no use. He freewheeled to a standstill. He was close to the farm-house . . . but not close enough.

Carl dumped the useless machine and began to run. He pulled off his helmet and threw it at the closest corpses, hitting one square in the chest and knocking it over. He was exhausted, but he sprinted further down the road. The turning onto the track was only a short distance away, but by the time he'd reached it, hundreds of corpses were in slow-motion pursuit, with more swarming out of the shadows up ahead of him. With lungs burn-ing, he charged up the hill in the direction of the farmhouse.

What the hell was going on?

Confused by the sudden appearance of an unexpectedly large crowd of bodies, Michael missed the turning and overshot the track. The sound of their engines had attracted the attention of plenty of cadavers along the way, but why were there so many of them here now? Had their collective interest been aroused by the noise from the Land Rover when they'd first left Penn Farm earlier that morning? Had they been standing there, just waiting for them to return?

Emma flashed her headlamps at Michael and blasted her horn,

not sure if he knew he'd passed the turning. Furious with himself, he slammed the brakes on, thumping into several corpses and sending them flying. Behind him he saw Emma disappear up the track and he reversed back, churning even more of the shambling creatures under the wheels of the Land Rover.

Emma powered through the rotting crowd and accelerated up the hill back towards the house. The rough track seemed more uneven than ever – the wheels of this car were smaller and the suspension less forgiving than either the Land Rover or the van had been, and each dip and trough caused her to lurch forward or threw her back in her seat. The defenceless corpses were smashed away to either side as they collided with the car, but they were never-ending, more and more of them up ahead.

She accelerated again, and this time as she glanced in the rear-view mirror she caught sight of Michael, finally on his way up the track behind her, his vehicle covered with gore.

Carl was tiring fast. He was still managing to outrun the bodies coming after him, but it was getting harder, and those coming down the hill towards him now were faster, helped by the slope. The air was dry, and he had a painful stitch in his side, a dagger jabbing into his gut every time he breathed. He knew he couldn't stop, but still he was struggling to keep going. For a second he thought he heard something. An engine? Some of the corpses dragging themselves up the hill after him began to break off their pursuit and stumble back down again, distracted by this new and unexpected sound. He looked back over his shoulder, but he couldn't see anything. In the distance up ahead he could see the gate and the barrier now, and, just beyond that, Penn Farm.

He had almost reached the gate across the stream now, but the number of bodies around him suddenly increased dramatically, the remnants of the vast crowds which had remained close to the farm. They were advancing towards him from all angles now, spindly, awkwardly moving shadows. He kicked out at the nearest few, then sprinted for the gate and hammered his fists against it.

'Emma! Michael!'

A corpse clawed at his back. He spun around, grabbed the soiled collar of its ragged clothes, then slammed it against the gate before lifting its insignificant weight and throwing it clear of the track. Another one hurled itself at him, then another and another, until he was surrounded by a virtually impenetrable swarm of the damn things – almost a single black mass, which had him pinned back against the gate. He looked up and, through their constantly shifting movements, thought he could see a car approaching.

Emma continued to accelerate up the track, blinded by the sheer number of bodies now surging towards her. She didn't dare slow down, fearing that the combined effect of the slope and the corpses would stop her reaching the farm. Instead she kept moving, barging many of the bodies away to either side, driving over still more of them and crushing them beneath her wheels. She thought she must be close to the gate now, but she couldn't see a damn thing. Up ahead was a densely packed throng of rotting figures. She had no choice but to punch her way through.

Carl didn't recognise the car, but he didn't care. He fought his way towards it, pushing the dead away, swinging his fists wildly and trying to batter his way through them. They continued herding towards him oblivious, fighting back with leaden, barely coordinated hands. On their own the bodies posed little real threat, but in these kinds of numbers it was a different matter altogether. He was tired and scared, and every time he got rid of one of them, several more took its place.

Emma braced herself as the car careered towards the mass of bodies. But then, just for a fraction of a second, she caught a glimpse of something unexpected – a flash of healthy, living flesh amongst the sea of green-brown decay; a fast, purposeful movement in the midst of the slow and clumsy fighting. Was that Carl? She'd already ploughed into the back of the crowd when she clearly saw his face, and her instinctive reaction was to steer hard left to avoid him. But still she didn't dare slow down. The front of the car smashed through more dead figures, then thumped hard into the gatepost, and the impact threw Emma forward in her seat, but she managed to straighten her arms in time to stop her head smashing against the wheel. Corpses were already swarming around the sides of the crashed vehicle. She'd barely managed to sit up straight when Michael, his vision equally obscured, smashed into the back of her. The sturdy Land Rover bounced back, almost shrugging off the impact, but Emma's car lurched forward again, glancing off the gatepost then rolling down into the stream nose-first.

Michael leapt out of the Land Rover and ran to the car, ignoring the dead now lurching towards him. He jumped down to the water, yanked the driver's door open and pulled Emma out.

She wasn't much hurt, and she scrambled back up the bank with him, climbed into the Land Rover and slid across into the passenger seat. Michael grabbed a corpse around its waist and hurled it away, then dived for his seat and pulled the door shut behind him.

'Carl,' Emma said breathlessly.

'What?'

She couldn't speak; she just pointed into the mass of writhing bodies now spilling around the front of the Land Rover.

'Drive,' Michael said, getting out again.

Emma started to protest, but stopped, knowing there was no point. She moved across to the driver's seat as Michael ran forward, disappearing deep into the bodies, and nudged the Land Rover forward slowly after him, steering around the back of the wreck of her car.

Michael dropped down and crawled along the ground, dragging himself through the dirt. The dumb bastards surrounding him were oblivious, their attention divided between the steadily approaching Land Rover and something else which was happening just ahead. Could that really be Carl? Between the forest of unsteady, festering legs he was sure he could see him, still dressed in his motorbike leathers, and he increased his speed, weaving around the feet of the corpses until he was close enough. Then he stood upright, but Carl didn't immediately see him.

Exhausted, barely able to keep moving, Carl was drenched with gore from the creatures which continued to attack him from all sides. His face was covered with blood where one of the bodies had slashed at him, slicing his skin with the exposed bone at the end of its rotten fingers.

'Carl, it's me,' Michael said, catching the other man's arm, arresting it in mid-punch.

It took a couple of seconds for Carl's panic to subside slightly, and for him to react. 'Michael?' he gasped, incredulous.

Michael pushed him towards the gate again, now weakened and leaning over at a precarious angle. He fumbled with the key and managed to remove the lock, then shoved it open. It scraped along the ground, carving an arc in the dirt. He pushed Carl towards the house, almost immediately grabbing his arm to pull him out of the way as Emma drove the Land Rover through after them.

Carl staggered after Emma, moving as slowly as one of the dead, while Michael tried to force the damaged gate shut again. Several bodies had already squeezed through and were crowding around him now like flies around rotting food, but he ignored them, concentrating instead on getting the gap closed. The wooden barrier rocked and shook as bodies threw themselves against it on the other side, but he managed to stand his ground and snap the padlock shut. He stepped back, shaking off one corpse that had grabbed hold of his leg, and wondered how long it would hold.

There were three more bodies in the yard. Michael dragged two of them into the stream and managed to force the third up and over the barrier around the house, then ran to Emma who was struggling to get Carl inside. He took Carl from her, leaving her free to get the front door open, and she moved to one side as he half-carried, half-pulled Carl inside, then slammed and locked it after them.

'Kitchen,' she ordered, and Michael dragged Carl through and laid him down on the tiled floor. His breathing was slow and laboured.

'Think he's going to be all right?'

'Don't know,' she said as she started to check him for injuries. There were no cuts too deep that she could see, nothing obviously serious, just flesh wounds. But his unblinking eyes stared up at the ceiling.

'You okay, Carl?' she asked. No reaction. 'He looks all right. It's just shock, I think. He's traumatised.'

'What the hell's he doing back here?'

'I don't know. Maybe he—' She stopped talking when she

looked back outside and saw the badly damaged gate rocking and shaking, the movement becoming increasingly violent.

'Will they . . . ?' she started to say when the barrier collapsed, unable to withstand the pressure of the immense crowd of corpses all surging in the same direction at once. The gatepost, already damaged by the impact of Emma's car, had been forced out of the ground, and the dead swarmed forward like an unstoppable flood. Within a few seconds a crowd of diseased bodies had gathered at the kitchen window, their dead faces pressed hard against the glass, their rotting fingers clawing to get inside.

'Upstairs, Emma, now!' Michael barked.

Emma didn't argue. Between the two of them they manhandled Carl into the hall and up to Emma's room. Michael kicked the door open so they could carry him through and laid him down on the bed. More concerned with their immediate safety than Carl's wellbeing, Michael ran to the window and looked down. His worst fears had been realised. The house was being surrounded.

42

Michael leant his head against the bedroom window and looked out over the yard below. He'd hardly moved since they'd come back to the house. 'Jesus Christ, there are more and more of those fucking things coming here by the second. There are bloody thousands of them down there.'

Emma had been sitting with Carl, who was lying on the bed, silent and motionless. She got up and walked over to where Michael stood and looked down over his shoulder. He wasn't exaggerating: below them there was an enormous crowd of the detestable figures surrounding the house, and their numbers were increasing by the minute as more continually poured in through the gap where the gate on the bridge had been.

'Why do they keep coming?' she asked, her voice little more than a whisper. 'We came here because we thought we'd be isolated and safe. Why do they keep coming?'

'It's the noise.'

'But we've not been making any noise. We've been careful . . .'

'Christ, how many times have we been through this? The whole planet is silent. Every time one of us moves, you must be able to hear it for miles around.'

'So the sound of the car engines . . . ?'

'Keeps attracting them. And even when the sound dies down, I think they're staying close because they know we're nearby.'

'Do you really think so?'

'Why else would there be so many of them?'

'So if we stay indoors and keep quiet and out of sight for a while then they should . . . ?'

He shook his head in resignation. 'I don't think that'll work any more.'

'Why not?'

Rather than answer her, Michael instead just opened the

bedroom window slightly. The sudden forcing noise as he pushed the sticking window open caused a ripple of excitement to quickly spread through the rotting crowd in the yard.

'Just listen to that.'

The shuffling of rotting feet, the occasional guttural groan, the sound of disintegrating bodies tripping and falling, the noise of the stream, the wind in the trees; a thousand individually insignificant sounds combined to create a constant, eerie noise.

'It's too late for us to just sit still and play dead now,' he explained. 'They're making enough noise themselves to keep bringing more and more of them here. And if it's not the noise, just the fact that there's *something* here will be enough. It doesn't matter how quiet we are now, the bastard things are going to keep coming regardless.'

Emma stepped back from the window, sat down on a chair and held her head in her hands. After a while she murmured despairingly, 'So what do we do?'

Michael didn't answer. He pulled the window shut again and the room became quiet, the only noise Carl's stertorous breathing – until he suddenly groaned in pain and they rushed to his side.

'Think he can hear us?'

'Maybe. I'm not sure.'

'How are you doing, Carl?' Michael asked, his voice still hushed. He gently shook Carl's shoulder, but he didn't respond.

Emma leant over him and looked him up and down, gently stroking his face. 'Poor bugger.'

'Has he said anything to you yet?'

'Nothing. I don't think we should pressure him by—'

'We need to know what happened in Northwich, if he ever got there. We need to know why he came back.'

'We need to be careful. If he's in shock the last thing we should do is—'

Michael wasn't listening. He shook Carl's shoulder again. 'Carl, mate, can you hear me?'

At first there was no reaction, then Carl swallowed painfully and tried to nod.

'Careful, Mike,' Emma warned.

Carl's eyes flickered shut and then opened again. He looked at Michael, his eyes blurred and unfocused, then he turned to Emma. Then he looked at Michael again, who asked, 'Did you get to Northwich? Did you—'

'I got there,' Carl rasped.

Michael anxiously glanced at Emma. 'So what happened? Why did you come back?'

Carl looked up at the ceiling again, licked his dry lips and swallowed hard. 'There was no one there,' he whispered.

'Where, at the community centre? Did you get back to the community centre . . . ?'

'They're gone. There was no one there.'

'Where did they go?'

Carl slowly lifted himself up onto his elbows and swallowed again. He took a deep breath. Every movement was obviously an effort. 'Didn't go anywhere,' he managed. 'Dead. All of them.'

'What?'

'Place was full of bodies—'

'What happened?' asked Emma, her voice hushed.

'They got inside,' Carl said sadly. 'There's so many of them still back there . . .'

'Christ,' Michael said quietly. 'And they wouldn't have stood much of a chance, not in that hall, with only one way in and out of the building . . .'

Carl slumped back onto the bed, exhausted from the effort of talking.

Michael stood up and stormed across the room. He kicked the bedroom door and it slammed shut, sending a sudden noise like a gunshot echoing through the house, causing the creatures outside to stir again, a wave of dead flesh and bone rippling through the crowd. He couldn't think straight. He didn't know what to do. They had reached a dead end and now they were rapidly running out of options. The farmhouse was under siege, and the only other place of refuge they knew was gone.

Emma, recognising his fear, walked over to him. 'What are we going to do, Michael?'

He didn't answer, but turned his face to the wall, not wanting her to see the frightened tears welling up in his eyes.

'We've got to do something,' she said firmly. 'Are we just supposed to sit here and wait, or do we—?'

'We don't have much of a fucking choice, do we?' he snarled. 'We can take our chances outside, or we can wait for them to get inside. We can barricade ourselves in this room and see if we can sit it out until it's safe again, but that's going to take for ever and we'll need food and water and—'

'The house is still secure—'

'I know it is, but what use is that to us any more? Go into any room downstairs and there will be a hundred of those fucking things staring in through the window. Once they see you they'll go fucking wild, and before you know it we're back to square one—'

'What do you mean?'

'I mean that it's only going to take a little bit of careless noise or for one of us to be seen and we'll be right back where we started. We could sit in this fucking house in silence for six months, until all but a handful of them have disappeared, and we'd still have a problem. All it needs is for one of them to react, then another will follow, then another and another, and—'

'So what are you saying?'

He wiped his eyes then turned around to face her. 'I don't know.'

'I think we have to leave. We can't stay here.'

He nodded. 'I don't know how we're going to get out . . .'

'But we don't really have any option, do we? We have to leave.'

Michael didn't answer. He wiped his eyes again and looked around the room. For almost a minute he said nothing. Then he started, 'We've got to keep out of sight and out of earshot of those bloody things as much as possible. We should try and get as much stuff together as we can. We're just going to have to fight our way through.'

'How are we going to get to the Land Rover?'

'Maybe we wait for a couple of hours, until it's dark. A few of them might disappear. And if I try and get the generator started—'

'Why?'

'It'll distract them – if there's a louder sound around the back of the house, they're more likely to go looking for us there, aren't they?' He sounded more positive with every sentence.

'We'll wait a bit, give Carl a chance to come round a bit more and pull himself together, then we'll just have to go for it.'

43

The days were getting shorter, but it seemed to take an eternity for darkness to fall. Each minute dragged unbearably, each second taking for ever to pass, but Carl didn't move. Emma wondered if he was aware of what was happening around them as he lay motionless on the bed, staring up at the ceiling, or whether he had become catatonic. Whatever his condition, she decided that she didn't want to take the risk of disturbing him again – at least while he was like this he was quiet. She worried that if she tried to talk to him or move him, he might react badly, and any such reaction might provoke another terrifying response from the vast crowds outside the house.

She and Michael had managed to pack their few belongings, and what was left of Carl's gear too, and they stockpiled the luggage in the shadows at the top of the staircase. They didn't dare to go downstairs yet, or get any closer to the front of the house, for fear of being seen, but that meant they had no way of getting to the more important supplies in the downstairs storeroom.

They passed on the landing close to the bedroom door and spoke to each other in hushed, anxious whispers.

'You okay?' Michael asked. Emma looked tired and frightened in the half-light.

'I'm all right.'

'Carl okay?'

'No change.'

'So is he going to be all right?'

'Don't know.'

'Christ, you were the one studying to be a doctor.'

'Piss off! This is way beyond anything I studied. I don't even know if *I'm* going to be all right any more, never mind anyone else.'

'Sorry.'

'Forget it.'

'You got much stuff together?'

'Got my clothes and a few odds and ends. What about you?'

'The same. We're going to have to get downstairs and get some of the stuff in the kitchen packed up.'

'So how are we going to do that? There are huge bloody windows in every room – we can't go anywhere without being seen from outside.'

'I know.'

'We're just going to have to leave with what we've got, aren't we?'

'I think we'll be lucky to get that much out, to be honest.'

'So what are we going to do?'

'We can find other stuff out there – we'll just have to start again somewhere else, I suppose, do what we did when we found this place. We'll find somewhere that looks half-decent, get ourselves settled, then get out and get supplies.'

'But won't the same thing happen again?'

'Probably.'

That wasn't the answer Emma wanted to hear, though it was what she'd been expecting. She'd just been hoping for a little more encouragement. She mentally shook herself, then whispered, 'So how do we get out? Have you thought about that?'

'Just have to make a run for it, I guess. We'll get Carl up and ready, get loaded up with stuff, and then go for it. We'll probably have to fight our way through.'

'Think we can do it?'

A third nonchalant shrug, and an uncomfortable silence followed.

'Are there still as many of them out there?' Emma asked after a bit.

'Can't tell,' Michael replied. 'Probably. I've seen a few walking away, but there are just as many still coming in over the bridge.'

'They can't get inside, can they?'

'We'd have to be bloody unlucky for them to get in. It's locked tight down there but . . .'

'But what?'

'But there are thousands of them, Emma. Their sheer numbers could do some real damage.'

'I don't think they'll be able to force their way in,' she said confidently.

'Neither do I – but then again, this time yesterday I never thought they'd get through the barrier . . .'

'But they didn't get through, we let them in.'

'Doesn't matter, does it? Fact is, they're through. Same as it wouldn't matter how they got inside if they manage to get in at all. Wouldn't matter if they put a window through or if we let them in through the front door. We'd be completely screwed, whatever.'

'When are we going to do this, Mike?'

'As soon as we can. We're kidding ourselves if we think we're going to gain anything by waiting.'

44

Carl felt much better. His body still hurt and his muscles ached, but lying alone in the darkness, things finally began to make sense again. He couldn't stand the thought of hiding in this house like a prisoner for the rest of his days. What kind of a life was that? What was the point of struggling to survive if that was all that they would be surviving for? He knew that something had to give, and it had to give soon.

He remembered running from the road back to the house. It had been hard, and it had taken every last ounce of energy he'd had, but he'd done it. He was faster than all the dead bodies, and he was much stronger too. He knew they were nothing – just useless bags of skin and bone. How could anything as weak as that hurt him?

He closed his eyes and pictured Sarah and Gemma. What would they have wanted him to do? Would they have wanted him to cower away in some dark corner, cold and starving, just waiting for the days to end? Of course not. He could hear her voice now. He could hear Sarah telling him that he needed to get up, he needed to be strong and make a stand.

He could hear Michael and Emma out on the landing, talking about trying to get away again. What good would it do? They'd just end up running and hiding somewhere else. The only way to deal with this situation, he decided, was to go out there and destroy every last one of the lamentable bastards outside.

He knew he could do it.

He was going to take them out. Every single one of them.

45

Quarter to ten. Pitch black outside. Michael sat in a chair in the corner of the bedroom with his eyes closed, ready to leave, but too scared to move.

Emma sat on the edge of the bed where Carl was still lying quietly. She had taken care to position herself so that even though it was dark, she could still clearly see both men. She watched them anxiously in the dull light, waiting either for Michael to open his eyes and decide that they should move or for Carl to return to full consciousness. She was less worried about Carl now. He seemed much calmer, and he'd briefly spoken to her a short while ago. He was sleeping now, his face untroubled and more relaxed.

Taking care not to make any more noise than was absolutely necessary, she stood up and walked over to the window. Cautiously peering down into the yard below, she saw that the seething mass of dark, heaving bodies remained undiminished, an apparently endless shuffling sea of rotting figures. Hundreds upon hundreds of them were trying to push ever nearer to the house. Individually the corpses were slow and dumb. While she was watching, she saw several of them lose their footing on the muddy bank and tumble helplessly into the stream, quite unable to stop themselves, or to get out again. She saw another get caught on a jagged shard of wood from the remains of the gate on the bridge, unable to pull itself free.

One or two of the bodies weren't a threat. A group of ten or fifteen, say, that was a concern, but nothing they couldn't deal with. They could outrun a hundred. But outside the farmhouse tonight, massing in the cold darkness, their numbers were incalculable.

'No better?' Michael asked from the shadows behind her, startling her momentarily, and she spun around quickly, her heart racing.

'They're still coming,' she replied.

'Sorry,' he said, his voice low. 'I didn't mean to scare you.'

She turned back to look out of the window again. 'Do you think they know we're in here?'

'I don't know,' he answered. 'I think they sense there's something different about this place. It might just be the noise we make, it might be the way we move . . .'

'But what do they want from us?'

'I don't think they want anything.'

'So why are they here?'

'Instinct, I guess.'

'Instinct?'

'We're different, that's all, and whatever's left of their brains is telling them we're not the same as they are. They're reacting to us because they think we're a threat.'

'*Us* a threat?'

'I think so, yes.'

Michael came closer and gently put his arms around Emma. For a second she involuntarily recoiled at his touch – she didn't mean to; she wanted to be close to him, but at the same time, she wanted to be alone. Actually, truth was, she didn't know what she wanted any more.

'You all right?'

'I'm okay,' she replied, turning around to face him, but not making eye contact. 'I'm just tired, that's all.'

'Sure?' he pressed, not convinced.

Her eyes filled with stinging tears. 'No,' she finally admitted, reaching out and grabbing hold of him. She pulled him closer and buried her face in his chest. 'I don't think we're ever going to get away from this house.'

'It's going to be okay,' he said instinctively, though without any degree of conviction in his words.

'You keep saying that,' she sobbed. 'You keep saying that, but you don't know if it's true, do you?'

She was right, and Michael decided it was better to say nothing. Still holding onto her tightly, he shuffled closer to the window and peered outside.

Nothing out there had changed.

'Come on,' he announced suddenly, 'we've got to go.'

'What?' Emma protested, pushing herself away from him. 'What the hell are you talking about? We're not ready to go yet—'

'It's not going to get any better,' he said, his voice surprisingly calm and unemotional. 'We could wait here for months, but we'd be fooling ourselves if we think it's ever going to get easier.'

'But what about Carl?' she snapped. 'We can't leave here until he's—'

'You're making excuses. We've both been doing it all night. We should have left already. We've got no choice, Emma, we've just got to go for it.'

She knew he was right; they'd both been trying to put off the inevitable. But now there was a newfound strength and conviction in Michael's voice which frightened her a little. This really was it – he was right, she knew that, and leaving was the only option, but that didn't make it any easier to deal with.

She watched as he pulled a thick jumper over his head and tightened the laces on his boots.

Michael looked up and noticed the concern on her face. 'You okay?'

She nodded quickly, but it was impossible to hide her fear. She was already shaking with nerves, and her legs felt leaden. She could hardly breathe.

'Look, I'm going to try and start the generator,' he continued. 'There are fewer of them out the back and—'

'What, only five hundred instead of a thousand?'

'There are fewer of them,' he continued, ignoring her. 'I'll see if the noise will distract them away from the Land Rover.' It was almost as if Michael had somehow switched off his emotions. Now he was concentrating all his attention and effort on the task to hand. He started walking towards the door, then he stopped and turned back to face Emma. He opened his mouth, as if to say something, then shut it again.

'You sure about this?' she whispered.

'No,' he replied with brutal honesty, 'but I can't sit here thinking about it all night. Do me a favour, will you, and try and get Carl up and ready to leave. As soon as I'm back inside we'll make a run for it.'

With that he turned and disappeared into the darkness, leaving Emma staring into the space where he had just been, trying desperately to make sense of the sudden confusion all around her.

Michael crept down the staircase, frightened that even the slightest noise might have a devastating effect on the vast crowd outside the house. Perhaps even something as insignificant as the creak of a loose floorboard might be the final straw, something to whip the rotting masses into a frenzy that would see them forcing their way into the house.

With his entire body drenched with a cold, clammy sweat, Michael lowered himself down onto his hands and knees and crawled along the hallway, keeping out of sight of every window and every door, his movements slow and deliberate. It didn't take long to reach the back of the house. He stood up carefully, keeping his body pressed tight against the wall, hiding in the shadows. Once upright he had a clear view of the back lawn through a small square pane of dirty glass. There were still many, many bodies outside, but on this side of the house their numbers were fewer and much more diffuse. He watched as a shadowy silhouette stumbled past, and as soon as it had gone he silently turned the key in the lock and pulled the door open. Holding his breath, he slipped through the narrowest gap he could and then shut the door quickly behind him.

He was outside.

He had seen thousands of these terrifying, pathetic corpses over the last few days, and yet, even at this most dangerous time, he still found himself unable to tear his eyes away from them. They were all deteriorating, and each one he saw looked more hideous than the last, until the next aberration staggered into view. Standing perfectly still he watched them lurch and sway around him, their limbs uncoordinated. For the most part their heads were bowed, hanging heavily, as if it would take far more effort than any of them could muster to look up.

The shed which housed the generator was some twenty yards away from where he now stood. He knew that running would attract more attention, so it made sense to try and walk slowly, matching the laboured pace of the cadavers around him . . . but moving slowly would be so hard, increasing the strain with every single step.

He was inches away from the nearest bodies, knowing one false move would set off a deadly chain-reaction throughout the enormous crowd. The monstrosity immediately ahead of him was horrific. Half of its clothes had been torn away, but so bad was the injury and decay that he couldn't even tell if it had been male or female. In the fleeting moonlight he could see most of the skin covering its face and neck had been lacerated. The wounds were dry – no blood seeped from them – but each slash and tear was filled with the teeming movement of hundreds of flies and maggots.

Step by painful, dragging step, Michael forced himself to move across the back lawn. Bodies stumbled past him, some even collided with him, and still he forced himself to remain focused, not to panic. The stench of rotting flesh was everywhere, and he wanted to run, more than he ever wanted anything in his life. He wanted to kick the bloody corpses out of his way, to smash his way through the hordes to the generator . . . but he didn't dare react. This was like playing with fire, like being forced to lie in a bath of scalding-hot water and not move: each second was agony, but every conceivable alternative was much, *much* worse.

Another cadaver lurched into his path and for a fraction of a second he looked into its clouded eyes before quickly looking down at the ground again. He winced with repulsion as the body crashed into him, instinctively lifting his hands to protect himself. Its torso was weak and his hands slid effortlessly through decayed flesh and into its chest cavity. Biting down on his lip to stop himself from shouting out in disgust, he carefully pulled himself free and carried on towards the generator.

Just a few yards to go.

The wind was cold, the air damp with spitting rain, but Michael didn't care. Three yards, then two yards. Almost there. With numb, trembling hands he reached out for the door handle, resisting the temptation to increase his speed by even a fraction. He pulled the door open and carefully slipped inside—

—and the gusting wind caught the door and slammed it shut

behind him, and he cursed the noise which rang out through the silence like a gunshot.

There was a torch in the shed which they had purposely left there for emergencies. Using the dull light from its dying bulb he scanned the control panel. It had been days since he'd used the generator and he prayed it would work tonight. Carl had taught both Michael and Emma how to operate the system; now, remembering his careful instructions, he began to prime the machine. When he looked up, he saw through the flapping door (which was constantly blowing open and shut in the wind) that there were bodies all around him now. He flicked the switch to start the generator, and as it coughed and spluttered and failed, every last one of the bodies he could see immediately turned and began to walk towards the shed. He tried to start the generator again, and again it died. Once more, and the same response. Terrified, unable to think straight, shaking so hard he could barely press the starter, he tried the machine for a fourth time, and finally it burst into life, beginning to chug and thump reassuringly. Clouds of dirty fumes billowed up into the swirling night air, smelling to him like the sweetest perfume.

All around the house, and throughout the surrounding countryside, more than a thousand bodies began to slowly surge towards the mechanical noise.

With no time to think, Michael kicked open the door and ran back towards the house, fighting his way through a thick sea of grotesque cadavers all advancing purposefully towards him. He kicked and punched his way through the masses, charging through to the back door. He desperately lunged for the handle as more than a dozen pairs of twisted hands clawed at him, grabbing hold of his hair, his clothes, his shoulders, his legs and arms, and he screamed and writhed, trying to free himself, but it was useless: no sooner had he managed to free himself from the grip of one corpse than he was caught again by countless others.

He felt himself beginning to be pulled back into the voracious crowd.

'Michael!' Emma screamed, and he looked up and saw that she was on the other side of the door. As she yanked it open, he managed to shuffle a couple of steps to his right and forced one arm inside the building, and Emma grabbed hold of him and pulled with all her strength, until he fell into the house. She'd dragged a body inside with him, and while he breathlessly kicked and punched at the tenacious cadaver, Emma slammed the door shut again, severing an emaciated arm in the process.

The body on the floor finally stopped moving, and Michael crouched down, struggling to catch his breath. He shook himself clean, brushing away scraps of flesh and splinters of bone.

'You okay?' Emma asked, shouting to make herself heard over the noise coming from the frenzied crowd outside who were throwing themselves bodily at the door.

'Think so. I think we need to—' Michael began, before being interrupted by another noise, this time from the front of the building. He looked at Emma for a split-second before standing up and running down the hallway. It was Carl.

'Shit!' Michael yelled. 'What the fuck are you doing?'

They watched helplessly as Carl unlocked the front door. He lifted his hand to the latch, then stopped and turned back to look over his shoulder at them.

'Ready?' he asked, grinning with excitement and misguided anticipation. His scratched, bloodied and bruised face was grotesque, almost unrecognisable, his features distorted even further by the dark shadows of the besieged house. A deranged smile belied the fact he was blissfully unaware of the danger of what waited on the other side of the door.

'Christ, no,' Michael shouted, running towards him, 'don't fucking open it, Carl!'

Emma was rooted to the spot with fear. She couldn't move, or even think, as her lips formed silent words of desperate prayer.

Carl lifted up the rusty rifle they had found and grinned again at Michael. 'Come on, Mike, let's take 'em. You and me'll have the fucking lot of 'em!'

Michael could hear the bodies fighting to get into the house, scrabbling against the windows and the door, whipped into an uncontrollable frenzy by the sound of raised voices.

'Don't do it, Carl,' he pleaded, 'just stop!'

It was too late.

Carl opened the door.

For a single second, which seemed to last for ever, nothing happened. The unexpected stillness was suddenly shattered by a tidal wave of rotting flesh and bone flooding into the house.

Michael turned and ran.

'Get upstairs!' he yelled at Emma, and grabbed hold of her arm, dragging her up the staircase, then pushing her ahead of him as they neared the top. He stopped and looked back down as the unstoppable surge of corpses continued, lifting Carl clean off his feet and smashing him back against the wall, watching as he tried to fight, but was dragged down under the weight of the dead. In seconds the hallway was completely filled and Carl had been swallowed up by the vast, still advancing crowd.

Turning quickly, Michael ran up the final few stairs after Emma into Carl's attic bedroom. He followed her inside and slammed the door shut behind him.

'The bed, quick! We need to push it in front of the door!' Taking one end each, the two of them shunted the heavy wooden bed down the length of the room and turned it sideways so that it completely blocked the entrance.

'Where's Carl?' Emma asked, although she thought she already knew the answer.

Michael didn't bother to reply. He ran over to the window and looked down. The bedroom was at the front of the house. It was dark, but he could make out the shape of the Land Rover in the yard below.

'We've got to get out,' he said, his voice trembling with panic. 'I've still got the keys to the Land Rover—'

'But what about our stuff? Christ, all our stuff's—'

'Forget it. We can always get more stuff.'

'But how are we going to get out? We can't just—'

Michael ignored Emma's nervous questions. He opened the window and leant out. A few of the bodies below caught the movement, and their ferocity increased when he climbed out onto the roof.

'Follow me,' he said, turning back to Emma.

She walked over to the window and looked down. 'I can't,' she whimpered, her voice trembling.

'Emma, you've got to,' Michael said desperately. 'You don't have any choice.'

Fighting to stay calm and in control of herself, she watched as Michael carefully turned around and lowered himself down the slanted roof until his feet were resting in the gutter. Lying flat with his stomach pressed against the tiles, he shuffled sideways until he was directly above the porch. Once there he stopped and looked up at the bedroom window again.

'Come on,' he hissed.

Emma looked at him, and then looked down at the mass of bodies in the yard. More and more of them were reacting to Michael's voice. Still unsure, she climbed up onto the windowsill and tentatively put one foot outside. Moving painfully slowly, she lowered herself down until she was hanging backwards out of the window. She stopped again, paralysed with fear.

'You can do it!' Michael hissed, seeing her terror, praying that she couldn't sense his. He lowered himself down the last few feet onto the roof of the porch and then stood still for a moment to regain his balance. He glanced down at the shifting sea of figures below. He was close enough to be able to see the faces of the hundreds of corpses gathered around the house. Just yards away from his feet an endless column of the dead struggled to force a way into the building.

Emma was still clinging for dear life onto the windowsill, too terrified to move a muscle. A sound from inside the house distracted her and she looked back through the open bedroom window to see that the door was opening, the heavy bed blocking it being shoved out of the way by the sheer weight of numbers. The massive number of bodies that had managed to squeeze into the house was simply astonishing.

The gap suddenly increased again, and she watched in horror as the first flood of disintegrating cadavers began to spill into the room.

'Move!' Michael shouted, distracting her, and she looked down and watched as he dropped ten feet from the roof of the porch onto the yard below. He landed awkwardly amongst the bodies, twisting his ankle, but he ignored the pain and the clumsy, grabbing hands which reached out for him and forced his way over to the Land Rover. Kicking and punching at the corpses holding onto him, he unlocked the door and fought his way inside, severing arms and fingers as he slammed the door. He started the engine, and another new sound meant another surge of bodies, this time all heading towards Michael.

Emma looked up. The bedroom was already half-full and the bodies were getting too close to her. She had to move. She stretched her legs out behind until she was lying on the sloping roof, then started moving her toes, feeling for the guttering so she could use it for support. Finally she let go and slid down until her feet caught the ledge, then she followed Michael's route across the roof.

She looked down for a moment, to see where the Land Rover was – and watched in horror and disbelief as Michael began to drive off.

'Michael!' she screamed, as the Land Rover moved away from the house, but it was okay; Michael was just driving around to get as close to her as he could possibly get. Only for a fraction of a second had Emma believed he was just going to leave her behind, but it left her shaking like a leaf.

She steeled herself and dropped down onto the roof of the porch – and caught her foot on a loose slate, which crashed to the ground beneath her. She struggled to keep her balance, and as she desperately fought to grab hold of something solid, she found herself lurching forward, loosening more slates, until the roof gave way under her weight and she fell down to the yard.

The mass of surging bodies below her broke her fall, but within seconds she was completely engulfed.

Michael jumped out of the Land Rover and dived into the scrum around Emma, grabbing at the constantly shifting mass, pulling one corpse after another up and out of the way until he found her. He hauled her up by the scruff of her neck and forcibly yanked her free and hauled her towards the Land Rover.

He manhandled her into the vehicle, and she slid across into the passenger seat, then reached back for his outstretched hand. She started pulling him towards her, but now the collective strength of the creatures was too much and they snatched him away, dragging him down amongst them.

Flat on his back, looking up at the crowd of bodies about to descend upon him, Michael realised he was about to die. The thought of Emma being left alone in this terrifying world of the dead hit him – and with the very last dregs of energy that he could summon from his battered and exhausted body, he pushed himself back onto his feet and started striking out at the corpses around him until he reached the Land Rover once again.

He reached inside, grabbed hold of the steering wheel and pulled himself in, yanking the door shut behind him.

'Okay?' he asked breathlessly, though he could hardly hear himself speak over the deafening noise of countless carcases smashing their decaying flesh and disintegrating bone against the metal and glass.

Emma swallowed hard. 'Just go.'

Michael forced the Land Rover into gear and lifted his foot off the clutch. His twisted ankle was agonising, but he scarcely felt it. For one desperate moment it looked like the impossible volume of dead bodies surrounding them was too much as the engine roared with effort.

Trying not to see Emma's face, white with terror, he accelerated again, this time increasing the power steadily until the engine was screaming to be released, and with one sudden, juddering movement they began to edge forward, carving a gory passage away from their home and out through the rotting masses.

Emma looked back over her shoulder at what remained of Penn Farm. Through her tears she could already see that the farmhouse was now just a shell. Dark figures were moving at every window.

Epilogue

Michael Collins

We drove for hours, only stopping once, to siphon more fuel from a crashed car we found on a deserted stretch of road.

We gave up for the night when I couldn't keep awake to drive any longer. We'd been following a twisting road which led along one exposed edge of a high mountain valley when I spotted an empty car park. Emma didn't want to drive. We decided we had to rest.

I parked the car, stopped the engine and got out – a stupid thing to do, perhaps, but it didn't seem to matter any more. If there were any bodies near (and I couldn't see any), then what could they do to us? What more could they take from us? We had nothing. And we could lock ourselves into the Land Rover if we needed to.

We were in a remote and beautiful place, miles from anywhere – but still not far enough from the dead. The moon was high and proud in the sky overhead tonight and the night was peaceful and still. Across the valley was a steep, jagged mountain-face, as harsh and inhospitable a place as we could have hoped to find.

Emma walked around the Land Rover to stand next to me. I pulled her close. The warmth of her body was comforting.

'Should we keep going?' she asked.

'I don't know,' I answered truthfully. 'What do you think?'

'Is there any point?'

'There's got to be somewhere we can go,' I said, 'somewhere they can't get to. Another Penn Farm . . . ?'

I looked down into her face and stopped talking. Her expression suggested that although she wanted to believe me, she couldn't bring herself to. Tears of pain and frustration were rolling down her soft cheeks.

In silence we clambered into the back of the Land Rover

together, locked the doors and lay there on the floor, holding each other tightly, hidden under blankets and coats.

'We'll be okay,' I heard myself say.

She smiled briefly, then buried her head in my chest. We had nothing left to lose but our lives. We lay there in the darkness and waited for morning.

THE END

The story continues in:

AUTUMN: THE CITY

Acknowledgments

The story behind this book has been pretty well documented: as a frustrated, unknown author I gave *Autumn* away for free via my website. Several years and several hundred thousand downloads later, it spawned a series of sequels, became a movie, and now, almost ten years since it first appeared online, the book has finally been 'officially' published.

Apart from thanking my family and friends for their love and support, and the various editors, publicists and others who have worked on the books around the world, I also have a very important group of people to thank – the people who discovered the *Autumn* series online and talked about it and promoted it and helped me along the way with everything from distribution and marketing to editing and design. If I was to draw up a full list of people to thank, it would take up a book by itself. I did start one, but stopped when I hit a hundred names and still had more to go!

You know who you are!

Thanks to each and every one of you for your input, feedback and encouragement. Without it, this book would never have happened.